Nathan Burrage lives in Sydney with his wife and two daughters. He is the author of FIVEFOLD, a supernatural thriller first published by Random House Australia, and subsequently translated into Russian as Code Kabbalah.

In 2005, Nathan graduated from Clarion South, an intensive, six-week residential writing program based on the famous workshops of the same name in the US. In 2011, he co-convened the Aurealis Awards in Sydney and remained part of the Organising Committee in 2012 and 2013.

Nathan has over twenty-five short story credits and has been shortlisted for both the Aurealis Awards and the Ditmar Awards. IFWG Australia will be releasing his duology—The Salt Lines—in 2023.

Irregular transmissions can be intercepted at www.nathanburrage. com

What Reviewers say of Burrage's *Almost Human*

"The stories in Nathan Burrage's *Almost Human* are both epic and familiar, magical and futuristic, but always deeply human. We are immersed in the grandest and the most intimate of struggles with the same sense of immediacy, the same feeling of being transported to another world. Sometimes, we almost recognise that world, it's so close to our own. Sometimes, it's so far, but no less real. Travelling with Nathan as he draws you through the stories in this collection is an intense journey, one that illuminates the very nature of what it means to be human... or almost."
–**Joanne Anderton**, award-winning author of *The Bone Chime Song and other Stories* and *The Veiled Worlds series*.

"Action-packed, compelling, and above all, humane. A wonderful collection."
–**Ian Irvine**, author of *The Three Worlds Cycle*.

"Nathan Burrage is a superbly gifted wordsmith and in *Almost Human*... Readers are catapulted from their comfort zones and chilled, thrilled and always entertained. From the end of the Middle Ages and a warring Europe, to the majesty and mystery of Istanbul, a cyberpunk nightclub, Bulgaria, Borneo and the suburbs of Sydney, this gripping collection is not only a journey through time and alternate and sometimes dark, mystical spaces, it's a lexical feast for the imagination and the ultimate in escapism."
–**Dr Karen Brooks**, author of *The Brewer's Tale, The Darkest Shore* and *The Good Wife of Bath*.

"Nathan Burrage's magic is to make the reader feel wiser for reading this transportive collection. The clever clockwork of lived travel, careful research and wild imagination are invisible—yet inevitable—in stories that are as thought-provoking as they are effortless to enjoy. This collection often had me reading late into the night saying to myself: Just *one* more!"
–**Stephen M Irwin**, author of *The Dead Path* and *The Broken Ones, and* screenwriter of *Harrow, Secrets & Lies*, and *Tidelands*.

"A collection of worlds under threat, doomed heroes and fated relationships—but ultimately with a message of hope."
–**Richard Harland**, award-winning author of *Song of the Slums, Liberator* and *Worldshaker*.

"In *Almost Human*, Nathan Burrage roams across snowy Transylvania, cyber booths, urban horrors and dark futures...culminating in his titular trilogy where he exercises his interest in history and mythology to consummate effect."
–**Jason Nahrung**, award-winning author of *Blood and Dust* and *The Big Smoke*.

"Nathan has been quietly putting out quality speculative fiction for years. This is a collection you do not want to miss."
–**Keith Stevenson**, author of *Horizon* and publisher at Coeur de Lion.

Almost Human

A Collection of Short Fiction

By Nathan Burrage

Almost Human: A Collection of Short Fiction

All Rights Reserved

ISBN-13: 978-1-922556-89-9

Copyright ©2022 Nathan Burrage

V1.0

Stories first publishing history at the end of each story.

Printed in Palatino Linotype and Amarante Regular.

IFWG Publishing International
Gold Coast

www.ifwgpublishing.com

For Liz, Liana and Brielle

Table of Contents

Remnants

With the snow easing at last—*thank the saints*—they could finally urge their horses to better speed in the moonlight. No point trying to obscure their tracks, thought Dumitru. Only further snowfalls could hide their passing and speed was more important now. Besides, the Ottomans had likely divined their destination. After their last disastrous raid, there was nowhere else to run.

The wound in Dumitru's hip still throbbed, although the pain was losing its edge as the cold deepened. He shifted in the saddle, taking more weight on his good leg, and pressed a hand to the sodden bandages. The arrowhead had not penetrated deep, but there had been no time to stitch him up once it was removed. Glancing over his shoulder, it looked like tiny red poppies had bloomed amidst the snow.

"We'll get that seen to once we reach White Church." Cosmin nodded at Dumitru's injured leg. "No doubt we'll find a willing seamstress who can knit you back together."

A bear of a man, Cosmin wore a ragged mail shirt crusted in Ottoman blood. A boyish grin split his bearded, forbidding face. Easy to forget how young they all were.

Dumitru smiled and tendrils of ice in his beard cracked. "Others need tending more than I."

"Maybe so," Cosmin replied, dropping his voice a notch, "but the men need a leader. So, you'll be first to the healers just the same."

"More than I deserve," Dumitru muttered.

Their party numbered just under a dozen now, less than half the men he had set out with. Most carried wounds of some description, although the cut to Cosmin's shoulder above his shield arm did not look too serious. They had captured their prize, but it had come at a terrible cost: Ciprian, Emilian, Marian and Serghei all face-down in the snow. The others were either captured or dying in winter's numbing embrace.

"Gave as good as we got," Cosmin muttered, his bravado fading away.

Dumitru forced the faces of the dead from his mind. "Let me know when Neculai returns. We can ill afford any more surprises."

Cosmin nodded. "You're going to check on the prisoners."

Dumitru sighed. "Yes, it's time I had words with my sister. As for the other, he'd better be worth the risk we took."

With snow falling heavily, their scouts had been unable to fully gauge the number of Ghazi soldiers escorting his sister. The advantage of surprise had quickly shifted as undetected Ghazi cavalry wheeled around and charged through the trees.

The raid had been fought in pockets of frenzied violence: men and horses screaming, arrows whirring beneath the branches of naked beech trees, the spray of blood, shockingly bright against the snow. It was Neculai and Stelian who'd managed to drag his sister back to her people, Ekaterina clawing and kicking all the way.

Dumitru reined in his horse and let his tired warriors pass. Few acknowledged him; most were either numb with pain or lost in their private thoughts.

Ekaterina had been stripped of her fine robes and jewellery and disguised in a thick monk's cassock. Her head was bowed and the cowl hid most of her face. Their second prisoner shivered in his foreign robes, the bottom of his turban wrapped around his face so that only a slit remained for his black eyes to stare out at the cold, hard Transylvanian landscape.

Silviu was keeping watch over the prisoners. Dumitru admired his bodyguard's features as they approached: a straight nose, strong jaw and hair as black as sin. He gave Silviu a brief smile before nodding towards the front of their column. Silviu handed over the reins of Ekaterina's pale mare, their gloves touching fractionally longer than necessary, before spurring his horse forward.

Ekaterina looked up at the sudden halt and her expression turned scornful. "Ah, the Captain of the New Varangian Guard. I'd curtsey if my hands weren't tied to the pommel." Her expression could not be less pleased if she'd just stepped in a steaming pile of horseshit.

Dumitru grinned. As Kat's younger brother, her scorn was like a comfortable, well-worn coat. "Sister, it's good to see your spirits remain undulled from your recent *misadventures*." An ugly bruise marred her cheek. He nudged his horse forward and tugged on the reins of her mount.

Ekaterina leaned forward in the saddle. "Rakosh will kill you for this. Every last one of you."

"Hardly news, Kat. The Emir's Ghazi have already tried a few times. It seems I'm destined to disappoint both of you."

Ekaterina made a noise of disgust. "So far, your resistance could be ignored in the name of largesse. Not now. Not after kidnapping his betrothed. Every person who has ever harboured you will die screaming. Don't you care about that?"

Now *that* sounded like the sister he remembered. The one from his childhood, not the woman who had unwisely chosen to dabble in politics. *Don't do this, don't do that, don't you realise what will happen, you idiot?*

"Is that why you chose to marry him?" Dumitru asked. "To protect us all?"

"Well, it wasn't for love!" Ekaterina snapped. "Rakosh and his Ghazi are too strong. Father fought and failed. He has learned to accept it. Why can't you?"

"So, if you can't kill a beast, tame it? Is that your strategy?" Dumitru glanced at Ekaterina. His sister wielded words with a deftness learned from their father. Even her expression was not to be trusted.

"At Rakosh's side, I can stay his hand. Do you have any idea how much our people have suffered for your petty raids?"

3

"There's no need to twist the knife, Kat."

She had the decency to look momentarily abashed. Dumitru pressed his advantage. "You err in assuming Rakosh will listen to you."

Ekaterina smiled. "I can be persuasive. And he needs me at his side if he wants to hold these lands. You've demonstrated that much."

"You're right. Rakosh will marry you to legitimise his claim, seed an heir or two, but listen to you? Never. Not with those cursed Djinndurum whispering in his ear."

Even Ekaterina's imperious expression faltered at the mention of those unholy brethren. Rakosh would be summoning them from whatever dark places they took their leisure. Combined with his highly trained Ghazi cavalry, Dumitru's remaining men stood no chance of winning a pitched battle.

"You may be right," Ekaterina conceded, "but at least my way only I suffer. Your campaign has achieved little and cost much."

"You're wrong. Our people know we reject the Ottoman yoke. And we have Rakosh's attention."

"Are you that eager for death?"

"The occupation began with Rakosh. It ends with him. It's that simple."

Ekaterina frowned as she studied Dumitru, her expression searching, as if she had glimpsed something she'd never seen before. "You're drawing him out, goading him."

"How can he command respect if he can't even protect his betrothed?"

Ekaterina shook her head. "You fool. He'll decorate a pike with your head and slaughter the entire village as an example."

"Perhaps, or he might prove overconfident. Either way, I'll not see our line joined with his."

Ekaterina scowled. "This man you're trying to be, it's not who you are, Dumitru. Don't forget I've known you before you learned duty and honour and all those other useless platitudes you New Varangians cling to. I know you have a…gentler side, a side that will never continue our line." She glanced in Silviu's direction.

Dumitru leaned in close to Ekaterina. "One more word—just

one—and you'll complete this journey in your smallclothes, your mouth gagged and slung over the saddle like the spoils of war. Am I clear?"

"As you wish, *brother*, but we both know you're lying when you talk of the future."

"Think what you like. It's not for either of us to decide. Father will be the judge."

All the blood drained from Ekaterina's face.

Dumitru chose that moment to summon her guard and he dropped back to the second prisoner.

The Ottoman was shivering as the horses picked their way through the denuded trees. Dumitru studied the thin foreigner, noting the soft hands scarred with old burns. Dumitru might be young in the grand scheme of things, but he had no difficulty recognising a man with secrets.

"Do you speak Saşi?"

"Well enough, Most Excellent." He tried to bow in the saddle.

"Good."

Keeping his voice low, Dumitru began his interrogation.

Night had fallen by the time they reached the remote village of Viscri. Unlit hamlets loomed without warning from the fog that had settled in the valley. The chill had deepened, lodging in Dumitru's lungs and seeping into his bones so that warmth was but a faint memory.

The Ottomans had no love for the cold. No matter how hot Rakosh's temper ran, he would be forced to camp for the night and search for firewood to keep his Ghazi from freezing.

They were safe.

For now.

Neculai had done his job, giving the villagers advance warning of the impending attack. The smallfolk would be huddling in the fortified church that overlooked the village.

The ache in his injured hip had faded and his left leg was stiff and almost numb. He was afraid to dismount for fear he might discover he could no longer walk.

"They're waiting for us." Neculai emerged from the shadow of the nearest hamlet. His face was almost ghostly in the moonlight, eye-sockets shrouded in shadow. "We made sure the villagers gathered what weapons they have. Mostly bows, a few spears and the odd axe. No armour, of course."

"It's the bows we'll need," Dumitru replied. "Spears and scythes will be no match for the Ghazi if they breach the walls."

Neculai nodded in agreement.

"Will they fight for us?"

Neculai spread his gloved hands. "Everyone fights, given no other choice."

"Then let's hope they aren't offered another one."

The horses plodded up a trail that wound out of the village and up the overlooking hill. Dumitru strained for a glimpse of light that would betray the church's location. He was pleased to discover he could find none.

The whitewashed walls from which the church took its name soon emerged from the gloom. Once, as a child, he had accompanied his father to White Church for a dedication ceremony. That boy remembered walls that towered overhead, grazing the bellies of clouds. The warrior that he had been forced to become was quietly dismayed.

The outer wall was roughly diamond in shape, with roofed towers protecting each corner. While the fortifications were pleasingly thick, they were hardly as high as he remembered; perhaps four times the height of a man. A Ghazi could approach on horseback, throw a grappling line and be over the parapet without too much difficulty. With insufficient warriors to man their perimeter, placing archers to make best use of the embrasures would be crucial.

A broad guardhouse overlooked the main gate. The church was set in the centre of the diamond and connected to a tower keep, which commanded views over the entire structure. That would be their final line of defence, should it be required.

He reined in his horse. "I am Dumitru, son of Lucian, rightful lord of Cohalm. I am known to you."

"What business do armed men have with the peaceful folk of Viscri?"

"As your Christian brethren, we seek sanctuary. As for myself, I would speak with my father."

No reply was forthcoming. Dumitru frowned: hardly the welcome he had hoped for. He caught the sound of boots pounding down wooden stairs. If he was forced to wait, he might as well assume the role of a penitent.

Dumitru dismounted carefully to keep most of his weight on his good leg. The dull pain in his hip sharpened considerably. Grimacing, he unbelted his scabbard and laid it in the soft snow. It was hard to make out faces beneath the eaves of the guardhouse, but he had no doubt he was being watched.

He sank stiffly to his knees, hiding the effort it cost him. "I will pray here, at your door, if I must."

Metal bolts screeched as they were drawn back, and the double gates swung open. A priest emerged from the gap, a lantern held aloft in a steady hand. He was clean-shaven and surprisingly young.

"My name is Father Petru. We were told to expect you." Petru hesitated before hurrying on. "Your father wanes, I am sorry to say."

Dumitru absorbed the news in silence. It had been months since he had last seen his father. Months since they had quarrelled about how to deal with Rakosh, his Ghazi, and the terrible Djinndurum.

Dumitru rose to his feet, biting back a groan. "We have injured. Can you tend them?"

"Of course." Petru took in the bloodstains on Dumitru's leg. "I gather we should include you amongst them. Best we hurry inside." His gaze darted downhill towards the village.

"The Ottomans will arrive tomorrow."

Father Petru met Dumitru's flat stare. "Then we have time to pray."

Most of the village had gathered inside the church. The hymn swelled as Dumitru did his best to walk normally across the courtyard. Ekaterina and the Ottoman prisoner followed, cords binding their wrists.

Dumitru flung open the main door to the church and limped inside. Light and heat rolled over him, blinding after hours in the chilly darkness. The hymn faltered and fell silent as frightened faces turned towards him.

"Reverend," Dumitru said, addressing the lean, elderly Abbot leading the devotion. "Please forgive me. I have men outside, good Christian folk who fight to protect our land. They are freezing and most—if not all—are injured. I humbly request shelter and succour."

The Abbot frowned. "I will not thank you for interrupting our devotion." He glanced at his congregation. "Nor will I turn my back on those in need. Place your men in the stables and we'll see what can be done for them once the service has concluded."

"Thank you, Reverend." Dumitru bowed from the waist and ground his teeth together at the pain in his hip.

"At the risk of further testing your patience, I wish to see Lucian, lord of Cohalm and my father."

If the Abbot was surprised by this statement, he hid it well. "Father Petru, please conduct this man and his...*companions*...to his father."

The smallfolk stared at the Ottoman prisoner. Angry mutters swirled around the room. That was good, thought Dumitru.

"This way," Petru murmured. They passed through an iron-banded door in the back of the church. Traversing a short, covered walkway, they entered the tower keep.

"I see no guards," Dumitru noted.

"They're at prayer," Petru replied with a mild note of rebuke.

Dumitru had a range of choice responses to that, all of which he wisely discarded. He tugged on the rope binding his prisoners. Ekaterina was strangely subdued, although knowing his sister, she would be hoarding her words for Father.

Petru led them up a tight staircase, across a landing, and stopped at a heavy wooden door. "You should prepare yourself. We've done all that we could, but I fear he'll be in God's keeping soon."

"He won't be the only one," Ekaterina muttered under her cowl.

"Is that a woman?" Petru asked in surprise.

"Thank you, Father Petru." Dumitru nudged him aside. "I'll

have some privacy now. Please ensure this Ottoman doesn't do anything foolish." Dumitru pushed the prisoner to his knees and opened the door.

Lucian lay on a low wooden pallet covered in furs. He was far too pale, and his cheekbones jutted from sunken flesh. A hearty fire burned in the grate. After the freezing cold outside, Dumitru found the room stiflingly hot.

Shrugging out of his fur cloak, he drew Ekaterina inside and closed the door firmly in Petru's face. Lucian murmured in his sleep but did not wake.

Dumitru's dismay was mirrored on Ekaterina's face.

"You should let him be."

"There isn't time, Kat."

Dumitru limped over and drew the furs back. His father had always been a lean, severe man. In the months since they had parted in anger, Lucian had wasted away. Ribs jutted from beneath his thin shift and sweat glistened on his brow.

"Father. Wake up." Dumitru gently shook him.

Lucian, formerly of Cohalm, groaned. It took far too long for his gaze to focus.

"Ah, the son who wouldn't listen," Lucian rasped. "And the daughter who couldn't hold her tongue. What a fine pair you make." He laughed, or at least tried to, and subsided into a fit of coughing instead.

"Father, we don't have much time."

"In the name of God," Ekaterina interrupted, "cut me loose so I can make him comfortable."

"Don't try anything rash, Kat."

She laughed, high-pitched and tight. "You inherited all the rashness in our family. None was left over for me."

No point arguing with her. Drawing his belt knife, Dumitru cut Ekaterina's bonds.

"Poor fool." Ekaterina rubbed her wrists and flexed her fingers. "Sit down before you fall down." Dumitru lacked the energy to argue. He sank onto a nearby stool and stretched out his injured leg. With the fire's warmth stealing over him, pain was stirring in his hip.

Ekaterina busied herself with pillows to prop up Lucian and a goblet of water to still his coughing. Once he was comfortable, albeit bleary-eyed from his fit, Ekaterina sank onto the floor at the foot of Lucian's pallet.

"Why have you come?" Lucian asked. "It's not to tend me, that much I know." His shrewd gaze took in Ekaterina's strange garb and Dumitru's injury. "If I didn't know the two of you, I could almost believe you've tried some ploy against those cursed Ottomans."

"Kat was going to marry Rakosh," Dumitru said hurriedly. Long and unhappy experience had taught him that when dealing with Ekaterina, it was critical to seize the initiative. "I prevented it."

"And killed half his followers in the process," Ekaterina snapped. "Rakosh is coming and he'll slaughter the entire village to crush any further resistance. I could've prevented that. I still might be able to…"

A deep sigh shuddered through Lucian's wasted frame. "My children." He shook his head sadly. "When you stand at the border of life, when all the doings have been done, some things become painfully clear. I wish you two could have been friends. Soon you'll be all that the other has. Your Mother—"

"Our Mother was killed by that Emir and his cursed Ghazi," Dumitru interrupted. "The same man Kat intended to marry."

"Not by choice, by necessity!" Ekaterina leapt to her feet. "Fighting Rakosh and his Djinndurum is madness. We can only endure by joining our house to his."

"That is not enduring," Dumitru snapped. "You'll be one of many wives, but the marriage gives him legitimate claim to our lands. Why can't you—"

"Peace!" Lucian growled. "I'm sick of your bickering and… expecting me to…choose sides." Lucian struggled for breath. Bright dots of colour infused his cheeks. "If you've told me true… Rakosh will finish…what he began at Cohalm. What is the point of deciding who is right…or who is wrong? It matters little. Both of you…have failed."

Ekaterina opened her mouth, but for once, words failed her. Dumitru chose to hold his tongue.

"If only my children fought together…instead of each other." Lucian slumped against his pillows, his accusing stare unwavering.

"We've all seen what the Djinndurum can do," Ekaterina said. "Rakosh is but a man. The Ghazi are formidable, but they bleed." She shook her head. "The Djinndurum though, they are beyond us."

"Perhaps not." Dumitru raised his voice. "Father Petru, I know you're listening at the door. Be so kind as to bring in the prisoner."

Floorboards creaked, and after a pause, the door swung open. Father Petru was flushed but his expression remained defiant. Dumitru gestured for Petru to bring in the Ottoman.

"What are you doing?" Ekaterina demanded. "He could be an assassin. Or a spy."

"Why don't you try listening for once, Kat? Tell them your name," Dumitru ordered the Ottoman.

The prisoner had lost his turban somewhere between entering the White Church and this chamber. His head was shaved in contrast to his thick beard. He sank to his knees and pressed his forehead to the floor. "If it pleases their Gracious Masters, my name is Diwan."

Dumitru noticed Diwan's accent had thickened.

"And what is your profession?"

"I am a humble merchant."

"Dumitru, why bring a heathen…onto this holy ground?" Lucian asked with a withering look of disgust.

Dumitru made a placating gesture. "Listen to what he has to say. What goods do you trade in, Diwan?"

Diwan's gaze slid into his lap. He knotted his fingers together nervously. "Antiquities, Most Excellent. Rarities from the East."

"And who are your customers, Diwan?"

He gave Dumitru a pleading look. "Please, Your Benevolence. There are worse things than death. I beg you."

"Answer the question."

Lucian leaned forward to get a better look at Diwan and Ekaterina shot a questioning look at Dumitru.

Dumitru ignored her. "Diwan, they know you've been captured. And they have your goods. What further need do they have of you?"

Diwan wrung his hands together. "You don't know what you ask. I beg you."

"No." Dumitru leaned forward. "Help me and I will set you free, as I promised."

Diwan searched the room desperately for a way to escape. His gaze lit upon the narrow, barred window, before dropping to the fire grate in defeat.

The shock of realisation spread across Lucian's gaunt face. "He serves the Djinndurum."

"Yes," Dumitru replied. "He supplies them with the materials they need for their magiks. Even more telling, he has some training in their dark arts. Tell them what Djinndurum means in your language."

Diwan grimaced. "Begging your pardon, but it doesn't properly translate."

"Tell them."

"Binder of spirits." Seeing their confusion, Diwan mimed a man wrapping a cloak around himself. "Like this, you see?"

"The Djinndurum wrap spirits around themselves," Ekaterina said. "We'd heard rumours but—"

"Blasphemy!" Father Petru cried.

"Silence, priest." Lucian scowled at Petru. "What else?" he demanded, shifting his attention back to Diwan.

"The Djinndurum work together," Dumitru said. "Individually, they're not as powerful. But when combined in certain…shapes, their magiks strengthen."

"Geometric alignment, Most Excellent." Diwan dipped his head in defeat. "Tapping into their djinni—the spirits they house—is but one part of their art. It's the sacred geometry that magnifies their stolen power."

"How does that help us?" Lucian demanded. "They're always cloaked in shadows. Arrows and spears never touch them."

Dumitru smiled. "That's because they're not where they appear to be. But Diwan here, he knows their structures, their patterns. He knows where they'll be when the attack comes."

"And without the Djinndurum, the Ghazi will be vulnerable." Ekaterina stared at Dumitru. "Did you know about this?"

"Not all of it. We received news of an Ottoman merchant who refused to trade his goods. And the Djinndurum hadn't been seen for a while, as if they were waiting for something. All soldiers require supplies, don't they?" He gestured to Diwan. "But this is more than I dared hope for."

Father Petru sank to his knees. "This is the Lord's work. His divine benevolence."

"I thought my days would end in disgrace," Lucian rasped. "Cast from my ancestral home. My people enslaved. This is a mighty gift." He reached out a shaking hand. Dumitru rose painfully and took it. Lucian reached out to Ekaterina. After a moment's hesitation, she rose and joined them.

"United," Lucian murmured. "For me. Your Mother. Our people. Promise me."

Ekaterina pursed her lips, no doubt swallowing a bitter retort. She gave a tight nod. With an inward sigh of relief, Dumitru nodded as well.

United with his sister. If such a thing were truly possible, he would greet the Lord with a content heart.

Silviu was waiting for him at the foot of the keep. To the casual observer, Silviu was simply standing guard, the butt of his spear grounded in the hard-packed earth. Dumitru wasn't fooled. They had not had a chance to talk since arriving at Viscri and they may not get another.

"Ekaterina?" Silviu asked, peering up the stairs.

"With my father." Dumitru leaned against the wall of the tower keep. The cold night air helped shake off some of his lethargy.

"And the Ottoman?"

"Locked away, although not before admitting his dealings with the Djinndurum."

Silviu studied Dumitru. He was slightly taller and wider in the shoulder. "You can't trust him. He'd say anything to keep breathing."

"Perhaps, although he's smart enough to realise he's become a problem for Rakosh. I can trust that."

Silviu frowned. "I'm not comfortable with placing our fates in his hands."

"It will be us defending the walls, not him. But we must unravel the Djinndurum's secrets."

Dumitru realised he was sweating despite the chill. He wiped his brow with the back of his hand and his bad leg buckled. Silviu was at his side instantly, a strong arm around his waist.

"The things I have to do to get your attention," Dumitru whispered.

Silviu grinned and glanced around guiltily. Seeing they were unobserved, he planted a quick kiss on Dumitru's mouth. Dumitru grabbed him by the neck and returned the kiss with fierce desperation.

Silviu pulled away reluctantly. "Enough. That leg needs attention."

"It's not the only part."

Silviu bit back a laugh. "That might be so, but you need stitching up. And rest as well for the morrow."

Dumitru sighed. "I suppose some problems really can't wait." He let Silviu help him limp towards the stables. By the Saints he needed a mulled wine, or even better, a dash or three of *tsuika*. The plum spirit would warm him from the inside and numb some of the pain he was about to endure.

Dumitru paused outside the stables. "You brought it?"

"Of course," Silviu murmured. "Hard to forget when you remind me a dozen times a day."

"And you've checked it," Dumitru pressed. "The mechanism is oiled. The bolts are true."

"Yes, 'Mitru. All is ready. I just need a real target."

"Oh, you'll have it," Dumitru promised. "Now let's get me stitched up." The smell of blood and the sound of men groaning in pain greeted him as he limped into the stables.

Cosmin hailed him: "Where have you been?"

Silviu followed, to all outward appearances a dutiful body-guard to his lord.

Ekaterina made Lucian as comfortable as she could after Dumitru left. They had been locked in, so there was little else to do.

While clearly exhausted, Lucian resisted sleep, shifting on his creaking pallet and shivering beneath his heavy furs. It pained her to see him reduced to this, a shell of what he had once been. Rakosh had done this to her father. She could not argue with Dumitru over that. But you could not change the past, only the future you stepped into.

Ekaterina hunched over the fire, prodding the embers to call forth more heat. With her hands busy, she turned over all that had been said like river stones, hoping to find new meanings on the hidden sides.

She was the subtle one of Lucian's children. *She* was the one who made plans, who thought through consequences and made decisions that would advance the interests of their family. Dumitru—ever the little brother—had always been the anxious one.

Anxious to please.

Anxious to avoid missing out.

Anxious to be accepted.

As a result, he always rushed in, heedless of the situation, mistaking swift decisions for decisive ones.

That's what had happened with the raid earlier today. Dumitru had rushed in, sword brandished, to save his sister with no thought for the deaths that ensued. Or at least that's what she had assumed. But after discovering the significance of the merchant, she realised that her supposed rescue was intended to conceal Dumitru's true target.

Did Rakosh realise what Dumitru had accomplished? Or did he merely assume Dumitru had tried to protect the honour of his family? Despite her earlier claims, she didn't know Rakosh well. The Emir struck her as both arrogant and vain. So, if she were forced to guess, Rakosh would probably assume Dumitru had acted impulsively.

"Clever, Dumitru. I'll give you that," she murmured to the flames.

"You should tell him," Lucian said.

Ekaterina turned in surprise. She thought her father had finally succumbed to sleep. Clearing her throat, she said, "He's reckless as it is. I see no reason to encourage him."

"Huh. So, you think being careful will rid us of the Ottomans."

Ekaterina pursed her lips. No point scowling at her father. It never did any good. "I never said that."

Lucian struggled up onto one elbow. "Then perhaps boldness is what we need?"

"If by boldness you mean risking all our lives, I'm not sure I agree."

"Rakosh is not a man to be controlled. In your heart, you know this. But you fight with the weapons you've been given. Dumitru is merely doing the same. Can you not respect that?"

"We already tried fighting them." Ekaterina flung her hand out. "Our fortress at Cohalm was better defended than this church. We had more men. Trained soldiers, not smallfolk. And we still lost."

"I remember," Lucian replied. "The ghost of that day haunts my every waking moment. Most of my dreams as well."

"Then why encourage this madness? Why can't you make Dumitru see what he's risking?"

"Oh, Kat. He knows what he's risking. If you were to have your way and you married that vile Emir, do you have any idea what you'd be risking?"

She tried to picture life with Rakosh: a squalling brat clutching her leg and another in her belly, one of but many wives, sequestered away in a harem. Persuasion required a man's attention, did it not? Could she really sway such a man?

"Ah. Now you understand. I see it in your face." Lucian subsided, whatever reserves of strength he had drawn upon now expended.

Ekaterina knelt next to his pallet and took his thin, dry hand. "Understand what, father?"

"Dumitru loves you too much to leave you to the fate you so rashly embrace." Lucian closed his eyes. His breathing deepened and became regular.

Ekaterina sat on her heels. She had never considered 'Mitru might be trying to protect her.

After a while, she returned to the fire. Now seemed like a good time to pray.

The sky was the colour of slate when he was shaken from his exhausted slumber. Dumitru struggled to his feet feeling like he had barely closed his eyes. Much of the night had been spent questioning Diwan in detail, poring over sketches of the church's walls and anticipating the Djinndurum's likely lines of attack. Now that day was almost upon them, he could only hope their preparations would suffice.

Lucian had recovered some semblance of his former self. With the aid of two sturdy priests, he was carried down to the nave of the church to address his former subjects, urging them to fight and warning of the likely slaughter should they fail. It was a greater contribution than Dumitru had hoped for.

When Dumitru emerged outside, the first blush of dawn silhouetted figures in thick furs manning the walls. The sentries numbered far more souls than the survivors of his band, so Lucian's pleas had been heeded.

Dumitru limped to the nearest set of stairs and climbed up to the battlements. His injured hip felt tight and unnaturally hot. That boded ill, but given his chances of living out the day were slim at best, it was hardly worth dwelling upon.

Cosmin was staring into the thick mist curling through the trees with two of the village elders.

"Can't see the bastards," Cosmin muttered. "Caught the muffled jingle of tack and a stray horseshoe on stone. They're mustering down there, no shadow of a doubt."

Dumitru peered in the direction Cosmin pointed. The fog was so thick the nearest trees were vague suggestions and the sun was a watery blur peeking over the horizon. Dumitru thought he caught snatches of whispered conversations in a foreign tongue.

Dumitru turned to the Viscri elders, nervous-looking men at least twice his age. One held a bow, the other a spear. Both weapons had seen better days. "The Djinndurum will try to sap our will. I can't say how, although I'm told every man experiences something different."

"Like what?" one of the elders asked.

Dumitru shrugged. "A sense of something creeping up behind you. Maybe the shade of a lost relative. Even insects crawling across your skin. Tell your men such things cannot touch them on this holy ground. Tell them to stand firm and put their faith in Christ. If they do, the Emir will be forced to demand our surrender. Don't waste arrows on him because they'll never find their mark. We need to draw the Djinndurum out so we can send them back to whatever hell they crawled from. Then all we must face is men, not demons. Understood?"

The two elders nodded, although neither looked convinced. Dumitru's people would need courage to resist the Djinndurum's magiks and faith was their most effective shield.

"Good. Pass the word. And tell your men to wait for solid targets." The elders hurried off in opposite directions along the wall.

"You really have a plan?" Cosmin cleared his throat. "To end the Djinndurum, I mean." It wasn't like Cosmin—usually so impassive—to seek reassurance.

Dumitru tried for a confident smile. "I do. Just hold the wall for me."

Cosmin grinned. "Hope I live long enough to piss on their carcasses."

"As do I." Dumitru clapped him on the shoulder. "Thank you, Cosmin. You've stood with me from the beginning and I won't forget that."

"No thanks needed for doing the right thing," Cosmin replied, his voice gruffer than usual.

Dumitru nodded and moved along the wall to the north-eastern guard tower. Silviu and Diwan were waiting for him, a wrapped bundle at Silviu's feet.

"Well?" Dumitru demanded.

"Any time now, Most Excellent," Diwan replied. "I have measured the length of your wall and double-checked my calculations. Your man here knows where to aim." Diwan bowed nervously. "I am a scholar, Gracious Master, not a warrior. I fear I'll only be in the way up here."

Silviu grabbed a fistful of the merchant's robe.

Dumitru studied the merchant. "Wouldn't a scholar be curious to see if his calculations were correct?"

Diwan's face paled in the weak sunlight. "Curiosity is not a virtue when the consequences of an error are so high."

"Then you may need to make some rapid adjustments," Dumitru replied.

"I sincerely hope not, Honoured Lord." Diwan lapsed into an unhappy silence. Silviu gave Dumitru a warning look. So much depended on the merchant. Dumitru had no choice but to trust in Diwan's instinct for self-preservation.

Long moments passed by. The sky gradually lightened. No birds welcomed the day, no dogs barked in the village below. The fog muffled all sound. Occasionally a sentry murmured to another or pointed out a half-glimpsed movement.

Dumitru felt alone despite the men standing within arm's reach. He had brought them to this point, to the brink of annihilation, all because he could not accept Rakosh's rule. Was that leadership or was it the worst kind of hubris? Would his people curse his name after today? Would Viscri become a byword for disaster, a warning to echo down the ages?

The thought was a thorn beneath his skin, gouging his conscience. He had never been the son his father had wanted, never the one born to rule. Surely all *this* was a belated attempt to win his father's approval…to prove all his doubters wrong. Maybe Ekaterina was right, maybe he *was* just pretending.

The frigid air dried Dumitru's throat. His ribs tightened, constricting his chest. Silviu moaned, whether in pain or fear Dumitru could not tell.

So alone.

So isolated.

Movement flickered through the fog. Dumitru stared, transfixed by the hint of wings. A prickling cold stole over him. Doom circled overhead, each pass bringing it ever closer.

A shape burst from the mist and swooped so low it barely cleared the battlements.

Dumitru ducked, terror coursing through his limbs. The

apparition circled and dove towards him again. Dumitru cowered, unable to hide from what surely must be the Angel of Death. Black-feathered wings fanned out from a sinuous body that was both woman and serpent. Tattered grey rags streamed from it, the tips crusted with dried blood.

The Angel screamed, and as it wheeled, he saw it wore Ekaterina's face. Dumitru knew—with absolute certainty—that she was his doom. She always had been.

Something tugged on his arm.

"These visions, they cannot touch you, Gracious Master. Not unless you let them." The heavily accented words were pained, as if ground out with great effort.

Dumitru blinked. The Angel—Ekaterina—was banking for another pass. Her body twisted like an eel through water. Rough hands dragged his gaze away. Diwan crouched next to him, pinching Dumitru's cheeks in desperation. Silviu remained upright, shaking head to foot, with God knew what horrors assailing him.

"The Djinndurum cannot tear down walls," Diwan said through clenched teeth. "They cannot burst open gates or slay a man with a word. But they can unlock your minds if you let them. Strike now, Honoured Master, or we have lost before we even begin."

Dumitru turned towards the main gate, expecting any moment to feel the Angel's talons sinking into his neck. His sentries had crumpled to the ground or thrown down their weapons and fled. The wall was undefended.

Anger stirred in the pit of Dumitru's belly. Rakosh must be laughing, assured of yet another victory.

The Angel screamed again and Dumitru flinched. He had a duty to his people. He must protect them, no matter the cost.

Duuuumitruuuu, the Angel taunted him.

"They cannot touch you." Diwan's voice was etched with desperation.

"Good folk of Viscri," called a new voice. "Why do you bar your gates against your lord?"

"He's here." Diwan dropped down behind a merlon.

Rakosh, Emir of the Ottoman Empire, strolled from the thick

mist encircling White Church. Beneath his peaked helmet, a thick moustache dominated his lean face. His long, dark hair was oiled and tied in a neat queue that hung past his shoulders. A polished mail shirt protected him from throat to knee and a red sash cinched his narrow waist.

Despite Dumitru's orders, at least one defiant archer loosed an arrow. It passed harmlessly above Rakosh's left shoulder and he dismissed it with a casual wave of his hand. The Angel pealed with laughter and circled Dumitru.

"You have been led astray by the son of a fallen lord. I do not blame you for this, people of Viscri. After all, your place is to obey."

Rakosh spread his hands in the universal gesture of peace. "Open your gates, surrender this Dumitru to me, and return my bride unharmed. Do this, and you may continue your day unmolested. Defy me and you will face my wrath. What shall it be?"

The few men still manning the walls looked askance at one another. The offer was reasonable, wasn't it? Even Dumitru saw the sense in it.

Diwan jabbed Dumitru's injured hip. A jolt of pain shot down his leg and Dumitru gasped. The unexpected agony broke Rakosh's hold over him. Somehow the Djinndurum had shifted the focus of their magiks from fear to persuasion. Already two villagers stumbled down the steps, weeping in their haste to throw open the main gate.

"Silviu, it's time."

Dumitru stood, his body trembling. A single tear leaked from the corner of Silviu's eye and ran unheeded down his bearded cheek.

"Silviu!" Dumitru shook his lover, but Silviu did not respond. His gaze was fixed inwards on whatever horror the Djinndurum had conjured. There was no time to be gentle. Dumitru backhanded Silviu across the face. His bodyguard stumbled and crashed into the side of a merlon.

"The crossbow," Dumitru snapped. "Now."

Silviu blinked in confusion, one hand touching his split lip. Dumitru unwrapped the bundle and thrust the heavy crossbow into Silviu's hands. Rays from the rising sun caught the silver filigree worked through the yew stock. "Now, for the love of God!"

Silviu nodded, his expression hardening. Planting the crossbow on the timber beams, he put one foot through the stirrup and drew the wax-coated string up until it locked against the nut. Quickly selecting a bolt, he placed it in the groove and hefted the crossbow.

While the mist obscured everything to the naked eye, the edge of the graveyard beneath the outer wall was just visible. Using his knowledge of the Djinndurum's sacred geometry, Diwan had calculated the spirit-binders would form a pentagram around the diamond-shaped church. If that was correct, then one of them should be positioned less than twenty-five strides from the tower directly in line with the wall.

"Well?" Rakosh called out. "I'm waiting."

Ekaterina emerged from the gatehouse. She had swapped her dress for a boiled leather vest, breeches and a small, recurved bow favoured by the Ghazi cavalry. Her back was rigid, suggesting she was not immune to the Djinndurum's influence. "Rakosh, there is no need for this. I am not a prisoner here."

Rakosh scowled. "I've lost six soldiers defending you. Their spirits would argue otherwise."

Ekaterina waved this detail aside. "I have communed with God in this holy church, and I believe it is His will that we should no longer marry."

"That is not for you to decide. Come down," Rakosh demanded. "Otherwise, everyone within these walls will die and I'll give you to the Djinndurum."

Ekaterina visibly paled. With shaking fingers, she drew an arrow from her quiver. "You would have been a poor excuse for a husband anyway."

"Silviu, now, while they're distracted," Dumitru murmured.

Silviu aimed at a target he could not see, took a long deep breath, held it, and squeezed the trigger. The bolt hissed through the mist.

Rakosh spun in their direction.

An unearthly scream, so high-pitched it was almost a whine, suddenly swirled around the walls of the church. The mist tore open, as if invisible beasts were ripping it to shreds. Rakosh's figure blurred and suddenly he was standing a dozen strides from where he had first appeared.

The Angel gave a shrill cry of despair. Its serpentine body coiled, tighter and tighter, until it became a blurring knot that devoured itself.

The mist exploded in a sudden rush of air. The whispering voices Dumitru had caught before swarmed past before fading into the distance.

With the fog gone, the nearest Djinndurum was exposed. He was naked, but for a loincloth, with skin so pale the web of blue veins and darker arteries were visible. Small, geometric tattoos stood out at various points on his body: feet, hands, the centre of his chest, his bare skull. Each pulsed with dark blood and emitted a sickly hue. If Dumitru had encountered an animal like this, he would have killed it without hesitation, burnt the remains, and called it a mercy.

Silviu's bolt had punched a hole through the Djinndurum's gut and emerged the far side, splattering the ground in foul blood that hissed as it congealed upon the snow. The Djinndurum sank to his knees with a hiss, although whether in pain or frustration, Dumitru could not tell. It looked up at the battlements with sunken eyes that reminded Dumitru of the sky reflected at the bottom of a deep well.

The Djinndurum's lips curved in a grotesque imitation of a smile and it toppled, face first, into the snow. Steam rose from around the body as the tattoos flickered and faded to the colour of ash.

Dumitru had expected to feel elation at this triumph, but he couldn't shake the feeling the Djinndurum was grateful for its death.

Stripped of the concealing fog, the Ghazi soldiers were suddenly exposed. They had deployed less than fifty strides from the main gate, well within bow shot. Dumitru quickly estimated their number at forty, maybe a handful more.

"You hit one," Diwan said, wonder in his voice.

"Hopefully, it won't be the last," Dumitru replied. "Go with Silviu. Run. Before they can regroup."

Silviu snatched up his bundle of bolts with his free hand and sprinted towards the next tower. Diwan ran after him, hunched over to avoid being seen.

According to Diwan, the Djinndurum would be dazed by the loss of one of their number. Something to do with lost anchors, inflection points and recoiling energies. None of that made any sense to Dumitru. What he did understand was they had gained a temporary advantage.

"You men," Dumitru shouted.

The two villagers struggling with the beam securing the front gate froze at the authority in Dumitru's voice.

He stabbed a finger at them. "Back to the wall. The lives of your families depend upon it."

An arrow whirred past Dumitru, only a few hands wide from its target. Rakosh was already marshalling his troops, no doubt furious one of his precious Djinndurum had fallen. Dumitru ducked out of sight and shouted at his men to loose.

A ragged volley of arrows dropped into the Ghazi camp, far fewer than Dumitru had hoped for. At least the defenders were no longer paralysed. He spotted Ekaterina drawing and releasing a shaft. That would shame the other defenders into finding their courage.

Another unearthly howl rose from the back of the church and unseen spirits streaked past. Silviu's bolt must have found another Djinndurum. For the first time in months, Dumitru felt real hope. Then the Ghazi began their assault and there was no more time to think.

The villagers were always going to be hard pressed to hold the wall. They lacked sufficient numbers to properly defend all the approaches. Worse still, they lacked the training. Arrows repeatedly missed their marks. Villagers armed with staves and rusted spears were no match for armoured Ghazi, even if the latter were scaling icy walls.

Dumitru rushed from skirmish to skirmish, forcing the Ghazi back with a spear that became slicked with blood. The ache in his hip almost became too fierce to bear and the wound reopened. His thirst intensified as the day wore on.

Yet despite all their deficiencies, they managed to repel the Ghazi as the weak sun climbed overhead and dipped back towards the far horizon. After each failed attack, the Ghazi regrouped and devised new approaches to stretch the defenders as thinly as possible. As the siege wore on, both sides suffered heavy casualties.

During a brief respite, Silviu confirmed the Djinndurum had fled, having lost a second member of their brethren. Diwan did not think they would return. At least not any time soon. After orchestrating victory after victory for Rakosh, the Djinndurum were unaccustomed to defiance, let alone losses.

There had been a faint hope that Rakosh might withdraw, deeming the price of the siege too high. That hope wilted during the course of battle. The Emir became more furious with every unsuccessful attempt to breach the walls.

The Ghazi conducted repeated raids, standing up in their stirrups as they approached the walls and hurling grappling irons over the battlements. Their archers peppered the defenders as the riders scaled up the icy sides of the outer wall. These attempts were usually masked by feints elsewhere.

They were being ground down, but there was nothing Dumitru could do about it. If they could hold out until nightfall, the Ghazi would be forced to endure another bitter night's cold without resupply. Scaling the walls at night would be virtually impossible and Dumitru's people would take heart from their success.

The breach, once it was finally established, claimed Cosmin's life. A well-placed arrow took him in the shoulder and nearly knocked him off the battlements. Stubborn as always, Cosmin caught his balance and rushed the first Ghazi squeezing through an embrasure. A second arrow caught Cosmin in the face as he brought his sword up for a double-handed blow. He toppled off the battlements, his body already limp.

A handful of villagers rushed to repel the attack. The first Ghazi over the wall was able to hold them at bay long enough for a second and then a third warrior to join him. Together, the Ottomans swept the villagers aside in a flurry of scimitars. Dumitru was too far away to prevent their surge towards the tower house guarding the main gate.

"Back to the church," Dumitru bellowed. "Get back now." Dumitru lurched to the nearest set of steps and limped down as quickly as he could manage. Many of the villagers threw down their weapons and fled for the temporary safety of the church.

Dumitru hooked the elbow of one of the elders. "Get archers in the tower," he snarled. "And barricade the doors to the church. We'll keep them out as long as we can."

The elder hurried off, his expression one of sheer terror. Dumitru doubted the man took in a single word.

The Ghazi had routed the defenders from the gatehouse and were lifting the heavy timbers barring the main gate. Villagers streamed past Dumitru into the church in panic. What had been a battle moments ago had become a rout.

"We almost had them, didn't we?"

Dumitru turned to find Silviu smiling ruefully at him. A cut had taken half of his lover's earlobe and left a nasty gash along the side of his neck. Blood caked his dark hair and more was spattered over his mail shirt. He still clutched the precious crossbow.

Weariness suddenly pressed its advantage. The world tilted and Dumitru stumbled, squeezing his eyes shut against the vertigo. Silviu caught his elbow. The weakness passed, leaving certainty in its wake.

"Almost isn't enough."

Silviu frowned.

"Do you have any bolts left?"

"Only one."

"Get up there." Dumitru pointed at the window slit where his father had been housed in the tower keep. "When Rakosh arrives, put it through his chest."

"I'm not leaving you."

"If you stay, who will avenge us? Now go." Dumitru gave him a hard shove. Silviu stumbled, caught his balance and let the cross-bow fall to the ground.

"No. That's not what we promised each other."

Dumitru shook his head, angry at the temptation he felt to let Silviu remain. "I know, but that promise was made when I thought our lives were ours to do with as we pleased. I see now that I was wrong."

Silviu remained unmoved, wrestling with whatever he wanted to say.

"Please, Silviu. I can't face Rakosh with you by my side. I need…to know there's a chance. Do you understand?"

Silviu shook his head.

"Besides, someone must see to my sister. Do this for me. Please." Dumitru staggered forward and quickly embraced his lover.

Silviu pressed his face into Dumitru's neck. "I can't watch you die."

"Then don't miss." Dumitru pushed him away. "Go." The Ghazi were deploying in the courtyard. Time had run out.

Unshed tears brimmed in Silviu's eyes. His gaze slid past Dumitru to the gate and his expression darkened. Angrily, he snatched up the crossbow and plunged into the depths of the church.

The stream of people rushing past Dumitru had dwindled. Stiffly, he knelt in the snow and offered a final prayer, asking that the Lord should excuse his failings and look kindly upon his soul when it arrived shortly. He lay his sword down, the hilt facing the gates.

The Ghazi found him that way, blood seeping into the snow, his head bowed. All the entrances to the church had been barricaded. Not a single man had chosen to stand with Dumitru. After all, he was the one Rakosh wanted.

Dumitru was counting on it.

Rakosh and his men approached cautiously, their round cavalry shields up, expecting a trap. Dumitru remained kneeling. His tired muscles were cramping in the chill and the blood leaking from his wound had left him feeling lightheaded. He just needed to hold on a little longer.

"So, they abandon you at the last." Rakosh approached warily, his dark eyes flickering across arrow slits and up to the roofline of the church.

Dumitru gathered the remnants of his dignity. "Your presence on this hallowed ground is an offence before God. Leave immediately or suffer His wrath."

"Let him strike me down then." Rakosh spat on the ground and shook his shield at the church.

Dumitru chose that moment to grab his knife, which he had hidden under a dusting of snow, and lunged forward, the blade aimed at the artery that ran down the inside of the leg just above the groin. Even with the advantage of surprise, the wiry Ottoman was too quick. Sidestepping Dumitru's desperate lunge, Rakosh parried and swung his sabre in a backhand arc that parted chainmail links and scored Dumitru's back.

Dumitru rolled onto his side before the pain could register and slashed at Rakosh's calf. The blow lacked strength and Rakosh leapt back. A spear tip lanced Dumitru's thigh, piercing his mail shirt and pinning him to the ground. A booted heel slammed into his shoulder. Something snapped and he lost all feeling in his arm. Dumitru cried out in anguish as the knife was wrenched from his grasp.

"Pathetic." Rakosh loomed over Dumitru and spat just as a crossbow bolt whistled past. It grazed Rakosh's helmet before thudding into the Ghazi standing behind him.

Dumitru fell back onto the snow. Silviu had missed. He would probably never forgive himself. Rakosh raised his shield belatedly.

"Get away from my son." Lucian emerged from the far side of the tower keep. He had found a sword somewhere, but was still dressed in his bed robe.

Rakosh laughed. "Yes, let's make a clean ending of this. As we should have done in Cohalm."

Lucian swung a tottering, double-handed blow at Rakosh's side. The Emir parried with ease. Squinting through the pain of his wounds, Dumitru was stunned to see his father block Rakosh's first riposte. Rakosh slashed with his sabre again and Lucian barely managed to parry. Off balance and stumbling backwards, Lucian raised his guard in anticipation of the next blow. Rakosh stepped in and shunted the blade aside with his shield. Almost casually, he slashed backhanded in a diagonal arc, slicing open Lucian's chest and catching the side of his throat.

Dumitru's father reeled backwards and tumbled to the ground. Rakosh rolled him over with the toe of his boot and stared into Lucian's face. "I see no God here."

Dumitru tried to curse, but he could only manage bubbles of blood.

"All hail Rakosh, slayer of old men and the injured."

Rakosh turned towards the new voice. Ekaterina stood at the top of the gatehouse. She had drawn her bow so deeply the arrow's fletching brushed her earlobe. Even as Dumitru registered her presence, the shaft leapt into flight and jutted from Rakosh's stomach before he could blink. The Emir stumbled backwards, a confused expression on his face. Ekaterina loosed two more arrows in quick succession. One lodged in Rakosh's leg, the other feathered his chest. The Emir toppled to the ground. He twitched for a moment and lay still.

The Ghazi stood frozen in astonishment. Ekaterina sent three more shafts into their midst, her hands a blur. Silviu must have found a bow, because arrows whistled down from the tower as well.

The Ghazi broke, fleeing the church without any sign of formation.

Dumitru could not move. The trampled snow eased the fire burning down his back. The sky above was a milky white.

More snow on the way, he thought.

It would be nice to drift like the clouds above. Unbound from the responsibilities of the world. Free to wander wherever the wind might take him.

Kat's face swam into view, her lips moving. Rain dripped on his cheeks. Or were they Kat's tears?

He felt he should say something.

Something…important.

Yes.

But the thought drifted away.

And Dumitru joined the clouds.

They carried Lucian and Dumitru into the church, laying them out on hastily prepared cots. While the mood was more of shock than grief, Kat was gratified her father and brother received the respect they were due.

Dumitru had killed at least two of the Djinndurum and routed the Ghazi. Father was dead, along with most of Dumitru's followers. And she had killed her betrothed. Kat shook her head.

It was too impossible to be believed. And too soon to be accepted.

As for now, well…she was the last of her line. Alone in a hostile world that did not embrace female rulers.

That thought was entirely too terrifying to encompass. She shied away from it, refused to consider its implications. "Later," she whispered.

"My lady?" Silviu knelt on Dumitru's other side. He had refused to let anyone carry Dumitru's body. Now he stood vigil over his lover, red-eyed and raw with a guilt that was painful to witness. Here was someone who had lost a person they loved deeply.

Well, they had that much in common at least.

"I didn't believe in him." Ekaterina caressed Dumitru's matted hair. "And now I can't tell him I was wrong." She was leaking. Leaking out all her pain and sorrow and regret. Would it ever end?

Silviu cleared his throat. "He said…told me, that is, to protect you."

Ekaterina bowed her head. Even after all she had put him through. "I don't deserve it."

"Even so." Silviu's voice was rough with emotion. "Now that's he gone, I need—" He couldn't finish the sentence.

"You need something to keep going." Kat nodded. Yet another thing they could agree upon.

Someone cleared their throat.

Kat turned. A small knot of men waited uncertainly at the far end of the church. They had caught Diwan.

Glad of the distraction, Kat walked over to face them. Hesitating, Silviu followed.

"Caught him trying to sneak off." The elder jabbed Diwan in the side.

"Please, Lovely Mistress. I did everything the Gracious Master asked. The remaining Djinndurum, they will look for me. They will realise I betrayed them."

"I expect you're right," Ekaterina replied. "But how long do you think you'll survive out there? A single Ottoman, unaccustomed to our winter, with word spreading of what happened here."

Diwan nodded. "That is why haste is called for. Every moment is precious. Will you honour your brother's pledge to free me?"

Father Petru and his priests were waiting. She could feel their impatience for the intrusions of the world to pass beyond their walls. And the villagers of Viscri had assembled outside to pay their final respects to their fallen lords. How many of the villagers had been killed? And who wept for them?

"These men you called spirit-binders," Ekaterina said. "They are demons, an abomination in the eyes of my God, and surely yours. I saw your courage in the face of the Djinndurums' magiks. Tell me truly, are you content serving such creatures?"

Diwan shook his head with a rueful expression. "Magnificent Lady, I was never given a choice."

Ekaterina stared into Diwan's eyes, into the eyes of a man she would have named an enemy only yesterday. "I grant you the gift of choice now. Will you accept it?"

He studied her, one hand twisting his beard between thumb and forefinger. All pretence of subservience fell away. "You have surprised me once today. I will admit I did not expect it to happen a second time."

"Is that a yes?"

"It is, my Ferocious Princess. I pledge myself to you." Diwan knelt on one knee and kissed the back of her hand.

Ekaterina's spirits lifted, which was a wonder in itself. What was her next move? Send emissaries across the Bran Pass into Wallachia in search of allies? Learn more of the Djinndurum, as much as Diwan knew, until every weakness was exposed? Then hunt them down. Every last one.

Silviu suddenly seized Ekaterina's arm in a fierce grip and pointed towards Dumitru's body. His mouth tried to shape words, but it was beyond him.

Ekaterina saw what he was pointing at and froze. A faint nimbus surrounded Dumitru's body, so pale it was only visible in the confines of the church.

They were waiting for him in the courtyard, arranged in a loose semicircle. Not as the men he had bled with but the essence of those men, all the humour and the hopes that had defined them in life made manifest in the shape of men.

He supposed he should have expected a reception of some kind, but dying has a way of occupying one's attention.

Ciprian. Emilian. Serghei. Neculai. Cosmin.

All his fallen comrades.

Even his father.

All waiting for him, radiating a sense of contentment and pride and love for him that was so intense it made him want to weep, if such a thing was still possible. He wanted to embrace them, to join their brotherhood, and never be parted from it again.

He took a step forward, or at least tried to. The very air seemed to resist him. His father smiled, the expression layered with so many emotions it was impossible to interpret. They were drawing apart, even though no one moved. The space between him and his comrades was changing, moving from unconditional acceptance into a reluctant leave-taking. The pride and love for him remained, but the world he had been allowed to glimpse was shutting him out.

A fleeting welcome followed by a parting of the ways.

He strained forward, reaching out, trying to hold onto that precious feeling of brotherhood. After all they had endured together, he could not let them just go.

His father smiled. Didn't Silviu wait for him on the other side of the veil? And what of Kat, who had sided with her brother when it really counted?

These tangled emotions weighed him down, drew him back to the earth, to the painful and flawed existence that is life.

His father sent a final outpouring of love and pride so intense it threatened to burst through every part of him, accompanied by a plea.

A plea for patience.

For the completing of things not finished.

For the closing of circles that had been broken before their time.

He did not want to take up burdens that had only just been set aside. Yet another part of him insisted that it was right. And besides, it was not entirely his choice. After everything his father and companions had sacrificed, did they not have a say in this?

The pull of responsibility intensified. And he did not resist.

Dumitru gasped, drawing in a shuddering breath. Pain sank its teeth into his flesh and flensed him to the very marrow. Dumitru moaned, too weak and disoriented to do anything else. The remnants of the communion he had experienced were already fading. He struggled to hold on to the feeling of belonging, of unity, but like a vivid dream, it burned away with the dawn of consciousness.

A sob escaped him. The parting felt so final. Alone, isolated, just as the Angel of Death had taunted him. Surely, he did not deserve this. Not after everything he had given.

A soft hand touched his brow. A face leaned over him, breathless words tumbling down, tears spilling.

He told his eyes to focus. Reluctantly, they obeyed.

Ekaterina swam into view. Her eyes were wild, the beautiful, poised mask she always wore finally discarded, so that her shock and wonder were naked and untempered. And Silviu. On his other side, kneeling it seemed. His head pressed against Dumitru's battered hand. Weeping uncontrollably. Tears enough for both of them.

Others rushed around behind them. A healer was called for.

And water and bandages. The world pressed in upon him, reass-erting its claim.

And at last he understood what his father and the others had wished for him. It was not forever, only a lifetime. And despite the pain, and the anguish of their loss, he accepted their decision. Accepted that perhaps he deserved this second chance, and all that he—no, *they*—might make of it.

Gently, Kat and Silviu drew him back from the brink and staunched his wounds.

Afterword

"Remnants" was first published in Issue 11 of *Dimension6* by independent publisher Coeur de Lion. You can find all the back issues of *Dimension6* at: https://coeurdelion.com.au/dimension6/.

"Remnants" was also shortlisted for Best Fantasy Novella in the 2018 Aurealis Awards.

The story is loosely set during the Turkish occupation of Transy-lvania—circa 1550—after the Ottomans invaded the Kingdom of Hungary. (While Transylvania is part of modern Romania, it belonged to the Hungarian kingdom back then.) The story was inspired by a visit to a remote fortified church in a town called Viscri in January 2016.

It was a bitterly cold day. Snow blanketed the ground, and we had the site entirely to ourselves. A picturesque graveyard guarded the approach to the main gates, and I remember it was terribly quiet. No sound of cars in the distance or planes flying overhead. Given the remoteness of the setting and the lack of modern intrusions, it wasn't long before my literary antennae started twitching.

The story you have just read is the result of that visit and subsequent research. I hope it transported you to a different place and time

Black & Bitter, Thanks

Two coffee mugs sit on the scratched, laminated table that is the centrepiece of my kitchen. One is blue and chipped in half a dozen places. You might say it has character. The other is green and unremarkable.

I pour filtered coffee into each mug. My hands are steady, but the joints in my fingers ache, as they often do these days. Milk goes into the green cup, followed by sugar. More than is good for me. I don't add anything to the blue one. Steam curls above its rim like an accusing finger. Memory is hard and unforgiving, like a metaphysical spoon stirring the bitterness in.

It's raining outside. The sky is grey and oppressive, matching my mood.

The letter from the Department of Welfare Services is still propped against the windowsill. I should take it down. Or burn it.

I sit this way for a long time. Watching the long black cool. Sipping my own diluted brew. Wishing I had the courage for something stronger. Remembering someone who did.

We met in a bar. One of those forgotten pubs that felt like an RSL, except it wasn't. Dozens of unemployed, many of them not much older than me, congregated within its walls. They'd stare at you, as if you'd interrupted a family gathering, clutching their form guides and their fourth beer of the morning.

It was a Thursday. The monotony of my administrative role had driven me out of the office. I wasn't quite so old then, although if you looked closely in the reflection of my life, you could see time was about to tap me on the shoulder.

Beer in hand, I wandered through the intermittent gloom and tired furniture, restless without knowing why. Sunlight angled through grubby windows, strips of light slatting across the floor. The carpet was sticky, the smell of dead cigarettes overpowering. Hopelessness filled the air, thick as incense. You breathed it in and it knew you, knew that you were divorced and had no family that gave a shit about you, knew that you belonged here. *Welcome brother*, it seemed to say. *Welcome to the rest of your days.*

The clack of billiard balls drew me deeper into the pub.

I've always loved pool. It's a skilful game when played on a full-sized table. Clarence was holding court, giving two other guys a lesson and earning some beer money along the way. My first impression of him was a lasting one—he leaned over the table, broad face intent as he focused on a long pot, pale blue eyes narrowed beneath thick white eyebrows.

"Bad luck, mate. Do you wanna play for double or nothin'?"

They say a face can tell you the story of someone's life, but I reckon only the honest ones do. Clarrie's face was like that— uncompromising in its honesty, almost naked in its refusal to hide the harsh lessons life had written there. You could see it in the crow's feet when he smiled and even more so when he frowned. The jutting chin was argumentative by nature, although tempered by his ready grin and open demeanour.

Clarrie was a man who had opinions. That was a given. And he wasn't prepared to change them for anyone. Perhaps that was why I was drawn to him.

Other challengers had left a row of coins on the edge of the table. I dropped two bucks at the end of the queue and waited, content to remain in the shadows while I watched. Clarrie's old flannelette shirt and faded jeans suggested a construction background, but he carried himself with unexpected grace. He toyed with each opponent in turn, never letting anyone get on the black before he potted it.

He always did like to win.

When my turn came, I was lucky enough to sink one off the

break. I potted another three in quick succession and snookered him when I couldn't get a clear shot at any of my remaining balls.

"What did you say your name was?" Clarrie asked, peering at me beneath the green lamp suspended over the table.

"Keith," I replied.

He concentrated after this exchange, narrowly losing a black ball game. After I won, he insisted we play again, and the other players drifted away beneath his impassive stare.

Clarrie won the next five games in a row and I accepted this with unusually good humour. He bought me a beer afterwards and we spent the rest of the day talking about the way our lives were meant to be, the reasons for our failed marriages, the state of the economy, anything except how we actually felt about those things.

We bumped into each other again at the pub a week later. Clarrie was dressed in the same clothes he had worn the first time we met, but his eyes were bloodshot, and his speech slurred. I offered to buy him a coffee and he accepted, so we went to a cheap cafe near my flat. He was in no condition to walk home and couldn't afford a cab, so I suggested he bunk down at my place.

We talked in that aimless fashion when only one person is drunk, the conversation turning in circles as Clarrie struggled for coherency and I struggled to keep up with his thoughts. Eventually he fell asleep, head slumped on the laminated table in my kitchen. I left him to it, too self-conscious to move him.

The next morning, I woke to the sound of the kettle boiling and cupboards banging. I found Clarrie shuffling around my kitchen, white hair sticking up like a pissed off cockatoo's crest. He clutched a chipped blue mug in one hand and gave me a wild, accusatory look.

"You got any decent coffee in this place? Because I could bloody well do with some."

"Of course." I took the ground coffee from the fridge and set about exorcising his hangover. Clarrie watched me, running a knotted hand over the stubble on his chin.

"How do you take it?"

"Black and bitter, like me soul," he replied with no hint of self-deprecation. I smiled and we sat down across the table.

"You don't have anywhere to go, do you?"

Clarrie took a sip from his mug and nodded, whether in approval at the coffee or in agreement, I couldn't tell.

"Do you?" I'm not one to push, but in my experience, pride stiffens with age.

"Made me choices," Clarrie said, cradling the cup in his hands. "Have to stick by 'em." A lesser man would've tried to explain, but not Clarrie. That's when I realised that I needed him to stay, not the other way around. I needed his casual decisiveness, his uncompromising certainty, in my life. Besides, if I was honest, I was lonely as hell.

"You could stay with me for a bit," I offered. "If you want."

"Reckon that'd be all right," he said, and that's how it began. The letter didn't arrive until much later.

"You seen this?" Clarrie thumped the newspaper on the table, almost knocking over my coffee. His colour was high, cheeks puffed out and white stubble bristling.

"Good morning. I slept well, thank you."

"Look." He shoved the paper at me. The front page contained an article on the *Pension and Social Service Assessment Act*, or *PiSSA*, as Clarrie dubbed it. He'd highlighted sections of it with a yellow marker.

…dropping ratio of workers to retirees…over-reliance on government pensions…falling superannuation returns…continued immigration to bolster the economy…withdrawal of welfare inevitable…humane solutions required…

"Well?" he demanded.

"Well what?" I sipped my coffee, unsure what he expected of me.

"You're in the government. You should do somethin' about this!"

"Clarrie, I work for the local council, not the federal government. They're hardly going to listen to someone so far down the food chain."

"But they're talkin' about old folks like they're some sort of burden on society. What about the buildin' sites I worked on? The taxes I paid? OK, so I didn't fight in the war, but I done me share." He banged the table with a clenched fist.

"Clarrie," I began, surprised by the violence.

"I never asked for nothin', you hear. They kicked me out of me apartment because I couldn't pay the rent and I copped that. But it's not right, this ballot system. It's not bloody humane at all. And you shouldn't be sittin' on the fence." A flush crept down from the white roots of his hairline.

"What ballot system?"

"I'm not a drain on resources," he said and stormed from the room.

Not knowing what else to do, I finished reading the article. The government's proposal had been leaked by an anonymous official from the Department of Welfare Services. Despite the apparent veracity, I re-read the article and still couldn't believe it.

I went looking for Clarrie to tell him the Bill would never get past the Senate, but he'd left, no doubt in search of a more sympathetic audience. The apartment felt empty with him gone. In the silence I wondered where my outrage was. Why wasn't I as passionate about this as Clarrie? Another ten years or so and I'd be part of the target demographic. And the answer, when it came to me, was more shameful still—a man should know his limitations, what he can and can't achieve, especially at my age.

And it had been a long time since I'd felt young.

Clarrie dragged me along to the demonstrations. It was the first time I'd left the ranks of the silent majority, and while I felt uncomfortable, I was exhilarated as well. People from all walks of life turned out. The media interviewed bawling grandchildren seated on the shoulders of their grandparents. A cavalcade of senior citizens swarmed down Commonwealth Avenue in Canberra, their motorised wheelchairs clogging traffic. It would've been hilarious if it wasn't so tragic.

A small contingent of the protestors argued the economic value of the aged. They pointed out caring for grandchildren allowed parents to work. They talked about the aged care industry and the number of people it employed.

It was enough to force a referendum.

Accountants and economists appeared in commercial breaks, explaining their pension forecasts and warning of economic disasters to come. Senior citizens and their supporters responded, invoking the ANZAC spirit and the sacrifices of earlier generations to keep our country free. The campaign was bloody and ruthless. It ravaged the face of the nation and divided people like nothing had ever before.

In the end though, a majority of Australians, across most states, voted in favour of PiSSA.

The Act was passed six months later to massive public outcry. It was challenged in the High Court, which deemed it constitutional four to three. An appeal was lodged with the International Court of Human Rights, but to no avail.

The first annual pension ballot was held four months later.

I made Clarrie wear a suit. He hated the stiff formality of it, but it made him look presentable. As an employee of the Council, I was required to assist with the local broadcast. I'll never forget that first group of candidates—retirees without independent income, scared and bewildered by how society had turned its back on them. I spent the day on the verge of tears, giving directions, handing out water, hating myself for being part of this, but wanting to provide comfort where I could.

The speeches were the worst.

A quivering, emaciated lady who could barely stand unassisted: "My name is Celia Leyton and I'm ninety-three. Please don't vote for me to lose my pension because I have seven grandchildren and eleven great-grandchildren."

An Asian gentleman with a thick accent: "I am Henry Ling. I am seventy-nine year of age. You not vote for me because I am still active member of community."

A florid-faced, portly fellow: "I'm Thomas Linton and I've lived in this electorate for the last sixty years. Paying me a pension is just returning some of the taxes I've paid over that time. What's that? Speak up, will you. Oh, I'm eighty-four."

And so it went, a parade of outraged, tearful or terrified senior citizens having to justify themselves to a faceless telecast.

Until it was Clarrie's turn.

He stomped into the broadcasting zone and glared at the camera. "I'm Clarence Lyndall. I'm seventy-nine years of age and you're all bastards for lettin' this happen." That was it. He had another forty-five seconds to plead his case but refused to dignify the whole process with another word.

I wanted to scream and cheer at the same time.

The next pensioner took his place, fumbling with the microphone and stuttering. I took Clarrie by the elbow and dragged him to one side. "What the hell was that?" I asked in a low voice.

"The voice of conscience," Clarrie replied, tilting his chin.

"Jesus, Clarrie, do you know what's at stake?"

"'Course I bloody do. A simple thing called human dignity. Reckon you should think about that." He glanced around the makeshift studio with a scornful expression and I released his arm.

"I'll see you back at the flat when you're done here." Clarrie walked off and all my arguments collapsed into self-loathing. Or perhaps that was just easier than doing something about the choices I hadn't made.

Ballot results were returned a week later. The letter from the Department of Welfare Services arrived three days after that.

"They're coming today, aren't they?"

Clarrie glanced up over the rim of his blue cup. "Yes." His voice was subdued, his eyes too bright.

"Why couldn't you just—"

He held his hand up, rebutting anything I might say. "Please. I never asked nothin' of you until now, Keith. Let's not fight about this."

But I couldn't let it go. "Are you trying to make a statement? Do you really think the world is listening?" My voice was rising, but I couldn't help it.

"Yes." His voice became softer as mine became louder, refusing to escalate the conflict.

"You're not that naïve."

"Reckon someone has to be."

"Clarrie, there aren't going to be any cameras. It won't be glorious, if that's what you're thinking."

"Then you must tell me story. Who else is gonna do it?" He drained his cup and left the room.

I picked up the mug and swirled the dregs, trying to find a way to dissuade him.

They rang the doorbell at precisely 8:00pm, just as the letter had promised. Under the cover of darkness, as Clarrie put it.

"Do you wanna get that?" Clarrie called in a breezy voice. I opened the door, my heart pounding. A young, clean-shaven man in a striped suit but no tie stood in the hall with a pair of armed security guards.

"Good evening. My name is Steven and I'm a private contractor working for the Department of Welfare Services." He checked his clipboard. "Is Mr Clarence Lyndall here?"

"No," I said, attempting to close the door. One of the guards caught the doorframe and gave me a warning look.

"Present," Clarrie called from the sofa in the lounge room.

"Show me your ID," I said, clutching at a breach in protocol.

Steven produced the required documentation, but still I hesitated.

"Sir, it's a federal offence to obstruct our work," Steven said. "We can force our way into your home if you prevent access to Mr Lyndall."

"Nothing would give you more pleasure, would it?"

"I'm just here to do a job," Steven the contractor replied. "It's up to you how unpleasant this has to be." The two guards shouldered past me and Steven followed them down the hallway into the living room.

Steven unplugged the TV at the socket and sat in a chair opposite Clarrie. "Mr Lyndall, do you understand why I'm here?" One of the guards took up position behind Clarrie. The other stood just behind my left elbow.

"Yeah, I know why you're here. Do you?" Clarrie gave him a wide smile and I could only admire his courage.

"Then you know that I am duly authorised by the government, under the Pension and Social Service Assessment Act, to enforce the pension ballot results," Steven said. "Do you understand these results?"

"Do you like your job, Steven?" Clarrie's expression didn't change, but I caught the subtle shift in his voice.

"That's not relevant, sir. Do you understand the results?"

"I'll answer your question if you answer mine first." The guard standing behind Clarrie shifted on his feet, but Steven shook his head.

"No sir, I don't particularly like my job. But the economics of our situation are irrefutable. I believe we have no choice but to allocate our resources to the future, not the past."

"Ah, the children." Clarrie smiled. "Really shoulda stuck with mine, in hindsight. I coulda watched them grow up to be like you."

Steven stiffened.

"Yeah, I understand the results," Clarrie said in a flat voice. "Let's get on with it."

"Very well." Steven opened his briefcase and withdrew a sheet of paper with a table of statistics. "These are the official results from the pension ballot, in descending order of votes. Is that your full name and date of birth?" Steven pointed at a row near the bottom of the page.

"It is." Clarrie's mouth had become a thin line and he began to tremble, finally. I bit my lip.

"And you understand the electorate has voted to discontinue your pension benefits effective immediately."

"Yep."

"Do you have any material assets to support yourself? Any foreign accounts or unrealised superannuation entitlements? An inheritance, perhaps?" Steven seemed to be reading an invisible script, distancing himself through professionalism.

"Nope."

I moved forward instinctively, but the guard's hand closed around my elbow. "Keep out of it," he murmured.

"Do you have anyone who can meet your financial obligations?" Steven asked.

"Yes," I said, straining against the guard's grip.

"No," Clarrie said at the same time. Steven hesitated, glancing between us.

"You can't afford it," Clarrie said in a gruff voice. "Not both of us. And I'll be buggered if I let you end up in me shoes."

"We can—"

"No." He turned back to Steven. "Keep going."

Steven had the decency to look uncomfortable before continuing. "Given the strain on the public welfare system and your lack of financial independence, it is government policy to relocate elderly citizens who lose the ballot to specialised care facilities. The nearest one is"—Steven made a show of consulting another sheet of paper—"just outside of Lithgow."

"You can't put him in a place like that," I protested. Being in local government, I knew the facility was once the Lithgow Correctional Centre, complete with unscalable walls and spotlights. During winter, it was one of the coldest and wettest places in the state. Hardly an ideal location for the aged and infirm. Other centres had been established around the country, the names synonymous with detention: Woomera, Villawood, Port Hedland.

"This is not America," Steven replied. "We don't abandon our people to the streets. Relocating senior citizens to a central facility is the only way the government can continue to support them."

"And heaven forbid the lucky country should be reminded what happens when you outlive your usefulness," I snapped.

"The referendum showed the majority of voters disagree," Steven said in a quiet voice. "We'll need your Medicare and Social Security cards," he said to Clarrie.

"Got 'em right here." Clarrie tossed the cards on the coffee table with a dismissive flick of the wrist. Unperturbed, Steven withdrew a compact card reader from his briefcase. He fed each card into the machine. It beeped once before spitting them out.

The magnetic strips were no doubt erased, just like Clarrie's future.

Steven put the reader back in his briefcase and snapped the locks. "Mr Lyndall, we're ready to transport you to the facility now. Do you have any belongings you can carry with you?"

Clarrie gave him a level stare.

"Mr Lyndall?"

"Got one bag in me room," Clarrie said with a nod in the direction of the second bedroom.

"Franks, get the bag," Steven said to the guard standing behind Clarrie.

"Christ, I can carry me own bloody bag." Clarrie stood and waved the guard off. "It's not like I got much, as you pointed out." Steven nodded at Franks, who followed Clarrie towards the bedroom.

Clarrie stopped in the doorway. "We can't help getting old, you know." Strangely, his gaze was fixed on me, not Steven.

I turned to Steven, assessing options for a last-minute reprieve—bribes, threats, an appeal to compassion—but he avoided my gaze. Clearly it had all been tried before.

Suddenly the lights in my apartment flickered and went out.

Someone cried out in the darkness, followed by a heavy thud. Steven and the guards shouted at each other. I rushed towards Clarrie's room, avoiding the furniture and flailing men. The smell of burning plastic filled my small apartment. Sparks arced into the darkness from the far wall of the bedroom.

A beam of light swept across the floor. Steven was at my shoulder, pushing me aside, as his torch probed the bedroom. I saw the knife first. One of my good butter knives, silver-plated, jammed into the power socket in the wall. Clarrie lay face-down on the floor, one hand twitching beneath the knife. Franks was swearing in a monotone voice that could've been mistaken for prayer, but he made no move to help.

Steven knelt next to Clarrie and checked his pulse. A minute later he stood, made a short call on his mobile and then ordered the guards out. "I'm sorry," was the most he could muster before he left.

Much later, after the ghastly circus of paramedics, counsellors and legal representatives had left with Clarrie's body, I collapsed on the couch.

I felt exhausted and abandoned, and then ashamed at being so selfish.

Time to go to work. Some stubborn, repetitive part of me knows this.

The funeral was held yesterday. Nobody came except me, the Reverend, and a government official, although he didn't stay very long. During the ceremony, I imagined composing a dozen different letters to the newspapers. I orchestrated a guerrilla campaign via the Internet. A letter drop in my electorate, vilifying them for killing the most honest man I've ever known.

None of these plans will be realised, of course. With Clarrie gone, it was past time for me to return to my place in the queue, to return to the silent, accepting masses. He'd made his protest and was met with a wall of indifference. Nothing had changed.

Clarrie's cup of cold coffee is still sitting on my kitchen table. I focus on it, channelling all the emotion I'm feeling, all the memories I hold.

C'mon, Clarrie. Give me a sign. Anything.

I don't know how long I sit that way, waiting for something to happen. My head is aching and I feel hollow.

Next week is my fifty-seventh birthday. The council's mandatory retirement age is sixty, but that policy might change once the older civil servants realise what "specialised care facilities" really means. I imagine my contemporaries planning their ballot speeches, wheedling their way into charities and philanthropic causes, justifying their existence.

The images make me nauseous.

The letter is waiting for me on the windowsill. Time to take it down, to let go of what's happened before it hurts too much. Too many of my protective fictions have already been stripped away.

I lurch to my feet and clutch the envelope. On the back of the letter is unfamiliar handwriting; large, rough letters that say *Look inside*. I've never seen Clarrie's handwriting, but it must be his.

The letter from the government advising that Clarrie's pension had been terminated is gone. In its place is a handwritten letter and Clarrie's Will.

Keith,

I wanna say thanks for taking me in. You didn't ask for nothing in return, and that's been a rare thing in me life, so I'm grateful.

I'm sorry to have put you through this. But I did tell you early on I stick by me choices. Thanks for respecting that.

I have some land and no one but you to give it to. All the details are in me Will. I want you to sell it and set yourself up. Stop working for those bastards. And if there's any money left over, I want you to fight for other people like me. Do you reckon you can do that?

You're probably wondering why I didn't do that meself. It's hard to explain. You never had kids, but I did. I can't tell you how bad it feels, seeing what they become and knowing you're responsible. And you can't take it back, can you? You can't change nothing. That's a hard thing, Keith.

Maybe that's what you should tell 'em. What it's like when you look back and it's too late to fix your mistakes.

Clarence.

I'm shaking as I read this. It's like he's standing next to me, hand on my shoulder, telling me to do the right thing. Asking me to find courage where he couldn't. Clarrie has brought me to the edge of my tolerance. And suddenly I'm so angry there's no room for doubt or fear, only a consuming need to extract some meaning from his death. In that moment, I finally understand who his protests were really for; not the children he'd failed, or the politicians who had fed us a culture of indifference and economic rationalism, but people who knew better and did nothing.

People like me.

I make another coffee, this one black and bitter, and start planning my campaign.

Afterword

The first draft of "Black and Bitter, Thanks" was written back in 2005. Here's what I had to say about it in 2007 after it was published in *The Workers' Paradise* by Ticonderoga Publications:

> "Black & Bitter, Thanks" was first drafted at the Clarion South writing workshop. It was one of those rare stories written in a single session, and based on the feedback received, seemed to capture the emotion I felt over how a future Australia might treat its senior citizens.
>
> Is this a speculative fiction story? I believe it is, but only just.
>
> Consider this: in 1960, every retiree over age 65 was supported by 7.3 working age Australians. Based on current population trends, this ratio is predicted to fall to 2.4 in 2040. It's not hard to imagine what this sort of statistic means for government pensions.
>
> Recognising the problem, the Australian government has effectively outsourced the future of welfare services to private industry, forcing employers to fund the retirement of their staff through compulsory superannuation. All well and good, unless the super funds collapse in value. If that happened, how would our country care for the elderly?

Now fast forward to 2020. The Royal Commission into the aged care industry has been running since 2018. Terrible stories of abuse and neglect have plagued the industry in recent times, and COVID-19 has posed an unprecedented crisis for the sector. I'm not usually one for social commentary, but I'm proud of how much this little story still has to say.

This story was also shortlisted for Best Science Fiction story in the 2008 Aurealis Awards.

The R Quotient

The first thing Tevet notices is the blood. It's running down cracks in the pavement, pooling in gutters and at the bottom of steps. The sight fascinates him, because the colour is so vivid in comparison to the concrete and bitumen. It's almost as if the city is bleeding.

A cold wind is blowing down Martin Place, sending foil wrappers and plastic bags tumbling before it. Bodies litter the ground, lying amongst shattered glass and chunks of debris. Tevet turns, wondering what happened here.

The old Commonwealth Bank building is a burnt-out shell, plumes of smoke rising from its once proud façade. Emergency vehicles are parked across the pavement. The sound of wailing washes over him, both artificial and human.

Tevet takes a step back, bewildered. He does not know how he came to be here.

The wind is cold on his skin and he shivers. The lycra shorts and garish shirt he's wearing are like those worn by bike couriers before digital execution of documents made them redundant.

Impossible.

Those days are long past. He has a lifetime of memories to prove it.

Tevet turns, seeking answers. Could he be connected to this carnage somehow?

The thought sends shockwaves through his body, triggering deeper questions and acute anxiety. He gulps in air, the smell of smoke and blood heavy on the wind. The sun retraces its path in the sky. Emergency vehicles screech out of sight. People run backwards down Martin Place and the Commonwealth Bank building implodes. Suddenly Tevet is standing outside the foyer.

Impossible again.

There is a weight in his hands that was not there before. He looks down to find a package, about the size of an old laptop computer. It has been carefully wrapped and is addressed to the bank. Tevet is still wearing his courier clothes as he enters the foyer.

A young woman wearing the black and gold corporate uniform smiles at him from behind the reception desk.

"Can I help you?" She is attractive and he smiles back.

"Yes. I have a delivery for"—he turns the package so he can read the name—"Graeme Massey in Retail Banking." She checks her screen, and he realises that his accent is not the same as hers. His speech is more guttural.

"Mr Massey is on level nine, but I can sign for it if you like."

"That would be great." She signs his clipboard, and he hands over the tightly wrapped bundle. He feels bad for some reason, wishing she wasn't so nice, but it doesn't stop him from making the delivery.

The world lurches and suddenly he's on his bike, riding through an inner-city street. It looks like Ultimo or Pyrmont, before they converted those suburbs into one huge apartment complex. The old, terraced houses are bunched together, only occasionally allowing sunlight through. He pedals, counting street numbers and strips of light criss-crossing the road.

Number 74 Bulwara Road is a decrepit looking building with large cracks and a worn door. The garden is in disarray and the house looks abandoned. He rings the bell, but no one comes. Normally he'd call back to base for instructions, but he cycles down a lane running parallel to the house instead. A door cut into the high paling fence opens before his touch.

Inside, the back yard is covered in rubbish. Twisted bits of metal jut out from piles of fast food packaging. The sight disgusts Tevet, but he doesn't move because the barrel of a gun presses against his skull.

"Password?" The voice is curt, the accent similar to his.

"Conflicts of interest." Tevet doesn't know where this springs from, but a fierce sense of determination accompanies it.

The gun is withdrawn and Tevet turns to face his assailant. The man is swarthy and his eyes glitter.

"Why are you here?"

"I've come to pick up a delivery. From Silvana." Tevet indicates his clothing and the bike, still uncertain where these words are coming from. Static on his radio punctuates the sentence, lending credibility to his claim.

"Of course," says the other man, smiling. He is not as tall as Tevet first thought.

"You will deliver our message then."

"Sure." Tevet returns the man's smile and shrugs, not sure how else to respond. The sense of unease he felt earlier—or was it later?—returns, stronger this time. There is a conflict within him, and the moment stretches out, as if time itself awaits the outcome. He leans against the fence, not understanding any of this, but feeling it is significant.

Then the yard is wrenched away and he's in a pub. It's dark and seedy, the sort of place where they don't bother washing the glasses. Cigarette smoke has stained everything. Tevet can smell it on his clothes, but he's very drunk, so he doesn't care.

Loud music dominates, bass riffs throbbing through the air, the singer's angst echoing his misery. He's upset about something, but not sure what. It doesn't seem to matter, because Sydney is not a place that cares about the needs of individuals, especially immigrants.

A woman next to him agrees and Tevet starts. He didn't realise he'd spoken aloud. She is attractive in a dark sort of way, although that might be the beer talking. Her name is Silvana, and she places a hand on his forearm when she asks where he's from—originally. It turns out they have common roots, a shared ancestry in this mercenary land that aligns itself with the fascist United States.

They share a few rounds together, Silvana doing most of the talking, low and fervent, while Tevet stares at her. Then they're outside, fumbling in the dark. She likes to talk, this one, but Tevet doesn't mind, too busy with her breasts. She's moaning and cursing, damning the politicians for their casual indifference, their policies, their conflicts of interest.

All of it washes over Tevet. There's only soft flesh and an urgent demand that must be served. At the last moment, Silvana turns him away, panting and wild in her refusal. This makes him angry and he considers forcing her, but then remembers she's a woman of his country. Perhaps if she'd been an Aussie...

Silvana presses a card in his hand, promising to see him again if he comes tomorrow. Alcohol is fogging his brain and he can't frame a response that might hold her. She bites his earlobe and then speaks, low and breathless, before disappearing into the night: "Remember, it's all about conflicts of interest."

Tevet leans against the pub, trying to find some point of stability. The card is still in his hand and he reads it with bleary eyes:

74 Bulwara Road, Pyrmont.

The darkness morphs into something else.

Tevet finds himself alone in one of the old cinemas where they used to show movies before the cost of public liability insurance shut them down. It's dark and light plays across the screen. He blinks and the colours resolve into words:

"You will remember."

No sound accompanies this announcement. He wants to leave but is strapped to the chair. Images rush at him from the screen. Sirens and Silvana. Explosions and receptionists. Bike couriers and emergency vehicles. Blood running across the ground. An ancestry of terrorism.

Tevet tries to look away, to avoid the connections, to evade the growing horror in his mind. The accusations appear as bullet points on the screen, shooting through his mind. You are:

- a terrorist
- a murderer of innocents
- an enemy of this democratically elected government.

"Bullshit!" The denial comes from deep within him, but the screen continues to flash its damning message. There is pain and light, and then they all fade to nothing, Tevet along with them.

"**A**mnesiac program Gamma-7.9 terminated. Initiating prisoner revival." The voice is flat and precise. Tevet blinks, wondering where he is this time. The images from the screen haunt him somewhere just behind his eyes.

Where am I?

He says the words, but they come out as an unintelligible croak. A paste coats his throat and tongue, astringent and burning. A retractable metallic arm appears overhead. It holds an empty syringe and the light behind it is harsh and artificial.

"You are in the Parole Portal of Incarceration Centre LB-351," says the mechanical voice. The arm withdraws and a large iris appears overhead, its ocular mechanism clicking as it focuses on his face. "How do you feel?"

Tevet stares in astonishment. What is going on? Part of him feels like he should know.

What am I doing here?

Again, he can't speak the words. He tries to touch his mouth, but his arm doesn't budge. The air is cold on his skin and abruptly he realises that he is naked and strapped to a gurney.

"This is your Parole Hearing."

Some form of AI.

The thought comes out of nowhere, yet Tevet knows it to be true. The iris is modern, state-of-the-art. He's not sure how he knows this.

"A chemical agent causing temporary amnesia has been introduced into your bloodstream. This allows me to calculate your R Quotient for the hearing."

R Quotient?

The sounds coming from his mouth do not resemble words, but the AI understands.

"The Remorse Quotient is calculated by stimulating scenes from your past, particularly the criminal acts that led to your incarceration, to determine whether you are eligible for parole. Your results will be available momentarily." The iris swings away, leaving Tevet groping for answers.

The ceiling far overhead is white and sterile. He flexes his muscles, but they are sluggish, and the restraints don't budge. The far wall is a towering sheet of metal, with regular drawers set into it like an enormous cabinet. Monitors display a range of data beneath each drawer: ECG, blood pressure, neurological activity and other incomprehensible information.

Tevet stares at the lights, the burnished steel wall, and memory begins to return, creeping into his mind like a cancer.

No! Don't put me back in there. I didn't know what was in the package. I had nothing to do with it!

The iris returns, zooming in so it can scan his vitals. "Please do not become over-stimulated or I will be forced to administer a sedative."

Tevet stills, breathing shallowly.

Please, I haven't done anything wrong. Not deliberately.

"The purpose of this hearing is not to determine guilt or innocence, only suitability for re-entry into society." A monitor appears, displaying a three-dimensional bar chart.

"Your R Quotient is insufficient for release," continues the AI. "You will now be returned to your incarceration chamber." The gurney shudders and moves toward the steel wall, which looms over him like the storage facility in a morgue.

No! Wait. I'm sorry. I never meant for any of it to happen.

The gurney stops at the base of the wall and begins to rise, the iris tracking his face.

"This is untrue. Your emotional response to the images presented indicates a strong denial of responsibility operating in tandem with a deep-seated sense of justification. You must be returned to Incarceration Centre LB-351 for further rehabilitation. However, you will be allowed to retain the engrams from this hearing for future reference."

Wait. I've changed. Really, I have. Please don't put me back in there.

The ceiling disappears as his gurney slides into the steel cell. It's a tight fit, wires and lights winking centimetres from his face. Claustrophobia settles over him in imaginary folds and Tevet screams, the gurgling sound horrific in the close confines. Something sharp jabs him in the buttocks and he goes limp, consciousness rapidly receding.

The last thing he remembers is the AI saying, "You will be eligible for parole again in seventy-seven years, which is the term of your natural life." He doesn't get the chance to remind the AI that this is his fourth failed hearing.

Tevet wakes and knows where he is.

Guards patrol the high walls of Long Bay Gaol, toting old-fashioned rifles. Overhead, the sky is cerulean blue, with dollops of cloud added for good measure. The ground is hard and dusty, and his fellow prisoners exercising in the courtyard are sweating. For some unknown reason, the AI administering their remedial program has decided it's going to be a hot summer. Tevet wonders whether the program is referencing actual conditions in a Sydney long past. The thought gives him unexpected pain.

Blister is the first to notice his return. The serial arsonist scampers over to Tevet, or *Bomber* as they call him here, bouncing on his toes in excitement.

"How it'd go? How'd it go? Didya find anything out, Bomber?" Tevet hasn't seen him this excited since he lit a fire in the laundry six months ago.

"I failed parole again," replies Tevet. "The AI didn't tell me shit, other than some psychological crap about deep-seated something or other." It's wise to admit to less than you know in this place.

Blister's face drops. "Fuck. I was hoping for *some* news. We don't even know what year it is anymore, let alone whether anyone's monitoring this friggin' program." His voice drops to match his expression. "Hey, the MBA's been looking for you. Says he's gonna take your parole."

Tevet looks around in fear. Reality is a malleable thing in Remedial Program LB-351 and brainpower, not brawn, determines the pecking order.

"Is he part of this exercise detail?" asks Tevet.

Everyone knows about the MBA. The corporate whiz kid graduated *cum laude* from Melbourne University at the age of 17, and then completed an MBA at the Australian Graduate School of Management in record time. The Commonwealth Bank recruited him, and his career skyrocketed until he decided to embezzle eighty-two million dollars from his employer. After a series of well-publicised trials and appeals, the MBA was given life imprisonment. It was an unprecedented sentence for white-collar crime, but an example had to be made. The MBA tried to commit suicide when they came to take him. It went wrong and he ended up killing a cop and taking two bullets himself. That earned him a permanent place in LB-351. But there was more to the story than anyone realised.

"Oh shit," whispers Blister, backing away. Tevet turns quickly, but it's too late. The MBA has him by the collar and belt, swinging him over his hip so Tevet hits the wall hard. He goes down and the MBA lays in, boots doing most of the damage. The guards laugh and point, but don't intervene.

"Welcome back," says the MBA, pausing to gloat. "I've missed my little bumboy. Do you have any presents for me?"

"I don't have shit for you, you big fuck." Tevet spits blood from his mouth and tries to twist the MBA's ankle, but it's useless. The other man's brain is too superior for him to contend with in this virtual hell. Tevet cowers under a hail of blows, wishing he'd pass out.

"All right, I'll give it to you," whimpers Tevet. The MBA stops, gasping for breath. He looks enormous standing over Tevet, eyes wild with fury, veins standing out from his neck.

Tevet knows what he wants. Memories from the real world are the only currency of any value in a virtual prison, and the worst form of violation.

He focuses on the hearing, visualising the memories as cocaine wrapped in a piece of aluminium foil. "Here, take them," he says, tossing it on the ground.

The MBA scoops it up and gives him a final kick before hurrying off. Blister and Raper help Tevet up, the latter's hands lingering on Tevet's groin as they dust him off. Tevet pushes the pervert away.

"Why didnya just give it to him?" asks Blister. "Woulda saved you a whole world of pain."

"The MBA would've been suspicious if I just rolled over.

C'mon. Let's watch the fun."

"Whaddaya mean?" asks Blister, fear lighting his face.

"It's payback time." Tevet limps after the MBA, knowing his destination. Blister follows, muttering and scratching at his bald head, as if there's an irritating thought that he can't get at. Raper drifts off toward the shade, hands busy in his pockets.

Tevet and Blister enter the outdoor toilets. The stench of urine is strong and flies swarm overhead, but Tevet can hear sniffing coming from the cubicles. He smiles. The MBA has snorted the memories he distilled from the hearing. That's good. He wants the MBA to experience it all.

Blister hesitates at the doorway, but Tevet limps past the crusting urinal and stops outside the occupied cubicle. The MBA's breathing is ragged, and Tevet knows he only has a little time before the mnemonic loop kicks in.

The latch bursts beneath the pressure of hip and shoulder and Tevet is on top of the MBA before he knows what hit him. The big man struggles and almost dislodges Tevet, but his mind is caught in two places now: here in LB-351 and in Martin Place on the day of the bombing. Even the MBA's oversized brain can't split its resources and maintain dominance in both places.

"Listen to me, you piece of shit," snarls Tevet. "Very soon you're going to be mind-fucked, but before that happens, I want you to know how it happened." The MBA struggles again, and Tevet uses the weight of his body to pin him to the toilet seat.

"I know you funded that terrorist attack on the bank after you lost your final appeal," continues Tevet. "It was your way of having the final say, wasn't it? Then along comes Silvana, pretending to be my fellow immigrant, and recruits me to be your patsy. Who would have guessed we'd wind up in the same incarceration centre, eh? The irony must have kept you sane all this time, you fucking prick."

The MBA's eyes are unfocused, but Tevet knows he can still hear him.

"Well now you're there, in my shoes, savouring your handi-work. How does it feel, walking through the rubble of Martin Place, blood soaking your shoes? Was it worth throwing your life away? Worth throwing mine away as well?"

The MBA grins, then his body goes limp, the smile sliding off his face. Tevet knows warning lights are flashing outside his enemy's cell. It's time to leave before they trace the mnemonic loop back to him.

"Well, I hope you enjoy it, because you'll get to relive the horror and disgust that I felt again and again, until it soaks into your very fucking DNA."

Tevet gives him a final shake that makes the MBA's skull bounce off the wall. Alarms start ringing and for a terrible moment, reality blurs and Tevet is afraid Martin Place is reaching out to claim him too. Then he's running from the cubicle, shaking off Blister who is panicking, and a past that never really belonged to him.

Afterword

"The R Quotient" is one of the earliest stories in this collection, having been first published in Issue 6 of *Orb Speculative Fiction*, way back in 2004. It started as an experiment in non-linear storytelling and evolved into the story you've just read.

"The R Quotient" was re-printed in *Orb's Greatest Hits* in 2010 and also received an Honorable Mention in *The Year's Best Fantasy & Horror (18th edition)*.

Blurring

She said she loved me. My quiet strength. The way I didn't try too hard.

Our first night together was a revelation. A mingling of olive skin, sweat and soft laughter.

She moved in with a handful of possessions. The boundary between where I ended and she began blurred. I learned to admire her quiet strength, the way she didn't try too hard. But I knew she'd leave, because that's what I'd intended.

I'm still clutching the pillow. Wisps of black hair poke out from beneath it, like a quenched fire. Blood drips from her fingernails, still now after clawing at my skin. I'm afraid to let go, afraid of whose face I might find.

She said she loved me.

Afterword

"Blurring" was published in the Shadow Box e-anthology released by Brimstone Press in 2005.

The brief to authors was simple: invoke a sense of horror within 120 words.

"Blurring" also received an Honourable Mention in *The Year's Best Fantasy & Horror (19th edition)*.

Fragments of the Fractured Forever

Club Continent is still packed, even though it's close to four on a Monday morning. Half-naked bodies twist through glittering dance cubes in the pit below. EgyptoGroove is closest to the main entrance, a golden block of sunlight the size of a house. Dancers pivot and strut through the haze, kohl eyes and white linen kilts a tribute to the ancient pyramid builders.

I clutch the railing of the catwalk suspended above dimly lit bars. In the gloom, I'm just another awkward guy watching from the sidelines. No one can tell I'm pale, shaking and needing my life to end.

The sharp smell of alcohol wafts up from the vats below. Lingering at the edge of perception is the sweet perfume of odour blockers and the metallic tang of heavy-duty electronics. But there's no music; it's all contained within the multicoloured cubes sliding around the pit.

A violet cube swings into view. Dancers weave and dip in a flurry of silks. Probably TurkoPop. Small lasers on lightweight gantries overhead zip around the heavier sonic-grid generators, knitting sound and light together.

"Are you ready?" a voice asks at my shoulder. Artoun's swarthy face splits into a grin. He's dressed in a black shirt with a refractive pinstripe and matching pants. The thin stripes change from silver to blue to purple as he shifts on his feet.

"You look like a waiter," I reply.

"And you look sick." He runs a hairy finger down my bicep and tastes the sweat. Blue veins stand out against my pale skin and the lasers emphasise how gaunt I've become. The black clingtee I'm wearing isn't tight anymore and cut-off fatigues hang loose from my hips.

"You're clean," he says. The smile disappears. "For now. But we both know it won't last, don't we, Raiko?"

"I told you before. My name is Richter, not Raiko."

"Whatever," Artoun says. "I know who you are."

Another cube swings into view, the floor rotating at random. This one's filled with orange haze and Bollywood wannabes rapping their way through IndiFunk. I can almost hear the sitars and the rap beat, fusing with nasal lyrics.

Artoun sneers. "I still can't believe she chose a useless addict like you."

I don't know who *she* is, so I say, "You said you could get me tangental if I stayed clean."

"I did, but I want you to understand something first," he says, anger flaring. I see it in his dark, moist eyes, in the tightening lines across his face. "I'm doing this for me, not you. Neither of you are forgiven, understood?"

"No, not really."

"Just remember what I said." He slides down the pole to the dance pit and I follow. The metal is cold against my bare skin, and pins and needles slide through my nerves. Pin-points of light flare and dart across my vision.

Coming down does strange things to me these days.

The Club looks fuller at ground level. The multicoloured sound-grids are enormous, towering over everyone. I purchase drinks from one of the autoservers lining the walls. Two glasses of Firebrand appear in the dispenser. Wisps of steam rise from the red liquid. I flick mirror-dreadlocks from my face and down my drink in one. Tequila and Tabasco sauce burn my throat.

"That'll hold off the chill," I say.

"It's not cold," Artoun replies absently. He sips his drink, eyes scanning the pit. I follow his gaze to a DJ suspended on wires above the EuroTronica cube. She's working her tray hard. Light from the monitors laps against her face, revealing narrow, almost elfin features. I can make out a severe, black bob and a long neck, but the rest of her remains in shadow.

"Do you know who she is?" A strange expression twists Artoun's face.

"Of course. That's Indra, one of the DJs who founded the Continent."

Artoun snorts into his glass. "I didn't think so. Let's get this over with."

We leave the bar for the bathroom. It's a long corridor with privacy cubicles running down each side. A few people linger in the hallway, spilling out of doors or smoking sticks of god-knows-what. Mist swirls through the translucent walls of synthetic glass. Artoun picks the first vacant one and we squeeze inside, not bothering to check whether anyone is watching.

Just another casual encounter. Nothing to see here.

The cubicle walls turn to the colour of storm clouds on the horizon when I lock the door. A plain mirror and washbasin above the toilet complete the ensemble.

"Show me the tangental," I say.

"Still eager for oblivion, Raiko?"

"Richter," I correct him, but my heart isn't in it.

The capsule of tangental is small, about two-thirds the length of my little finger. The liquid, when he holds it up to the light, is pale yellow, like anaemic piss.

Promises, promises, the drug whispers to me. I grin, stupid in my anticipation.

"How much?"

"You can't put a price on freedom," Artoun replies.

"Cut the shit. How much?"

"Think of it as a gift, not an apology."

I give him a don't-fuck-with-me look, but he just shrugs. A half-smile plays across his face. I fish out a universal tester hidden in my dreads. It's rolled up like a tiny scroll, so I flatten it on top of the toilet seat. Artoun releases a pale drop from the capsule. Stripes of green fan out across the tester, lightening to shades of amber. The tangental is clean of contaminants, though potent, judging by the number of lines.

"This is what you've been looking for, Raiko." Artoun's teeth are bright in his dark face.

"How can I trust you?"

Artoun frowns. "You said you wanted answers. Answers to questions you couldn't even define. You said you'd given up hope of ever finding peace. That you wanted your life to end."

"People say crazy shit when they're high." I lean against the basin, folding my arms and trying to match his intensity.

"Indra is your answer," Artoun says, "but only tangental can help you pose the right question." He takes a deep breath, like someone doing something they really don't want to do. "Only you can decide when all this ends."

And with that he unlocks the door and walks out. The walls change from liquid ash to milk and back again as I lock the door behind him. I hold the drug up to the light, staring at the gold flecks floating in the liquid. A haggard guy with dark shadows beneath his eyes and silver snakes for hair imitates me in the mirror.

I've never done tangental before, but I've heard the stories: a kaleidoscope of images, a rush of dreams and memories you never knew you had, all blurring into reality. Apparently, it makes sense at the time, but leaves you brain-fucked for days afterwards.

Perhaps tangental *is* my answer, the solution to the sense of incompletion that's been my constant companion.

The liquid is cold and smooth on my tongue, not gritty like I'd expected. It's tasteless, but the moment I register this, I think of warm custard, which I haven't had since I was a kid. And that's tangental: thoughts sliding sideways, one tenuous connection to the next, ricocheting off the sides of your skull. But for now, it starts small, the tangents making sense.

I need to dance.

Artoun is gone when I leave the cubicle. Instead, some dickhead is giving one of the EgyptoGirls a hard time. She's upset. Tendrils of kohl run down her cheeks. The flood of rage takes me by surprise. I lunge, grabbing the guy by the arm and belt. He struggles, but I pivot, using my hip to lift him off his feet. Twist and throw. He slams into the back of the cubicle. Blood smears the cracked mirror as he slides to the floor. The rage dissipates, leaving me trembling.

The girl blinks at me in astonishment.

"I hate men who pick on women," I say. She backs away, more frightened than before.

Alone again. The universal constant of my life.

The DreamtimeTrance cube is nearest when I enter the pit. Swirls of ochre, beige and sapphire symbolise the Australian landscape. I blunder into the sound-grid. A chill burns across my skin and the call of the didgeridoo takes over, sliding through powerful tribal beats. The hardcore fans are decked out in traditional gear: yellows and sunburnt orange spirals curling around the dotted white spirit lines. I'm into it, letting my body and feet follow the rhythm, not worrying about the complicated hand gestures or poses.

Tangental and trance work well together, but I won't find Indra here. I jump across to the EuroTronica cube as it slides by. Flickering blue lasers create a deliberate retro effect from the early rave days. Bass riffs tear through the sound-grid, deep and funky. My hands zoom through the air, riding currents of sound. The melody, when it comes, is a cascade of notes pouring through my brain. I'm twisting and turning, head back and howling, not giving a fuck what anyone thinks.

Heat surges up the back of my skull. It floods my brain and sears the back of my eyes. My arms feel weightless, floating on sound. Cold shivers down my legs. Pressure is building under my ribs, forcing my lungs aside and squeezing my heart with cruel fingers. Pain splinters down my nerves, pumping to the 'tronica beat. It feels wonderful and I dance my death, spinning and funking to a heart attack.

Indra is suspended above us, our guardian angel of sound, dispensing music upon her followers. She looks down at me, blue eyes wide with shock. Closer now, I admire how her pale skin is offset by full, dark red lips.

They shape a word, a question. I can't hear it over the music, but all of my attention is focused on the curve of her mouth, the movement of her lips. And so I know what that word is.

Raiko?

A second surge of heat flares behind my eyes, less intense than the first. I'm rising up, floating, climbing a stairway of light and sound. My body's still pumping, music and tangental the twin overlords of my nervous system.

Tears shimmer in Indra's eyes and she reaches for me. Her aura flares, a pulse of white light forming a nimbus about her head. It refracts into a full-body rainbow. Shades of yellow and orange cascade down her shoulders, merging into streaks of blue and green running down her torso, and turning purple and brown as they reach her legs.

I glide towards her and we touch. Recognition shatters the barrier of memory.

I know her.

I know her history because it's mine.

Her name is *Ina*.

And I've lost her too many times before.

Ina crept from her sleeping pallet in the wagon so she could eavesdrop on the men. Her mother stirred in her sleep, but thankfully didn't wake.

"We're agreed then," Milosh said from the other side of the curtain. "The dowry is fair." Ina imagined her imminent father-in-law fingering his long, greying locks now that the negotiations were almost complete.

"For my daughter?" her father said. "No price could ever be fair." She could hear the mock distress in his voice.

Milosh laughed. "Branko, please, no more. That's how we started three hours ago." *Three hours and at least two bottles of wine,* thought Ina.

"Wait until it's your turn," Ina's father replied. "Gaining daughters is much easier than giving them away." A chair scraped on the floor of the wagon and a cork popped.

"To our families," Milosh said.

"To Raiko and Ina," Branko replied. Glasses clinked in the darkness.

"You can come out now," Branko called. Ina emerged from

behind the curtain with a grin. She had chosen her best green blouse and the necklace of gold coins her mother had given her.

"I see you've dressed to meet your new father despite the hour," Milosh said. He stood and opened his arms to accept her into his family. Ina embraced him and stepped back, returning his warm smile. He was tall, like Raiko, but not as handsome.

"Shall I tell my son your father has accepted our proposal?" Milosh asked.

Ina cocked her head and tapped her lip with one finger. "Perhaps Raiko can wait a little longer. My back is aching from listening to you two arguing for so long."

"So, you would have him share in your misery," Milosh replied.

"Well, not when you put it like that." Ina gave him a cheeky smile.

"You didn't mention she's mischievous," Milosh said to her father. "Perhaps we should discuss this further."

"Too late," Branko replied, grinning behind the rim of his glass. "She's your problem now."

Milosh laughed. "Come. Raiko won't be far away."

Ina lit a candle and placed it inside a copper lantern. They descended the steps and entered the circle formed by the five wagons of the Sunset Glow family.

"Father?" Raiko emerged from the trees. Ina lifted the lantern so she could see his face. His moustache was thin and he had let his hair grow to shoulder length in the time they had known each other. She must do something about that once they were married. He wore a simple blue shirt and grey trousers, cinched at the waist by a brown belt.

"I was worried it was taking too long." He stopped when he saw her. "Hello, Ina."

"Hello, husband."

He glanced at Milosh and then said, "Is this another one of your jokes?"

Milosh grinned. "Branko accepted our proposal, despite the difference in status between our families. You can breathe now."

"He did?" Raiko picked her up and spun Ina around in a joyful circle.

"Steady," Milosh said. "You're not married yet."

"No," Ina agreed, "but tomorrow we must start planning the ceremony." She could smell alcohol on Raiko's breath, and he seemed unsteady on his feet.

A slow smile crept across Raiko's face. "I'd like that."

"Well, I'll leave you two to celebrate," Milosh said. "Don't do anything to dishonour our family," he warned Raiko.

"I won't, Father." They held each other as Milosh walked back along the river to his campsite. Raiko's hands were on her hips and his leg brushed against her thigh. She leaned against his side, breathing in the scent of him: dust and sweat, and something more elusive.

"Soon, my love," Raiko said, whispering into her hair. "Soon."

"I can't believe it," Ina said, her voice soft. "After waiting so long."

"I always knew," he replied. "We were just kids, but even then, I knew." One hand stroked her hair while the other circled her waist. "What did I always say?"

Ina leaned back in his arms and shrugged. "Can't remember."

He snorted in mock disgust. "Yes, you can. Say it for me now."

She laughed.

"Say it."

She pulled Raiko's head down and caressed his earlobe with her lips. "You said I was going to be your wife and that you would love no other. Then you tried to kiss me, which is why I hit you."

"What's going on here?" A man's deep voice cut through the darkness. Ina jumped at the intrusion. She turned to find Artani and his father, Kolev, from the River Sheen family. Artani had a thin face framed by dark brown hair. Deep-set eyes and a full moustache gave him a commanding look. Kolev carried a lantern and had similar features, but greying hair.

"Artani, what are you doing here?" Ina stepped in front of Raiko. "I thought the River Sheen were heading north into Armenia."

"Ina, who is this man?"

Raiko pushed her to one side. "I'm Raiko, of the Green Wheel."

"The Green Wheel are very poor," Kolev said. "You shouldn't be talking to him, Ina. Where's your father?"

"Please don't insult my new family, Kolev," Ina replied.

Artani grabbed Ina by the arm. "You agreed a dowry with *them* when you knew my family was preparing a proposal?"

Ina shook his hand off. "Raiko and I have been pledged in our hearts for years and my father has accepted their offer."

"How much?" Kolev asked. "We'll offer more rather than be shamed by the Green Wheel."

"You're too late," Raiko said in a rising voice. "She's mine and there's no shame to be had in it."

"It's not too late until the ceremony," Artani snapped. "Where's Branko? Branko! Get out here."

Ina's father emerged from his wagon holding a glass in one hand. "What's all this noise?"

"We wish to discuss the dowry for your daughter," Kolev said, mounting the first step of the wagon.

"Too late," Branko said. "Ina's made her choice."

"You'll hear our proposal," Kolev said in a low, dangerous voice.

"I've already chosen my husband," Ina cried.

"Silence, you stupid girl," Artani snapped.

"'Enough," Raiko said. "Your manners are an embarrassment to all of the Roma. Go back to your wagons before you taint us with your bad luck."

Artani lunged at Raiko, a knife flashing in the darkness. Raiko grappled for the knife and twisted Artani's arm. The two men struggled and fell. Artani landed on top of Raiko and one of them gasped. Branko staggered down the steps and with Kolev's help, pulled the young men apart.

"Ina?" Raiko's voice was weak and afraid. Kolev lifted his lantern. The hilt of a knife protruded from Raiko's chest. A dark stain spread from the wound.

"No," she whispered. Ina sank to her knees, cradling Raiko's hand.

"Raiko! Listen to me," Branko said. "Breathe slowly and all will be well. Kolev, get the healer." The older man dashed off, shouting for help.

"It was an accident," Artani said as he backed away. Even in the dim light his face was pale. "I only meant to—"

"Be silent," Branko commanded.

"You will pay for this," Ina said, spitting the words at Artani. "Bad luck will follow wherever you go. Your family will be forced to expel you."

Raiko tried to speak, but the words were unintelligible.

"Hold my hand, my love," she said. "The healer is coming." She kissed his hand, but his fingers didn't respond. "Raiko?" She listened against his chest, but he was no longer breathing.

Ina clutched his hand, too stunned for tears or grief.

"I didn't mean it," Artani said into the grim silence. His eyes were white in the moonlight and he licked his lips.

Ina tore the blade from Raiko's body and plunged it into Artani's stomach. He screamed and staggered against one of the wagons. Her father's strong hands closed about her, but she didn't struggle. All of her energy had gone into that single act of revenge.

Artani collapsed against a wheel, plucking at the hilt and moaning. "I curse you," he shrieked. "On my blood I swear... always will you find...the one you love...but never will he know or love you." Flecks of Artani's blood spattered across her dress.

Kolev and the healer came running. They carried Artani away, still swearing and cursing her entire family. Ina stood in a daze. She could feel the curse settling over her. In her mind's eye, it was a triangle of blood, binding the three of them together.

According to whispered reports delivered to her father, it took more than two days for Artani to die. The healers could do nothing to stem the bleeding or ease his pain. Towards the end, when fever and delirium held sway, it was said he called out her name, asking for forgiveness. But this didn't save him. Nor could Ina find it in her heart to forgive Artani.

The court of the Roma met two months later and expelled Ina for the murder of Artani. She stood in the centre of the gathering, proud and upright as the River Sheen family called for her execution. Only in the privacy of her father's wagon did she succumb to tears, as expulsion from the wagons was effectively a death sentence, given how the Roma were persecuted in these lands.

On the morning of her exile, Ina woke early. The sun was just a promise on the eastern horizon and fog covered the ground. She walked through the forest and it seemed to her that Raiko walked beside her. She could hear him sigh in the breeze that whispered through the trees. His laughter echoed in the crunch of leaves and he called to her in the murmur of the river.

She sat on the bank and unbound her hair. Long had she dreamed of her marriage to Raiko, imagining it in intricate detail. The words of the ceremony came to her now from the deepest places of her heart. Tears accompanied them as she undressed and entered the river.

The water was cold, almost more than she could bear. She thought of her parents, of Raiko, of the life that she had lost, and surrendered to the river's icy embrace. Soon she became numb, her limbs heavy and unresponsive. The last thing she saw before the water closed over her face was the first rays of dawn striking the river, turning it into a glittering path to the next life.

The call to prayer from the Blue Mosque drifted over the wooden houses of Istanbul. Izmira listened from the balcony, guilt and regret churning through her because she could not respond. The sun was setting, its dying rays glinting across the Golden Horn and lighting up the merchant buildings of distant Galata. A ferry plied across the water, steam rising from its stack as it churned towards the Bosphorus. The Hayratiye—or Charity Bridge—was just visible, pontoons rocking with the tide. She could smell incense, and beneath it, the putrid scent of refuse. The cries of merchants filled the night, a different call to prayer for the foreigners who could be coaxed out of hiding as the heat subsided.

"Izmira! Where are you?" Artaç's voice shattered the moment.

"Over here," she replied, plumping the scarlet and purple cushions that lined the balcony.

"What are you doing, stupid woman?" Artaç bustled into the room, dressed in the latest western fashion: tailored coat and trousers, a waistcoat with an expensive fob watch, and the ubiquitous fez that had replaced the turban of their ancestors.

"I'm cleaning up, sahip, as instructed." She kept her eyes downcast so his slap to the side of her head caught her by surprise. She staggered in a flutter of silks and tassels.

"You stupid bitch!" His thin moustachioed face was red as he leaned over her. "Your job is to look pretty for the rich Englishmen. Now get down there. They'll be arriving soon."

"Yes, sahip." She left the balcony, eyes down, back rigid. No matter what her family's debts, this vile man *did not* own her soul.

Izmira stalked across the smoking room, stepping over pillows and low divans scattered about the floor. The lingering smell of opium, like roasted nuts, clung to the fixtures. She descended the stairs to ground level. Bright, expensive rugs covered the hallway. Fine kilim hid the plain wooden walls with symmetrical patterns of red, blue and yellow. Individual rooms opened off the central corridor, smoky gateways to oblivion.

A full-length mirror covered one wall, framed by exotic Chinese characters and a twisting red dragon. She caught a glimpse of her full figure and long black hair flickering in the corner of her eye, but couldn't bear to examine her face, not when Artaç's touch still burned her skin.

She opened the front door and let the dusk in. Salt and lavender incense mixed with the distant scent of roasting meat. A steamer whistled in the distance while horseshoes clattered on cobblestones nearer to hand. The city stirred beneath her, both ancient and modern, but she was part of neither, only bound to this house.

Izmira lit a lamp. Distant, English voices carried on the breeze. They laughed and called to each other with the confidence of their Empire. Izmira stilled.

Would *he* come again? She had seen him with the others, tall and fair-haired, with startling blue eyes and a generous smile. What had they called him?

Richard.

She savoured the taste of it, rolling it around in her mouth, enjoying the strange flavour of his name.

The heavy stomp of Artaç's feet down the stairs called her back to reality. "Ekrem! Fazil!" he called. "Light the lamps, you lazy salaks!"

Izmira lit a second lamp, cradling it between her hands. "Artaç, the Englishmen approach."

"Well don't just stand—"

She passed through the carved doorway with the poppy etched into it, taking pleasure in insulting Artaç in the guise of obedience. The breeze was strengthening, tugging at her silks and tassels. The chimes in her hair sang and the touch of the cooling air on her skin was soothing.

The Englishmen strode down the street, their sweeping black jackets and laughing antics too brazen for any other nationality. She loved their confidence, their absolute faith in their superiority. Merchants and diplomats from around the globe negotiated with the Ottomans of Istanbul, but the English were unique in their indefatigability.

"Good evening to you, effendis," Izmira called in her best English. She smiled, knowing the angle of the lamp was just right, lending her face beauty and mystery in equal measure. As Artaç always said, everything follows from the first invitation.

"And good evening to you, Miss," one of the men replied.

"Would you care to try the forbidden delights of my country, good sir?" Izmira shifted the lamp, letting it drop to expose the trough of her cleavage. The Englishmen smiled, bright and predatory.

"And what are they, exactly?" asked one.

Another said, "Careful Phillip, she looks like one of those djinni we've been hearing about." They laughed and more Englishmen joined them, staring down at her. Such a tall people.

She scanned pale faces, looking for Richard. He was near the back, watching with a smile on his face. A surge of delight shot through her, all the more powerful for having to keep it secret.

"The delights of which I speak," she continued, "are grown on the southern hills of the Black Sea. They are harvested and taken to Smyrna, where they are crushed and ground into a paste. The smoke of it has medicinal properties for both body and spirit. Perhaps you are familiar with it, sir?"

This speech had taken months to learn. Artaç constantly prompted her, raging when she mispronounced a word or used the wrong inflection. It had become second nature to her now, as had the delicate dance of avoiding provoking his temper.

"Opium, yes I do believe I've heard of it." The men laughed. She dipped her head, outwardly subservient.

"Please follow me if you'd like to become reacquainted." She turned and ascended the steps, giving the men a clear view of her swaying hips and smooth back. They followed, voices loud to compensate for their conscience. Most would have wives back in Galata, or cold England, so far from Istanbul in geography and culture.

This was the part she liked, this power over men.

Artaç was waiting inside the hallway, unctuous and efficient. "Good evening, sirs. And to you. A pleasant evening, is it not? I agree. The heat is most terrific and almost impossible for a gentleman to abide."

The words flowed from Artaç, easing the Englishmen into the premises. His command of English spread a veneer of legitimacy over his establishment. Though she hated him, Izmira acknowledged his genius. An Armenian refugee, he had come to Istanbul less than a dozen years ago. His voracious business acumen and ruthlessness allowed him to rise quickly in the opium trade.

The downstairs rooms filled with noisy, restless Englishmen. Artaç called to Izmira, motioning the stragglers upstairs. She saw Richard in this group, glancing about uncertainly. Izmira nodded to Artaç and led the remaining men upstairs.

They spread out on the cushions and divans, moaning about the heat and their aching feet. But they did not undo their cravats or remove their shoes. A strange people indeed.

Izmira served apple tea and knelt before each of them, speaking soothing Turkish as to a baby, unlacing their shoes and washing their feet in scented water. Some groaned in pleasure. Others watched intently, their avid gaze revelling in her subservience. The mood had changed, and they talked in quiet voices.

74

She left Richard until last. He smiled at her and tried to wave her away. She smiled in return, shaking her head so the chimes in her hair tinkled. Gently she took his pale hands in her darker ones and put them together, like a Christian at prayer.

Please let me serve you.

His smile widened and the corners of his eyes crinkled. Izmira returned to his shoes, unlacing them and easing the leather from his feet. He sighed when she immersed them, even though the water was not cold. She marvelled at the softness of his skin and the fair hair on his calves.

By the time she finished, Ekrem had laden the low tables separating the divans and cushions with the tools of their trade. The men's attention shifted to the bowls of opium paste and pipes. It was obvious some of them frequented other opium dens because dense, curling smoke soon filled the air.

Richard hesitated, uncertain what to do. Izmira wavered, not wanting to initiate him into the addictive practices of opium. It would ruin him, but if he did not smoke, she might never see him again.

Feeling selfish, she knelt at his side. *First the wire*, she said in Turkish.

She dipped it into the thick black opium paste and then twisted it so that a small blob attached to the end.

Next the flame.

Izmira turned the wire above the flame of the lamp. The opium hardened until it smoked from the heat.

Now the pipe.

She gave Richard the long stem and she forced the burning mass into the small, curved opening at the base of the pipe. He inhaled but coughed most of it out.

Good. Don't like it too much.

He grimaced, drawing in a smaller amount this time. White smoke curled from his nostrils. This time he did not cough.

All of the Englishmen were puffing on pipes. Their faces became paler and the cravats were finally torn away. Izmira attended to them, watching their eyes glaze over as they saw visions beyond this world. The mood changed again. No longer foreign merchant princes, they were simply men in need of release.

Izmira went downstairs to assist Ekrem and Fazil with the larger group. An hour later, many of the Englishmen upstairs had succumbed to the smoke. Richard was still partly awake, his skin pale and eyes wandering. His nerveless hand dropped the pipe. She quickly put out the burning ember of opium paste. When she finished cleaning up, his head lolled to one side, mouth parted.

Izmira glanced around the room. All the men were stupefied, and she would hear anyone climbing the stairs. Richard's soft, red lips, so different to the darker ones she had known, were an irresistible temptation.

She knelt and pressed her mouth against his, ignoring the nutty taste of opium. He did not move or respond, but cold lanced her nerves, burning in its intensity. A deep and instinctual recognition chimed through her body, and she pulled back, frightened by the reaction.

Richard moaned but remained unconscious. Light flared above his head, illuminating his blonde hair. It cascaded down his body, running like all the colours of the rainbow to fall at the feet she had washed. Heat radiated from her skin, pulsing in waves like the wake of a steamer. She felt like a bell that had been struck, vibrating in his presence.

It was then Izmira *knew* this man.

She knew his history because it was her own.

His name was Raiko, and he was the half of her that had always ached with loss.

She shook the Englishman—*no, Raiko!*—but he was lost to the poppy. She wailed and beat his chest, trying to rouse him but he fell to the floor. Red embers fell onto a bright green cushion. They flared and darker smoke mingled with the white of opium. That brought her back to her senses; the risk of fire in a wooden house was an ever-present danger. She smothered the flames with other cushions, knowing Artaç would beat her for this, even if she blamed it on the Englishmen.

Ekrem helped her clean up the mess, promising not to tell Artaç in exchange for a kiss, which was his second-favourite currency. Hours later, the Englishmen roused themselves and left. Richard departed with them, stumbling and disoriented, oblivious to her presence.

The pain of his indifference was greater than anything Artaç had ever inflicted.

Richard returned a month later, with a smaller group of men this time. Izmira curtsied to him and he laughed, but she could tell he was impatient. Once seated, he handled the pipe with assurance, even instructing others in an affable manner. Her adoring ministrations to his feet went unnoticed.

She spoke his true name, but he only frowned in confusion. Her attempts to explain in Turkish and broken English made the other Englishmen laugh. His expression turned to amusement and she could not bear that, not when she knew what they were to each other.

Richard's visits became more frequent, sometimes with groups, but increasingly alone. Each time he greeted Izmira with courtesy, exchanging awkward phrases in Turkish for her uncertain forays into English. But it was obvious what drew him back. He became gaunt and his skin lost all trace of colour. As time went by, Izmira dreaded his visits, lacking any defence against the slow destruction of the man she knew was part of her.

She refused him entry once, railing at him in Turkish. Artaç emerged from one of the back rooms and struck her so hard she bled on the floor. Richard flew into a rage, striking Artaç repeatedly. Ekrem and Fazil were forced to drag Richard off Artaç and throw him out. Later, Artaç beat her so badly she could not rise from bed for three days.

But Richard returned a week later, asking for Artaç. Her bruises were still visible, and tears glistened in Richard's eyes. He touched the contusions, saying something incomprehensible in English and she wept at the tenderness in his voice. Artaç appeared and Richard spoke, offering him money. The Armenian let him inside and they remained cloistered in one of the private rooms for hours, talking and drinking apple tea. Izmira eavesdropped, but she could not understand their quiet, earnest exchanges.

The next evening Richard returned to resume his addiction.

After he left, Izmira cried the rest of the night. He returned three days later, barely recovered from his last bout and unsteady on his feet. His face was the colour of ivory and he traced her tears as she helped him into one of the downstairs rooms, trying to soothe her with his soft English words.

His visits became more frequent, sometimes running together into two or three days at a time. Izmira fed him dates and baklava, but his appetite waned, and she knew that she was losing him.

Once, in the depths of his opium dreams, she thought she heard him moan "Ina". An intense, painful hope flared within her. But everything she tried—cajoling, pleading, even striking him—could not force him to say her original name again, or recall his.

One morning, he failed to wake up.

She found him sprawled among the bright cushions, clutching an envelope addressed to her.

Artaç found her sitting with Richard's body, stroking his hand. He did not enter the room but remained in the doorway, blinking sleepily in the morning sunlight. "Have Ekrem and Fazil leave his body outside the English consulate. The staff will know what to do."

Izmira looked up at him. "That's all you have to say?" She could not muster any anger. All of her emotion had died with Richard.

"No." Artaç looked past her shoulder and stroked his narrow moustache, a strange expression on his face. "Don't come back when you take him."

"What? Why not?"

"The Englishman bought your freedom last week." Artaç walked out and she never saw him again.

Izmira did not return Richard to the consulate. She arranged to have him buried in the hills to the south of the Black Sea instead, overlooking the Bosphorus. The envelope contained two hundred pounds. She used this money to build a cottage near Richard's grave, where she spent the rest of her days. Sometimes she would walk among the hills, collecting wild poppies. These she would burn in great bonfires, blinking at the clouds of smoke and the memories they contained.

Indra cuts the music feed and rappels down to the pit. Clubbers stare at Raiko lying on the floor. Lights swirl, bass thrums, but a cocoon of shock has settled over the scene. No one moves to help him.

"Outta the way," she yells, shoving people aside. Indra drops to her knees and checks his pulse. It's erratic and his skin is clammy. "Raiko? Raiko! Can you hear me?"

"Tangental," a voice at her elbow says. She starts, glancing up at the speaker. It's Artoun, the Club Manager. Laser light splinters across the refractive pinstripes of his shirt. His face is almost disembodied between the spray of colour and his black clothing. "Tell the medics when they get here."

"How do you know that? Did you give it to him?" He crouches next to her, dark eyes searching her face.

"Yes."

"Why? Why would you do that?"

His eyes narrow. "I loved you, Ina. In spilling my blood and committing suicide, you bound the three of us together in unending misery. Every lifetime, every single reincarnation, I've remembered who both of you are. I want an end to it. The tangental was the only way to make him remember."

Raiko convulses on the floor. White liquid bubbles from his nose and froths at the corners of his mouth. Indra rolls him onto one side and shoves two fingers down his throat to clear his airway. When she glances up again, Artoun is gone.

The Club medics arrive, bristling with efficiency. People part before their red jumpsuits with the white cross running from neck to crotch. Indra gives them the run-down and they go to work on Raiko, checking his pulse and pupil dilation. The music cubes continue to rotate around them, an endless game that ignores a fallen pawn.

"Gimme a blocker," one of the medics says. The second medic loads up the syringe with a clear liquid and injects it into Raiko's thigh. The convulsions continue for almost a minute, only gradually easing.

"Can't give him anything stronger," the first medic says. "Too dangerous to mess with the tangental."

"It'll have to work itself out," the second medic agrees.

"Can I do anything to help?" Indra asks. She's hovering in the background, feeling useless. The past throbs through her nerve endings, the tingle both familiar and disturbing.

"We need to move him as soon as he's stable," the first medic replies.

"Shit, he's awake!"

Pale blue eyes blink beneath curling, silver snakes. Raiko's Medusa gaze turns her to stone. She can't move, can't speak.

"Ina?" His voice is hoarse, but it pierces her brain like a needle.

"Raiko," she says through numb lips.

"I'm sorry…" He shudders. "Oblivion's…only way back…to you."

"It's all right," she whispers.

Indra kneels and kisses his face. Memories flood her mind as their lips touch: *Istanbul and a steamer plying waters lined with wooden houses. A poppy carved into a wooden door. A wagon with green wheels and knives flashing. The glittering touch of dawn on a river. Crying as the water closes over her face.*

Emotions accompany these images: pain, regret, sadness. Indra struggles to ride the torrent flowing through her while heat pours from her skin. Raiko smiles, as if he can feel it.

"Next time…" he sighs, and his chest stills.

"Not again," she cries.

The medics push her aside and start CPR. The first breathes into Raiko's mouth. *Exhale-inhale-exhale.* The second takes over, compressing Raiko's chest with the palm of one hand on top of the other. *Fifteen beats.*

Oxygen again. Compression.

Exhale-inhale-exhale. Fifteen beats. Exhale-inhale-exhale. Fifteen beats.

Raiko doesn't respond. The medics stand up. One of them says something to Indra, but she can't hear him. All she can focus on is Raiko lying on the floor. The scene blurs and she sees a knife protruding from his chest. Then he lies pale and unmoving, surrounded by purple and scarlet cushions.

"No," she says. Indra pushes the medics aside and drops to her knees. She is the strong one. The one who always endured. Raiko has always needed her, now more than ever.

She pinches Raiko's nose and breathes into his mouth. The heat, the memories, the lifetimes they've lived and lost, enter Raiko. Indra wills him to remember. To stay. To keep his promise to love her. She demands it with everything she has suffered, with all that she has lost.

Exhale-inhale-exhale.

He gasps. The sound is horrible, rasping. Eyelids flutter and the blue of his eyes flickers and returns. His gaze focuses, locks onto her. A word forms on his lips and she knows it's her name, her original name. Pain contorts his face but he fights, jaw clenching, teeth grinding. She takes his hand and their fingers interlock. He arches off the floor, the veins in his neck bulging. His grip is crushing her fingers but she doesn't let go. The spasm eases and he collapses, breathing fast and shallow.

"My love," he says. Barely a whisper, but the words ricochet through her, setting off a cascade of conflicting emotions. A smile touches his face and then blurs as her tears finally come.

Indra holds Raiko's hand and feels their forever, a thousand lifetimes that might have been, fracture and fall away.

There is only now.

Finally.

Afterword

My wife likes to remind me, now and again, that romance outsells every other genre. I haven't checked industry sales in recent years, but I have no doubt she's right.

"Fragments" was my first attempt at telling a love story. Not content with stepping outside my comfort zone, I decided to tell the story in three different time periods, dabbling with the historical fantasy and cyberpunk subgenres along the way.

I certainly enjoyed writing this story, although I admit it was a struggle to wrestle it into a short story length. Thankfully the first draft was written at Clarion South in 2005, so there was no shortage of suggestions on how the story could be improved.

I'll let you decide whether I should be looking to include more romance in future stories or not.

"Fragments" was first published in Issue 43 of *Aurealis Magazine* and is reprinted here with their kind permission.

In the Arms of Medusa

The auditor offered his hand and said, "Josh Halliday. Thanks for letting me sit in, Mr Rheinbeck." Wolfgang Rheinbeck gave it a perfunctory shake and wiped his hand on his leg.

At first glance, Halliday was the youthful idealist he'd been expecting: athletic build, tidy brown hair and a tan that complemented the beige coveralls worn by all staff in the lab. Looking past the exterior, Rheinbeck saw a man who moved with calm assurance and had learned enough to know when his easy charm wouldn't suffice.

Rheinbeck smiled. Overconfidence was a cage he loved to rattle.

"First of all," Rheinbeck said, ticking off a pale, fleshy finger, "it's *Doctor* in the lab—we never use surnames. Second, it's not like the Parole Board gave me much choice."

"Well, there *have* been complaints, Doctor." Halliday's tone was reasonable, his frown perplexed, not condemning. *Surely this is all just a misunderstanding*, his body language said.

"From ignorant people who don't understand the intrinsic value of my program," Rheinbeck said with a dismissive flick of one hand. "Does no one appreciate what I'm trying to do here?"

"Of course, we do," Halliday replied. "The Medusa Rehabilitation Program would never have been funded if it didn't have such promising potential."

"It's about much more than that."

"Then why don't you educate me?" Halliday's smile had become a little too fixed.

Rheinbeck sucked his bottom teeth. "So, you can decide whether to shut me down or not?"

"Not you, the program. But essentially, yes." Halliday didn't flinch from the accusation in Rheinbeck's voice.

"Well, at least you're honest," Rheinbeck replied. "More than I can say for the Board, who withdrew their support at the slightest setback."

"Enduring psychotic behaviours in your subjects is more than just a setback."

Any response to that statement was likely to further incriminate him, so Rheinbeck said nothing.

"Why don't you tell me about Medusa?" Halliday nodded towards the ball of three interlocking titanium circles that stood twice the height of an average man. Thin black transceiver boxes peppered the metallic rings, the blinking LED lights resembling electrons orbiting a nucleus. In the centre of the machine, a bright red thermoplast harness was attached to each ring. Thick black straps of reinforced latex dangled from the harness, glistening snakes waiting to coil around the subject.

"Don't insult me," Rheinbeck replied. "You wouldn't be here without becoming familiar with its principles."

"True," Halliday agreed amiably, "but that's just theory. I'm here to assess the mechanics." He moved closer to inspect the machine. "What's that for?" Halliday pointed at the drainpipe in the tiled floor beneath Medusa.

"That's where theory ends and experience begins," Rheinbeck said in a grim voice. "You can have the honour of hosing down afterwards."

He waved Halliday over to the console. "Our subject's name is Cordello. Twenty-seven years old. Convicted of second-degree murder. Profiling indicates a high guilt quotient, so he was eligible for the program."

"You think he's got a shot at rehabilitation then?" Halliday asked with what seemed to be genuine interest.

"We're about to find out." Rheinbeck keyed in the authorisation sequence and the entrance to the holding cell irised open. Two guards guided the subject to Medusa. Cordello was five foot ten, medium build, dark of eye and hair, and unusually calm, aloof even. Most subjects became highly agitated when they saw the flashing Medusa with its red maw and black snakes.

The guards lifted Cordello into the harness and fastened the straps. Rheinbeck pressed the locking button. The reinforced latex sealed against the subject's wrists and ankles as the vacuum lock pumped the air out. Cordello didn't even flinch, his dark brown eyes calmly following Rheinbeck's ministrations. A slight smile, almost a smirk, played across his face. Most unusual.

The latex helmet, with its delicate anemone of wires, moulded to the subject's head. Finally, a thick belt secured his body to the harness.

"You can go," Rheinbeck said to the guards. They left via the prisoner entrance.

"Can I help?" Halliday asked.

"No," Rheinbeck replied, knowing men like Halliday abhorred feeling useless. He spun one of Medusa's rings. The subject, spread-eagled on the titanium loops, rolled with the motion. Virtually frictionless, Medusa could move in any direction—up, down, sideways, backwards—even quickly enough to almost simulate weightlessness. He stopped Medusa with a light touch.

Cordello hung upside down, roughly at a sixty-degree incline. The grin remained, although it had become part grimace or sneer, Rheinbeck couldn't tell which.

He rotated the subject to vertical and activated the voice signature. "Sir, I need you to read this declaration."

The man didn't hesitate. "I, Anton Cordello, confirm that I have (a) read and understood the conditions of Medusa Conglomerate contract AC-11159; (b) consent to the application of neurotopography stimulation as a condition of my parole; and (c) will in no way hold the Conglomerate, or its subsidiaries, responsible for any harmful side-effects."

The v-sig beeped, and its status light turned to red to indicate analysis. Rheinbeck waited, already knowing the outcome. The light flicked to green as it confirmed voice stress levels were within tolerance. No coercion detected.

"Ready when you are," Cordello said in a soft voice.

Rheinbeck ignored the comment and drew three ccs of myrhanzonol into a syringe. He locked Medusa and administered the hallucinogen to the base of the subject's brain stem. Cordello convulsed, his brown eyes rolled back, and he sighed. Was that *relief* softening his expression?

"What is it?" Halliday asked. He glanced between Rheinbeck and the subject.

Rheinbeck cursed inwardly. Something wasn't right here, but he could hardly admit that to Halliday. Not with the entire program under review. He needed a definitive result. "The subject's fine. Let me show you the monitoring process."

Rheinbeck directed Halliday back to the console. "These columns indicate the electromagnetic feed from Medusa." Rheinbeck adjusted the microscopic flanges until they aligned with the spines on the helmet, which were linked in turn to subdermal implants. An array of numbers scrolled across the screen.

"What does that mean?" Halliday pointed at the reading.

"No anomalies in neurotopography, apart from elevated levels of serotonin."

"Is that normal?"

"Of course. Serotonin's a common by-product of myrhanzonol."

"No stay of sentence then," Halliday joked.

"No," Rheinbeck replied. Brain activity was elevated above the expected baseline, but to abort now was unthinkable. "We proceed once the subject's neurological activity mimics REM sleep."

"And you participate via the beholder." Halliday nodded towards a metallic chamber that owed much of its design to now-antiquated MRIs. A simple trundle bed would retract into the metallic cylinder, sealing Rheinbeck off from all external stimuli. A temporary anaesthetic would dull his body's senses and the curved VR panels would feed direct from the cerebral interface. Rheinbeck would be completely immersed in the subject's world.

"I *observe*," Rheinbeck corrected. "The subject is in full control of the session."

Two minutes later, Rheinbeck activated the synaptic simulation and Medusa began to whirl.

Anton opens his eyes. The first thing he notices is that he's different. The knotted shoulders, the sick feeling in his gut, the tension headache, all gone.

So, it's before she died.

The thought summons her into existence. Savannah enters the lounge room from the study. Anton drinks in her appearance: hair cut in a neat black bob, square, almost mannish face, softened by wide, generous lips. Today she's dressed as a drogy. Steel and bitumen coloured urboflague hide her figure, the overlapping plates of padded prylene lending her a blockish appearance. The look is designed to eliminate gender bias, but it doesn't work for Anton. He can still visualize her femininity.

"It's been a long time," Anton murmurs.

His voice inadvertently activates the program. She turns, makes eye contact and smiles. The move from memory to synaptic projection is seamless.

"A long time since what?" Savannah touches his arm in concern and cocks her head just the way he remembers. He isn't prepared for the depth of awareness, the captured intelligence, in her eyes.

Anton glances around their apartment. A faux-leather red sofa dominates the room. It's the one she insisted they buy together, reproduced right down to the scrape on the back leg as the removalists forced it through the front door. A kilim-plasma drapes across the far wall; the same model as the one he'd demanded in exchange for the sofa.

"A long time since I felt anything." Anton says it to both of them. "Anything good, that is."

She frowns, but her tone remains light. "Well, I mustn't be taking very good care of you then." And the way she says it, combining both pout and concern, is too much.

"No, Savannah." He takes her hand. It feels cold and shockingly real. He must be squeezing too hard, or the look on his face is too intense, or perhaps even here, in the heart of a simulation, she still knows him too well. Whatever the reason, she flinches. And the reaction hurts. Even now, more than ever, he needs her to understand.

"*I'm* supposed to take care of *you*, not the other way around."

Confusion flowers across her face. "Anton? What's wrong?"

He places a finger on her lips. "Shush. Let me do this," he says.

God, all the pain he felt after she died, all the bleakness he'd endured, they paled before the agony of facing her again.

He needs a moment.

Anton says, "Anarchic."

Savannah turns rigid as Medusa accepts the activation code. A cursor flashes in the depths of her blue eyes. She says in a cold, artificial voice:

[Awaiting input]

"Command String," Anton says. "Estimate current timepoint, where termination event is defined as T."

[Timepoint is T minus 2.73 months.]

Almost three months before she dies. Before his stupidity kills her. Anton resents the program using Savannah to say this. A disembodied voice would've been more humane.

"C-String: move timepoint to T-minus 30 minutes."

The scene shifts.

TurkoPop weaves through sound panels in their apartment. The strident, wailing beat wends around the red sofa. Savannah's dressed in a sheer, black night robe. The privacy shutters are down and she's dancing, slow and complex, glass in hand, to the music.

They've only had a few drinks so far. Still working their way up to bigger and better things. Two lines of tangental gleam on the clear silicate of their coffee table, a chemical equals sign for bliss.

"Savannah." The raggedness in his voice shunts her from the music. He drops to his knees. Not how he imagined doing it during the trial, but his legs will no longer support him. "I have to tell you something."

"Anton? You look like you've seen a ghost." She hurries over, frowning and brushing a lock behind one ear. Streaks of blue gleam in her hair. Anton remembers she'd only had the colour done that morning. A small thing, but something he'd forgotten.

"I have," he murmurs, too soft to hear over the music. She sits cross-legged in front of him, worried but tipsy. The hem of her shift rides up pale thighs. He aches to follow it to the most natural of conclusions.

"What's up, sweetheart?"

"The gear," Anton says. "It's going to kill you."

Her frown deepens. "Are you trying to score it all for yourself? Because if you are, that's a shitty thing to do."

"No." He takes her by the shoulders. "Gustavo was short, so I bought it from this guy he recommended. In about five minutes, I'm going to take a shower and you're going to do half your line. A little surprise for me, you'll say. Then the convulsions will start. Within twenty minutes you'll be dead. The paramedics will arrive about an hour after that, too fucking late to help either of us."

"Why are you saying this?" Savannah stands, a little unsteady on her feet. Arms cross beneath her breasts. "Just because you're feeling crappy doesn't mean you have to send me on a downer too."

Not the reaction he'd imagined during the inquest and the dark days that followed. After all, he'd only made one mistake, one tiny error in judgment that resulted in a lifetime without her. Medusa is the only chance he has to glimpse the life that had been stripped away. Surely if he'd warned her, if he'd admitted his mistake, everything would've worked out.

Surely…

"But it's the truth." Anton struggles to his feet, desperate for her to understand.

"The truth." She laughs. "Let's say it really was the truth for a change. What am I supposed to do? Forgive you? Say it's all OK? Like you wanted when I found out about Jacinta? For Christ's sake Anton, just how much shit do you think I'm gonna take?"

Her glass shatters against the wall.

Not like this, he thinks. *Please, not like this.*

"Savannah, I love you. I know that now."

"Yeah, well I'm not so fucken sure anymore."

"Look, this isn't easy for me either. You don't know what I've been through, why I have to tell you this." He takes her hand, but she pulls away.

"Savannah, I cut the gear." He licks his lips. "It was too good to waste on just the two of us. The profit from onselling would've funded half as much again."

Her expression is changing from anger to something far worse.

"So, I mixed it with phetagrin. It should've given us a nice buzz. I swear I had no idea the combination was unstable. It was wrong and I'm sorry. I'm sorry for everything and I need you to forgive me." He says it all in a rush, hoping she can hear the plea in his voice.

"You—" She chokes on whatever she's about to say. Horror and disgust twist her features. "I can't believe…even as a joke."

Her voice is too soft for him to catch all of it. Blue highlights lash her jaw as she shakes her head. She won't look at him. He takes her by the shoulders again. The light dusting of her freckles blurs through the mist of his unshed tears.

"As usual, it's all about you." Savannah looks up. The pain of betrayal pinches her face. Her bottom lip trembles. "I can't do this anymore." She shrugs him off and walks into the bedroom.

The slump of her shoulders, the quiet closing of the door, the snick of the lock, all of these things tell him she's gone. If she'd stormed around the apartment, raged at him, then there was passion left to salvage. Her desolate acceptance of his ability to disappoint is far worse.

And now Anton feels like himself again. The familiar, sick feeling is back in his gut. The throbbing ache of guilt renews its tenancy in his temples. Only now they're joined by something new. Doubt pours into a cold cavity that has opened in his chest.

Did she mean she couldn't talk to him now, or she couldn't do the relationship any more?

No. Medusa is wrong, the simulation flawed. It had dangled the wrong outcome in front of him. She wouldn't have said that. They were in love. They'd still be together if she hadn't been tragically taken from him.

Wrong. Wrong. Wrong.

"Anarchic," Anton says into the empty room.

The TurkoPop stops.

[Awaiting input] emanates from the sound panels.

"C-string: beta rollback."

[Authorization code:]

"Ginseng-zero-omega." The administrator password cost over six months' rent and more prison favours than he cared to remember, but none of it mattered now. He couldn't lose Savannah twice.

[Accepted]

"C-string: conduct diagnostic."

[Verify]

"C-string: diagnostic topography *Cordello_Anton*."

[Accepted]

The room melts into a pool of colours that drain into a single pixel. It's like gazing into a cloudless night sky, except there's only one star.

Images whip through Anton's mind, a kaleidoscope of memory, as Medusa analyses his brain-map. The simulation is supposed to use a combination of his memories and knowledge of Savannah's behaviour to construct plausible exchanges. Like any program, the output was only as good as the input. He'd forgotten about Savannah's blue hair. What else had he forgotten?

[Diagnostic complete]

Without a construct to use, the system voice is disembodied. Some vestige of inherited Christianity from his forbears makes Anton think of God. He sneers at the thought, but the voice still sounds judgmental.

[Synaptic simulation integrity 0.9783]

Almost ninety eight percent accuracy. Savannah was going to leave him if she hadn't died.

Anton flounders in the emptiness, trying to anchor his life to something. Savannah is lost, both in life and memory.

No.

He can't face that.

Won't.

The void surrounds him, a vast emptiness like the loss seeping into his heart. Anton focuses on the solitary pixel that remains. It throbs, a full stop in the depths of his mind.

This is the original version of Medusa. The one they wrote before all the security protocols and fancy mnemonic overlays. Somehow he must've known absolution would elude him. Why else did he purchase the backdoor to the program?

"C-String: display Ginseng."

[Secondary authorization:]

"The root of all self."

[Accepted]

A small plant flowers from the pixel. Bright green, diamond-shaped leaves emerge from the narrow stem. A cluster of bright red berries bunch from the centre of the leaves. It's so delicate. He'd expected something more robust, but he knows better now.

Ginseng. The ancient Chinese believed it improved vitality, potency, and qi. Perhaps that's why Medusa's architects had chosen the herb to symbolize system integrity.

"C-String: locate root folder *Natal_Cordello_Anton*."

[Located]

Anton pauses, straining in the darkness for something to hold back the final command. Unfinished business. The promise of a future. Anything.

The numbness that had insulated him from the world since Savannah's death is thicker here, isolating him from hope. Stripped of all illusions, Medusa has finally made him face the truth of his existence. With Savannah gone, his life will amount to nothing more than a futile attempt to fill the void.

"C-String: delete all files and sub-folders."

[Are you sure you want to delete?]

"Yes."

Medusa wheels into motion, overwriting the most recent files and working its way back. The original software is much faster, unencumbered by security protocols designed to protect the subject. Anton has a few moments to watch the leaves of the ginseng plant turn brown, the stem wither, the berries shrivel, before it's completely uprooted.

The beholder hissed open and the cold air of the lab whispered across Rheinbeck's face.

He rolled off the trundle and approached Medusa in a daze, the mirror of his life's work cracking with every step. The subject (*no, Anton!*) lay face down, almost in a horizontal position, toes slightly higher than cranium. A thin strand of drool hung from one corner of his mouth and vomit has splattered across the floor. Rheinbeck smothered his disgust and checked Anton's pulse. It fluttered in the carotid artery, but soon stilled.

The heart often took a bit longer to shut down once brain activity ceased.

When he first initiated the program, Rheinbeck had wondered whether this phenomenon was proof that who we are is defined by what we feel, not what we think. The question felt unnecessarily...*existentialist* these days.

"What just happened?" Halliday asked. A recorder had appeared in his fist. Rheinbeck noted the operating light was active.

Rheinbeck sighed. "Hackers penetrated Medusa's security protocols more than a year ago. You can purchase the access codes for the right price, despite the fact we keep changing them." He glanced at Anton. "Even in prison."

"And you admit you covered it up? Despite the risks?" The recorder whined as it zoomed in on Rheinbeck's face.

This was the one opportunity he'd get to make them all understand.

"Twenty-seven years ago, Mr. Halliday, my mother was raped and murdered by a man released from prison." Rheinbeck struggled to keep his voice level. He must, at all cost, appear rational.

"Eighteen months after that, my father was killed by a drunk motorist. I survived the accident but spent eleven months in rehabilitation. You see the irony in the victim being rehabilitated, don't you Mr. Halliday?"

"So, you're exacting an elaborate revenge on prisoners. Is that it?" The lens of the recorder never wavered.

"Don't be an idiot," Rheinbeck snapped. "Medusa only works where subjects feel some level of remorse. It's not meant to be pleasant."

"And you think this excuses the death of patients in your care." Halliday's face turned red with outrage.

"They're not patients," Rheinbeck said with more vehemence than he'd intended. "They're criminals. And before you accuse me of anything else, independent controls ensure my impartiality."

Rheinbeck activated the v-sig and said, "Parole hearing carried out at 16:17. Safety protocols failed at 16:29. Initial analysis indicates the subject subordinated therapy objectives. Neurotopography flatlined at 16:31. Brain activity ceased at 16:32. Report ends."

The red light on the v-sig switched to green as it authenticated the objectivity of his statement.

"Those are the facts." Rheinbeck shrugged. "Anything else is mere conjecture."

"You just killed a man," Halliday said in an appalled voice. "Doesn't that bother you?"

Rheinbeck met Halliday's accusing stare. He'd been like this once, believing in the nobility of the human spirit.

"The man killed himself," Rheinbeck said in a quiet voice. "But I will say this much: one could be excused for hoping Medusa could show us the brain topography that causes criminal behaviour. If so, maybe we could even find a way to eliminate it." Rheinbeck shook his head. "Isn't that worth striving for?"

"Save it for the trial," Halliday warned. "I can guarantee you one."

"And I'll welcome it," Rheinbeck replied. "But tell me, who is qualified to defend humanity?"

"It'll take more than sound bites to save you, *Doctor*." Halliday stormed from the lab, stripping off his coveralls as if they burned his skin.

Rheinbeck squatted in front of Anton and searched his features. His dark eyes were half-open, lips parted, but nothing remained of the man. Not even a lingering sense of peace.

This would be his last, Rheinbeck knew. He pressed the *unlock* button and the restraints hissed as the vacuum dissipated. The body that was once Anton fell onto the tiles like a bundle of wet rags.

Rheinbeck walked over to the console and keyed the delete sequence for the last session. The server hummed as it erased Anton's desperate attempt to find reconciliation with Savannah. He suppressed the desire to visit her grave. The remorse of so many subjects swirled through him; it was hard to know whether any of it truly belonged to him.

He stared at the screen, mind replaying the exchange with Halliday. Was the auditor right? Had he become the very thing he was trying to eradicate? If so, where had he gone wrong? Perhaps at the very beginning, after his mother died.

Only one way to find out.

Rheinbeck rotated the empty Medusa to vertical and hefted his bulk into the harness. The locking button was difficult to reach, but he managed with the help of a stylus he always carried in his breast pocket.

Black snakes hissed around his pale skin and Medusa began to whirl.

Afterword

"In the Arms of Medusa" was first published in 2007 in Issue 7 of *Orb Speculative Fiction*, and was subsequently reprinted in *Orb Speculative Fiction—Greatest Hits* in 2010.

The story is reprinted here with kind permission from Sarah Endacott, publisher of *Orb Speculation Fiction* and principal of Edit or Die: www.editordie.com.au.

I don't have a lot to say about this story, other than that it has always made sense to me that technological progress would inevitably lead to a deeper understanding of the human psyche. Having said that, I also think human beings are inherently unpredictable, and we have an innate talent for finding loopholes in any system (or simulation).

The Ties of Blood, Hair & Bone

*B*link.

Pain: an excruciating spike that runs up his arm and nails the back of his skull to the floor.

Blink.

His right hand, throbbing and bandaged, the little finger gone, severed at the first joint.

Blink.

Police peppering him with questions. Answers eluding his mangled grasp.

Blink.

Jared tries to divide his confusion into pieces that might—in time—be assembled together.

*E*arlier…

A flashy car parked in the driveway, its sleek steely blue lines glinting in the autumn sunshine. Jared studied it, the first flickers of rage stirring in the pit of his stomach. A Mercedes E250 Cabriolet.

His dream car.

In his favourite colour.

Fucking Annika.

She must have bought it with money from the settlement, rubbing his nose in the court decision, as if being forced to move to this shithole of a rental on the outskirts of Sydney's north-west wasn't bad enough.

Jared uncurled his fingers. His nails, chewed and uneven as they were, had left welts in his palms. Annika was talking to Ellette in the front passenger seat. It wasn't difficult to guess the conversation: Elli would be complaining about having to stay. Annika would be reassuring her that it was only for a few days. Elli would pout, Annika would frown, a tiny crease in her forehead that held all the threat of a thundercloud. Elli would find her composure, adopt that bright smile she had perfected during the separation...

...and the passenger door opened.

Elli emerged from the Merc. "Hi, Dad." Her long black hair was pulled back into a single ponytail near the crown of her head. While Elli was only eleven, the resemblance to her mother was becoming starker with each passing day. Not only did they share the same hairstyle, Elli's taste in clothing was moving towards black as well.

"Hi, sweetheart." A hesitant smile crept across Jared's face. The boot opened silently and Elli retrieved her bag.

Jared hurried down the steps from his porch. "Here, let me."

"I can do it." Elli tottered under the weight of her backpack. Jared lifted the bag from her protesting grasp.

"Dads like to be useful. At least now and then."

Elli let go, her hazel eyes searching his face. Far too much awareness in that gaze. She was slipping away from him, just like Annika had, and he was powerless to prevent it.

"There's apple juice in the fridge. Why don't you go inside? I'll be with you in a minute."

"Are you sure?" Elli glanced at Annika, concern fluttering across her delicate features.

"Yes, I'm sure." He was pleased that his tone remained level.

"Don't be long."

"I won't." He walked her to the front door and deposited the backpack next to the umbrella stand. Elli slipped inside the house without a backward glance.

The boot closed automatically with a click. Jared walked up to the passenger window and tapped. By now, his rage was well alight. If Elli wasn't here, he might have taken a mattock to the sleek lines of the Cabriolet. Just to make a point.

The window slid down. Annika peered over the top of her sunglasses. He was looking into Elli's eyes, except Annika's lashes were fuller and longer. She hadn't aged since he met her a dozen years ago; no grey strands nestled in her black hair, no blemishes had dared touch her fair skin.

When he and Annika first started dating, his mates had labelled her a stunner, a real catch. His female buddies were notably less enthusiastic, branding her haughty or worse, after a few drinks. Mitch, his oldest mate from primary school, was brutally honest: "Don't chase this one, mate. She's toxic."

He hadn't listened, of course. Annika was beautiful, intelligent and constantly surprising him with her worldliness. Life with her had held so many possibilities.

"Morning, Jared." Annika's voice was light with just a hint of impatience.

Jared grabbed the handle and yanked the door open. Anger was good. It had sustained him this long. He slid into the leather seat and slammed the door.

"Nice car."

Annika sighed. "Do we have to do this every time?"

"Do what?" His nails dug into his palms again.

Annika thumbed her sunnies back up her nose, retreating behind the dark lenses. "Elli will be watching. Can't you pretend to be civil for her?"

Jared glanced at the living room window. Did the curtains just ripple? Sitting in the Merc, immersed in the cloying smell of *new car* and Annika's perfume that always made him think of lilies, his anger faltered. At least Elli would get to enjoy this luxury: lifts to school, shopping excursions, a weekend cruise down the old Pacific Highway. He could choose to be happy for his daughter, couldn't he?

Annika nodded as his mood shifted. She had always understood him, even from the very beginning. He was the ignorant one, the one who always needed more, especially once her "retreats" became more regular. He'd tried hard to find the bloke who had split them up, but had never succeeded. Now he wondered whether Annika was right; that man was only a mirror away.

"I take it you have something to say." Annika's manicured nails drummed on the soft leather of the steering wheel.

"The new school," Jared muttered.

"Ravens Grammar. What of it?"

"They called me. Said Elli's attendance has been erratic."

Annika's lips thinned to a slash of red lipstick. "I'm sorry, Jared. They should have contacted me. It won't happen again."

"What won't happen again: the school calling, or me having any involvement with my daughter's education?"

Annika *tsked*. Jared detested the sound.

"Why do you have to make everything about you?"

"I'm not. This is about Elli."

"Of course it is, which is why I will visit the school and sort this out."

"We should go together."

Annika finally lifted her hands off the steering wheel. "That's not necessary."

"Why not?"

"It would send the wrong message." A note of irritation had crept into Annika's voice.

"What message would it send, Annika? That I am interested in the welfare of my daughter? Would that be so bad?"

"No. It would suggest we're still together. And that *would* be bad." Annika's gaze flicked to the front door.

Elli stood in the shadow of the lintel, her arms folded across her chest.

"If you're so worried about Elli, you'll get out of the car and act like everything is fine."

Jared knew he'd taken this as far as he could. At least for now. He climbed out of the Merc meekly, wondering why he let her boss him about.

Because she's out of your league, mate. Always has been.

"Dad? Everything OK?"

"Yes." Jared mounted the steps and gave her a belated hug. "How would you like pancakes? I've been practising."

"Dad, it's four thirty in the afternoon. You can't have pancakes for dinner!"

"I know that. I just thought you'd like a treat."

"What's for dinner then?" Elli's gaze narrowed in suspicion.

"I don't know yet." Jared shrugged as if it wasn't a big deal. "I'll rustle something up."

"You haven't been shopping, have you?" Suspicion shifted to something far more complicated on such a young face. "If you need money, I can give you one hundred dollars from my savings."

"No!" Jared retrieved Elli's backpack so she wouldn't see the shame that flushed his face. "That's good of you, but I'm fine. Let's just go inside. You can tell me if I'm flipping the pancakes the wrong way, eh?"

Elli rolled her eyes. At least that was normal, Jared thought with a smile.

Later that night, Jared stopped outside the door to his office. He liked to refer to it as that, rather than the second bedroom, although it was Elli's room when she stayed with him. Having an office reminded him of when he still owned his landscaping business, *Terrace, Lawn and Tree*. A bit like *Surf, Dive and Ski*, he used to joke with potential clients. At its zenith, TLT had thirty employees and there had been talk of franchising. The future had been bright before the divorce. He might be clinging to past glories, but there *was* a desk, along with a stack of unpaid bills and a sofa bed.

Jared took a step closer to listen at the door and grazed his bare foot against the doorframe. "Fuck." Bending down to rub the scratch, he noticed a strand of hair wedged between the wall and the skirting board. It was brown and short, so definitely not Elli's. Must be his.

"Bit clumsy, mate. Must have been that last Scotch." Whenever he talked to himself, it was Mitch's voice he heard. Shame he'd moved to Melbourne. Jared placed a steadying hand against the wall.

Elli should be asleep by now. He had no idea what time it was. At least four fingers of Scotch had followed the last quarter of the Swans game he'd been watching. He should check on her.

This dump he was renting had its share of draughts, and it was chilly outside. Turning the handle slowly, he did his best to slip inside quietly. A sudden chill prickled across the nape of Jared's neck as he entered the room.

Elli was curled up on the fold-out sofa, only a sliver of her face visible between the edge of the doona and her long hair. A rare smile settled over Jared's face. His life might have turned to shit, but he still had Elli.

Edging around the sofa, he adjusted the doona so it wouldn't slide off during the night. Jared's fingers brushed against a hard surface. Peering closer, he saw a book was hidden underneath Elli's pillow. It was a hardback, not one of the thin paperbacks that Elli usually liked to read. Lifting the pillow gently, Jared eased the book out. Elli stirred, but didn't wake. Jared held the cover up, expecting to find a picture of horses or funky urban princesses. Instead, he could just make out the silvery letters: "My Diary".

A diary? Wasn't she a little young for that? Then again, maybe not. Girls were more inclined to write about their feelings, weren't they? Jared knew Elli wouldn't want him reading it. And yet he couldn't help wondering what she'd written, especially since the divorce was still fresh. Any insight into her frame of mind would only help him be a better father, right? And he could return it without her ever knowing.

Decision made—even though it weighed on his conscience—he tucked the diary under one arm and retreated to his bedroom. Collapsing into bed, Jared switched on his bedside lamp and studied the diary. The red leather was soft beneath his fingers. Annika had undoubtedly bought it. Had they written something in there together? The thought of them sharing this secret overwhelmed any lingering reluctance.

The first few pages were just sketches: a love heart, a horse, and a surprisingly good castle. The early pictures showed signs of adult help, but as he flicked through the images, Jared could see Elli's technique was improving.

He stopped at an unusual picture. It looked like an arched doorway in an old wall. The blocks of stone were particularly vivid, with shadowing that suggested a light source just above Jared's left shoulder. A faint triangle—so lightly drawn Jared had to squint to make it out—connected three symbols. A tiny bone shape had been etched into the keystone at the top of the arch. The foundation stone to the right of the doorway bore a curling shape, while the image on the left foundation stone was a teardrop. A severed hand lay in front of the archway, the grasping fingers reaching towards whatever lay beyond.

"What the hell?"

Jared shook his head. Annika had always let Elli watch whatever shows she wanted. It was one of many areas where they had disagreed on parenting. Clearly some of them had affected his daughter.

Jared flicked through the remaining pages. They were all blank, except for the very last one. Elli's large, immature script covered the page. Jared's conscience made a feeble protest. Diaries were meant to be private, yet gaining an insight into Elli's inner thoughts might help him bridge the steadily widening gap between them.

Setting his concerns aside, he began to read:

Dear Diary,

This is my first entry. I'm starting at the back because that's how my life is—all messed up.

I feel funny inside ever since Mum left. Is that normal? I don't know. Maybe.

I am staying with Dad. He gets angry sometimes. When he drinks alkahole. But he doesn't mean to.

I know Dad loves me. But he scares me too. Sometimes he even pretends I'm not there. The school councellor gave me a phone!!! For emergincys trouble. I'm not to tell Dad. But I won't need it.

Mood = Anxious

Elli ☹

Jared closed the book gently and squeezed his eyes shut. He regretted reading the diary now. Things had been difficult over the last few weeks and…well, he hadn't always been attentive. But he would never ignore Elli. Sometimes he just lost track of time. Who didn't? As for being afraid of him…Jared's mind shied away from pursuing that line of thought.

Closing the diary, he retraced his steps and slipped it back under her pillow. Staring down at the one part of his failed marriage that would last, he silently vowed to do better.

A dark shadow drifted past. Jared jerked awake.

"I can't sleep." Elli stood next to his bed.

Rubbing his eyes, Jared sat up. His head felt stuffed with rocks that shifted painfully every time he moved.

"What time is it?"

Elli glanced at the digital clock on the bedside table. "Three seventeen. In the morning."

Jared peered at her blearily. "What have you got there?"

Elli looked at the purple scissors in her right hand and shrugged. "My Smiggle scissors."

"What for?"

"To cut away the threads of dreams."

That made no sense, but Jared was too tired to debate the matter. "Do you want to sleep in my bed?"

"No. Can I have a glass of water?"

"Sure, then straight back to sleep."

His dreams, when they finally descended, were filled with squealing tyres and a horrible tumbling that refused to end.

Having insisted on dropping Elli off at school and enduring the peak hour traffic on his way home, Jared didn't start making calls until ten thirty. That was pretty late for tradies, but hopefully he'd catch them on a break. The first couple of calls rang out and he left brief messages. Finally, someone answered their mobile.

"Yeah, g'day Tom. My name is Jared. I'm an experienced landscaper and was wondering whether you were looking for more crew?"

"Sorry, mate. Business is pretty slow. I'm not looking to take anyone on at the moment."

Jared suppressed a curse. "I understand, but maybe I can leave my number with you in case one of your blokes isn't available? I've got plenty of experience. You just need to point me in the right direction and I'll get on with it."

"Yeah, sure. Your number's come up on my phone. What's your surname?"

"Hills. Jared Hills."

"Wait, like that bloke on the news?" A note of caution had crept into Tom's voice. "He was a landscaper, wasn't he?"

Panic clawed at the insides of Jared's gut. He thumbed the disconnect button and dropped the phone, his breathing fast and shallow.

He mustn't think about the reporters…or any of that. Incessant questions and camera flashes snapped behind his eyes.

All he wanted was work. *Focus on that*, Mitch said in his head.

Jared stared at the list of numbers he'd circled in the local directory. He'd already contacted two-thirds of them and either left messages or been palmed off. All his contacts were in the inner west, not up here in the north. Still, the bills were mounting and he was too proud to go on the dole. What would Elli think of him? All he needed was one chance to show what he could do.

Jared marched out of the office, trembling with a restless energy. His feet led him down the hallway and into the kitchen. The half-empty bottle of Scotch sat on top of the fridge where he'd left it the night before. He stared at the bottle, torn between the desire to pour a few fingers and to smash it against the wall.

Reaching up, he unscrewed the lid and held the bottle at a slight angle over the sink. He might be in a hole, but he wasn't going to sink any lower. *But what if you do, mate?* Mitch's voice whispered treasonously in his head. Jared trembled, caught between opposing desires. Gritting his teeth, he tipped the bottle over and poured the Scotch down the drain.

Jared marched into his bedroom, stripped down to his trunks and stared at himself in the mirror. His chest and shoulders were still broad and sharply defined, although he'd put on some weight around his middle.

It took a bit of a search, but eventually he located his boxing gloves. The punching bag was stuffed in a storage container under the house. He scratched one shoulder on the head of an old nail retrieving it. A thin trickle of blood ran down his triceps, but Jared ignored it.

Hanging the bag on a hook in the carport, Jared took an experimental swing. The heavy thud and accompanying shudder were deeply satisfying. He threw a few more combinations until the bag swung wildly.

"I. Will. Get. Through. This." Each word was punctuated by a punishing blow. This might not be the life he'd imagined, but he'd turn things around. A grin lit Jared's face as he began to sweat.

Dear Diary,

Dad hit me today. He didn't mean to. He said I got in the way of his punching bag.

Dad was very sorry. He cried a lot and couldn't look at me. I told him it was OK, but that made it worse.

It's Mum that makes him angry. Sometimes I think maybe he sees her, instead of me.

Mum told me that being caught between two worlds is never easy. I think I'm beginning to understand.

Mood = Hurting

Elli ☹

Jared stared at the page. A dark brown smudge marred the bottom corner. Was that blood? He ran a shaky hand through his hair. He didn't hit Elli, did he? Surely he'd remember something horrible like that. Yes, he'd worked the bag over, but Elli was at school. Doubt flickered through his mind, as it did so often these days.

At least Elli was sleeping peacefully now. A week had passed since her last visit and there had been no more calls from Ravens Grammar, just as Annika had promised. Jared had picked up some casual days of labour digging trenches for the footings of retaining walls. It was hard work, but he'd enjoyed the exercise. The other blokes had been stand-offish, eyeing him and muttering under their breath. Jared didn't care. All that mattered was the cash in hand. Things were finally looking up, but now Elli was making up new stories about him.

What should he do? If Annika saw the diary, she might try to revoke the custody agreement. He could talk to Elli, but she'd realise that he'd read her diary and that could only end badly.

What he needed was sound advice. Jared picked up the phone and dialled Mitch's mobile.

"Hey Mitch, it's Jared."

"Jared? Mate, it's been a long time. It's great to hear from you. Hang on a sec. I'm on night shift and it's bloody noisy." Jared caught the whine of a circular saw in the background.

"There. That's better. So how are things?" Mitch sounded more cautious than Jared remembered.

"Yeah, OK." Jared flopped on the lounge. "Haven't found steady work yet, but I've picked up some casual jobs here and there. Keeps me going."

"That's good. I wasn't sure if you got my messages." Mitch paused before saying, "Our move to Melbourne was a bit bumpy, but the job is good and the kids are settling. Janine's not entirely happy, but she's met a few mums through school. Reckon it will work out."

"Great. I'm really happy for you."

Mitch laughed. "I know that voice. You never were a good liar."

Jared chuckled. "Look, I know it's been a while. Maybe this isn't the best time."

"Nah, it's fine. What's on your mind?"

Jared sighed. "It's Elli. I found her diary the other day. She's writing stuff in it that's, you know, make believe."

"O-kay. Is that a problem?"

Jared could picture the puzzled expression on Mitch's honest face. "Guess not. But she's said some stuff about me that's not very...kind."

Mitch hesitated. "Like what?"

Jared bit the inside of his lip. "Just stuff. Who knows what Annika said to her?"

Silence on the phone. "Look, about this business with Annika—" Mitch began.

"All right, don't start down that road again. I don't need a 'I told you so'. All I wanted to know was whether Tim or Maddy keep diaries and if so," Jared shrugged, "whether they made up shit about you and Janine?"

"Mate, you know that's not what I meant."

Jared hated hearing the hurt in Mitch's voice. The phone trembled against his ear. "Please, just answer the bloody question."

After a long pause, Mitch said, "Well, Tim's always on his Xbox, so I can't imagine him writing anything. Maddy's a bit younger than Elli, of course, but she's beginning to demand a bit of privacy. If she's got a diary though, I've never seen it. Have you thought about talking to Elli about this? She's a pretty mature kid."

"Of course, but I don't want her thinking I've been snooping through her stuff. Things are strained as it is. She might stop talking to me altogether."

"True. How long have you been in your new place?"

"Dunno. Five, maybe six weeks."

"Well, that's not very long. Give her some time to settle, eh? And if she's using a diary to work through some difficult emotions, well, that's probably healthy, right?"

"I suppose." Mitch had his head screwed on right, but that didn't explain what Elli had written. Or drawn.

"Listen, I need to get back. But we'll catch up properly on the weekend, yeah?"

"Sure, sure," Jared muttered. "Look forward to it."

Mitch disconnected and Jared stared at the blinking digital display. It didn't feel like things were settling. If anything, it felt like his life was tipping over in slow motion.

A piercing scream split the night. Jared lurched upright, layers of sleep sloughing away.

"Mum," Elli wailed from the office. Jared rolled out of bed and hurried into the makeshift bedroom. Elli was thrashing about, struggling with her doona. Her pillow had fallen onto the floor, along with her diary.

"Elli. Sweetheart. Daddy's here." Jared gently stroked her forehead. "It's all right. You're just dreaming."

"Noooo," Elli moaned. "I don't want to. I don't want to!"

"Shhh. It's just a dream. You're safe." Jared kept stroking her hair until she drifted into a deep, untroubled sleep. He retrieved the fallen pillow and diary. The book lay face down and Jared noticed a page had been torn out when he picked it up. That was odd. Elli had never ripped a page out before. He turned the pages, a dark suspicion taking root in his mind. The page with the stone archway and the weird triangle had been removed. But why?

Shifting Elli carefully, he placed the pillow under her head. After a moment's hesitation, he slipped the diary under the pillow as well.

Jared padded out of the room and into the kitchen. The digital display on the microwave told him it was 2:37 in the morning.

Why rip out that page? Had Elli been creeped out by what she'd drawn? Or was there something else at play?

He pulled the plastic garbage bag out of the bin and rummaged through the trash. Fortunately it was only half full. Jared found a scrunched up ball of paper at the bottom, as if it had been deliberately shoved down there.

The torn page *was* the one he remembered, complete with the strange symbols in each corner of the triangle. Only now, written along each side of the triangle was Annika's familiar, cramped script. Jared turned on the fluorescent light over the oven and strained to make out the words: *Our hair marks us. Our blood defines us. Our bones remember.* In the centre of the triangle was a small, bloody fingerprint.

What the hell was going on? Was Annika actually encouraging Elli to indulge in these fantasies?

Jared snatched up his phone and sent a quick text to Annika: *Family conference. 2moro nite. My place. Make time b/c urgent.*

"**O**ne cup of Earl Grey, black, no sugar." Jared passed the steaming cup to Annika. She was particularly pale tonight and Jared wondered if she was unwell. Not that he could remember her ever being sick. As usual, Annika was clad all in black, from her ankle-high boots, all the way to her long-sleeved top, which was just transparent enough to reveal her black bra.

"And one hot chocolate."

Elli accepted her mug with a tentative smile. She was dressed in purple pyjamas dotted with Halloween pumpkins.

Jared settled into his chair, one hand clasped around his steaming cup of coffee. After the interrupted night's sleep and a day digging holes for timber posts, he was pretty buggered.

"You said it was urgent," Annika prompted.

Jared glanced at Elli, who was sipping her hot chocolate. He'd spent most of today thinking about how to approach this conversation. Now the moment had arrived, all of the phrases he'd prepared felt awkward or inappropriate. "Look, I know the last few weeks have been difficult."

"Try the last year, Dad."

Had it really been that long since he and Annika announced they were splitting up?

"Fine, Elli. The last year. Still, we have to make the best of the situation." Jared cut Annika off with a warning hand. "I'm not saying that I hope to get back together with your mum. That horse has bolted. But there's no reason to pretend I'm something I'm not."

Elli glanced at Annika. It was impossible to interpret the look that passed between them.

"What are you saying exactly?" Annika's eyes had narrowed and she hadn't touched her tea.

"I'm saying that I'm doing my best." Jared shifted his attention to Elli. "I'm saying that I'm trying hard to be better than I was, and that I need you to give me a chance."

"I *know* that, Dad." At least Elli didn't roll her eyes.

"Then why are you writing such terrible things about me in your diary?"

Elli's eyes widened and a flush bloomed across the pale skin of her neck. "You read my diary?"

"It fell out of your bed when I was tucking you in after a nightmare," Jared replied, "but that's not the point."

"It's exactly the point," Annika snapped. "You've never respected anyone's privacy."

"Stop changing the subject," Jared fired back. "I want to know why Elli is writing these horrible things about me."

"Show him," Annika said to Elli.

"Mummmm."

"Stop whining and show him."

Elli reluctantly pulled her sleeve back to reveal an ugly bruise on her upper arm. A large Band-Aid, dark with congealed blood, covered a scrape on her elbow.

Jared gaped. "Elli, who did this to you?"

"Dad, please." Elli's beautiful hazel eyes had filled with tears. "I know it wasn't you. Not really."

Annika pushed away from the table. "You're sick, Jared. You're hurting our child and you can't even admit it."

"No! I'd never do that." Jared reeled at the accusation. He'd lost chunks of time before, but that was just the booze, wasn't it?

"Who was it, Elli?" Jared asked in desperation. "You can tell me. Does it have something to do with this?" Jared pulled the torn page of Elli's diary from his back pocket.

Another swift look passed between mother and daughter.

"What is this?" Jared demanded, shaking the scrap of paper.

"Your father asked you a question." Annika was staring intently at Elli, not him.

Elli glanced miserably between the two of them. "Why are you doing this to me?"

"Doing what? I just want a straight answer." Jared's temper was rising. It was a struggle to hold it in check.

Elli shook her head, unable to voice whatever she was feeling.

"See? Even your father wants you to choose."

"Whatever is going on, I deserve to know," Jared said in the calmest voice he could manage.

Elli covered her face with her hands. Annika's expression was cold and remote. Until this moment, Jared had assumed that whatever she'd felt for him had retreated over the last few years. Seeing her now, he wondered if she had ever cared for him at all.

"I can't really explain, Dad. I can only show you." Elli glanced at Annika, who nodded deliberately.

"This way."

Jared followed Elli out of the kitchen and down the hallway towards the office, his confusion growing with each step. As Jared passed through the doorway, an invisible skein brushed against his face. At first Jared thought he'd walked into a spider web, but an unexpected current pulsed through his limbs and up his spine. Silver spots flared across his vision and heat prickled through his flesh. He tried to cry out, but his jaw was locked.

Elli stared at him, her eyes enormous in her face. "I'm sorry, Dad. This…it's the only way."

"Well done, Ellette." Annika walked straight through Jared, a chill crackling through his body.

Jared would have gaped if he wasn't paralysed. Seams were splitting down the sides of his brain and deeply suppressed truths were threatening to spill free. Jared tried to shake his head and failed. The current ran up both feet and exited through the follicles in his scalp. He remembered the patch of hair he'd found wedged into the skirting board and the same image on the triangle.

What the fuck?

Annika patted Jared's cheek, the tips of her fingers like feathers rimmed with ice. "Poor Jared. You must have so many questions. Yet there's no point answering them. Your memory is so, so unreliable."

"Isn't there another way?" Elli pleaded.

Annika turned slowly, her boots gliding over the carpet. "We've discussed this, Ellette. My time on this plane has ended prematurely thanks to your father. You must complete the invocation if you wish to become a Bride of the Eternal. Fail now and you'll be condemned to the ranks of the mundane just like your father. Is that what you want?"

Elli glanced between them. Jared didn't understand what was happening, but it was clear Annika wanted to take Elli away. He pleaded with his eyes, hoping that she could read the depth of his feelings for her. Whatever he'd done to Elli, whatever sins he'd committed, he was sorry. Tears welled in his eyes.

"No," Elli said heavily. "I want to claim my birthright."

Annika drew up to her full height. "Then fetch the burner."

Elli hurried over to her bag and returned with a small case of burgundy velvet that Jared had never seen before. Opening the case, Elli removed a long, thin blade, a pair of wicked looking tin snips, a capped bottle and a small, iron flask in the shape of a three-sided pyramid.

Sweat beaded across Jared's forehead and his armpits became damp. He tried to break this unnatural paralysis, but his body didn't budge.

Elli left the room and returned with the portable gas burner they used on camping trips. Removing the cap from the pyramid flask, she poured the contents of the glass bottle into it. Setting the flask on the burner, Elli sat back on her haunches.

"I know this is difficult," Annika said, "but this is why I chose your father. His anima is strong. It will help you ascend from the physical plane."

Elli nodded, her gaze on the unused implements. Jared made a herculean effort to wrench free from the accursed doorway. All he could manage was a hiss of breath through his clenched teeth.

"You won't remember any of this. I promise, Dad." Elli held the thin knife in trembling fingers.

Jared screamed in fear and frustration, but the sound never passed his lips.

"Our hair marks us," Elli said. Standing on her tiptoes, she cut a lock from the back of Jared's head. Elli placed the hair in her mouth and then spat it into the bubbling solution. One face of the pyramid flask turned a dull red.

"Our blood defines us." Elli ran the blade along Jared's little finger and squeezed the cut. Sucking the blood from Jared's wound, she spat it into the pyramid as well. Another side glowed the colour of a cooling ember.

Jared tried to call for help, but it only echoed inside his skull.

Elli picked up the tin snips. Her face had turned ashen and Jared's blood trickled from the corner of her mouth. Tears leaked from Jared's eyes as he willed her to stop. Elli shuddered and wrenched her gaze from his face. "Our bones remember," Elli said hoarsely. The cutting edges settled around the first knuckle of Jared's little finger. He moaned in his distress and Elli's hands shook.

"Focus," Annika whispered.

Elli took a calming breath and squeezed the handles of the tin snips together with all her strength. Jared howled silently. Even though the edges gleamed, Elli had to squeeze a second time to sever his finger. Blood spurted on the floor and the urge to cradle his injured finger was so strong, Jared's other hand twitched.

With a look of revulsion, Elli popped the severed finger into her mouth and spat it into the flask. She dry retched, and somewhere beyond his blinding pain, Jared actually felt sorry for her. His little girl didn't want to do this. Annika was forcing her.

All three sides of the flask now glowed a sullen red.

"Well done," Annika crowed.

Elli turned off the burner and replaced the cap on the pyramid. Taking a paintbrush from her case, she quickly drew a large equilateral triangle on the carpet around the pyramid using the puddle of Jared's blood. Once complete, she said, "Three faces we wear. The first we show the world, and so are ruled by it." With this, she drew the curling symbol inside one corner of the triangle.

"The second face is worn within, and so we must master our inner selves." Elli painted the teardrop in the next corner.

Reaching the final corner, Elli said, "And the third face belongs to the Eternal, from whom we all spring and ultimately return." A quick set of brush strokes produced the stylised image of a bone.

A thin mist coalesced inside the borders of the triangle. The pyramid had dulled to the colour of charcoal and a slow hiss escaped a narrow hole in the cap.

Elli put the brush aside, a look of apprehension tightening her young face. Annika drifted across the carpet. Her body became translucent as she entered the triangle. Lifting the pyramid in both hands, Annika offered it to Elli. "Drink, Bride of the Eternal."

Elli joined her inside the triangle and accepted the pyramid. If it was still hot, she gave no sign. Removing the cap, Elli drank the contents, gulping it down without pause.

A triumphant smile lit Annika's ethereal features. "You're ready to join us, my Ellette."

Elli's skin turned a shade of ivory and her eyes blazed with a frightening luminosity. "Yes, Mother. I'm ready to be my own person." Elli backed out of the triangle. Annika's eyes bulged in surprise. She flung a hand out towards Elli, but it couldn't pass beyond the border of the blood triangle.

"What are you doing?"

"I'm choosing," Elli replied, "just as you said I must. I'm choosing a mortal existence, but I will be anything but mundane."

"No," Annika cried. "I suffered for you, I debased myself so that you could be made. We only visit this plane once a century. By then, your bones will be leaching into the ground!"

"I'm tired of trying to be like you," Elli replied. "Dad is far from perfect, but at least he loves me in his own way. Tell your sisters...tell them that girls today want to be more than just brides. Goodbye, Mother." Elli smudged one corner of the triangle with her shoe. The mist dissipated, taking Annika with it. A faint wail of anger hung in the air, before it too, faded.

Elli looked up at Jared. She appeared taller somehow, although perhaps he'd diminished, Jared thought wildly.

"I'm sorry, Dad. This was the only way for us to escape. And what's the point of eternity if you never care about anything?"

Jared stared, unable to reconcile this self-possessed girl with the child he thought he knew. Annika was gone...somewhere... wherever she'd come from. He felt no sense of loss, only relief.

Pressing her index finger against his bloody stump, Elli then smeared a horizontal line of blood across Jared's forehead. "When you wake, Dad, you won't remember what you've seen in this room. Nor will you remember what you saw in my diary."

Elli joined the end of the first line to the bridge of Jared's nose. "You'll be free of the veil Mum has drawn across your mind, so you won't drink, you won't neglect me, and you'll never, ever, lash out again in your pain."

She drew the final side of the inverted triangle. "And from now on, you'll see the best in people, including yourself. Three times have I sacrificed, three times are you bound; from without, from within, and from beyond. Now sleep, Dad." Elli pressed her thumb into the centre of his forehead.

Jared's limbs collapsed. He was falling, falling backwards into a darkness that rose up on all sides and swallowed his bewilderment and pain.

Blink.

"Mr Hills? Can you hear me?"

Jared blinks, trying to focus.

"He's coming around."

Jared is lying on his back. He tries to sit up. No one prevents him. Pain shoots up his arm and two faces swim into view.

"Mr Hills, can you hear me?"

Jared tries to reply. Really, he does. All he can manage is a croak.

"Give him some water."

A bottle is pressed against Jared's lips and he gulps greedily.

"Mr Hills, it's Detective Andrews and Detective Mayberry."

Jared blinks and some of the blurriness retreats. Andrews is in his late forties with a thickening waist and thinning hair. Mayberry is female and hatchet-faced, her flat eyes and pinched mouth suggesting she's the harder of the two. For some reason, they look vaguely familiar.

"Mr Hills, we received a report that your daughter hasn't attended school in three days and they've been unable to reach you. Can you tell me where your daughter is?"

"Elli?" Jared frowns. "She was just here." Didn't he make her a hot chocolate last night?

Andrews and Mayberry swap a look before Mayberry says, "Why

didn't you report her as missing?"

"Have you contacted my wife? I mean, my ex-wife?"

Andrews and Mayberry share a puzzled frown. Slowly, almost gently, Andrews says, "Annika Hills died in a car accident over a fortnight ago. We're still investigating the circumstances of her death, as you well know, given you were the driver."

An icy feeling of shock slithers down Jared's spine. "No. That's not what happened. Her car is parked outside. Look!" He struggles to his feet and points at the E250 parked in the driveway. Only it isn't there. His battered 2003 Hilux is sitting there instead.

Connections are forming in his head; memories seeping back in, colours replacing sketchy greys. Elli! She'd been with him ever since they moved here, yet he'd only paid her attention when he thought she was in his custody. And Annika…Annika was gone, killed while they'd been arguing as he took her new Merc for a spin.

"Have you taken any medication recently? Or recreational drugs?" Andrews asks.

"What? No, of course not." Jared looks around in bewilderment. Two paramedics are packing up their equipment. Both are listening, but they avoid meeting his gaze.

"Can you tell us what happened to your hand?" Andrews presses.

"My hand? What do you—" He lifts his arm and sees a bandage wrapped around his hand and what remains of his little finger. The sight is accompanied by a deep, stabbing pain. "I—I don't remember."

"And what about the blood in the spare bedroom?" Mayberry is holding an iPhone to capture his responses. Had they been recording the whole time?

"Blood? What blood? Look, I don't understand what's going on."

"On the carpet," Mayberry replies. "Is it your blood, Mr Hills? Or does it belong to someone else?"

"I don't know what you're talking about." Jared glances between the two detectives in confusion. "Where's my daughter? Where's Elli?"

Andrews glances at Mayberry, who nods and pockets her iPhone. "We'd like to know as well. Let's continue this conversation down at the station." Andrews takes Jared by the elbow.

Jared lets them guide him outside. He feels weak and... unbalanced. Something precious is missing, yet he can't say what it is. He can only identify it by its absence, like trying to guess an object by its shadow.

They're almost at the squad car when Elli appears at the bottom of the driveway. Tears glisten across her pale cheeks and she's shaking. "Dad!" Elli launches into Jared's arms. He holds her tight, a desperate relief rushing through him. The police are right, he'd almost lost her. Somehow.

"Where have you been, Miss?" Andrews demands.

"I was at the mall," Elli replies. "Dad said he'd come get me, but he never did."

Andrews and Mayberry look unimpressed.

"I had an accident." Jared studies his bandaged hand. He has no memory of the injury, although the pain is real enough.

"I'll look after you," Elli says, squeezing his ribs tight. "After all, it's just us now."

Jared clings to her, still trying to assemble all the scattered pieces in his mind. One thought towers over all else: Elli is the most precious thing in the universe, and she deserves the very best he can possibly give. Everything else is just incidental.

Afterword

"The Ties of Blood, Hair and Bone" was published in *Bloodlines*, an anthology edited by Amanda Pillar and published by Ticonderoga Publications. Bloodlines was awarded Best Anthology at the 2015 Aurealis Awards. Here's what I had to say about the story when it was first released:

When it comes to stories, inspiration can be found in the most bizarre places...and sometimes in the most mundane. My story started with a scene every parent can identify with: waking suddenly in the early hours of the morning to find their child standing next to the bed, studying them in their sleep.

I'm sure we've all read stories about creepy children, so I wasn't convinced this scene, and the questions it raised, contained sufficient originality to carry a short story. And that's the thing I've discovered about short stories over the years: one good idea, one good character, even a good setting, is not enough to sustain a story. You need a collision of ideas, an unexpected, even improbable, juxtaposition of characters and situations that sets the story down rarely travelled paths. Think of half-glimpsed alleyways in the shadows of high-rise buildings or overgrown lanes with crumbling houses looming on either side.

Those are the places I like to creep towards in my stories.

For "Ties", the collision of ideas occurred when I recognised that I had been wanting to write a story with an unreliable narrator for some time. I took another look at the child staring at her father lying in bed and realised it was the father who was disturbed, not the child. The roles had suddenly been reversed and there I was standing at the mouth of one of those unexpected alleys. And what if the father was not the only unreliable narrator, I wondered? What if all my main characters in this twisted little family had an uneasy relationship with the truth, each deceiving the other?

Well, I had taken the first step and there was no turning back.

The Sidpa Bardo

No bright light for me when I transitioned.
No tunnel, no welcoming relatives, not even full consciousness. Only the haunted look on Jocelyn's face as she upped my morphine dosage…

Night—thick, black, impenetrable.
Stars glimmer between clouds, but the moon is coy.

A bonfire blazes. Wood pops, leaves crackle, and sparks soar into the darkness. Trees waver at the edge of the firelight. Away from the fire, the air is cold.

Jocelyn and the twins appear in the flames. She's been crying. A doctor talks to her, something about the inevitability of pancreatic cancer, but she ignores him. She kneels, gathers Jack and Cynthia into an embrace, and presses her face against their heads.

"Daddy's gone to a better place."

Her voice catches as she speaks and something inside me splinters. I reach for my family. Flames lick my fingers, not burning, but not permitting me to touch them either.

They'll be OK. Now I'm gone, they have to be.

I watch as my life burns—the triumphs, the humiliations, the unfulfilled desires of what might have been.

The sky brightens as the fire dies. My family fades into the embers, try as I might to hold on to them. It's then, with my old life receding, I have the clarity to know this place, to know I've been here before. Tibetan Buddhists call it *Sidpa Bardo*—the place where you wait between lives, the place where the next one is chosen.

Sunlight crests the horizon. From a ridge, I overlook a valley blanketed in mist. The pale, twisted trunks of snow gums jut through, grasping at the light.

A crack echoes through the valley. The gums split open and pale bodies emerge, shedding bark from their pulpy skin. Their naked forms lack hair or gender. The ground swarms with them, a false dawn of pale shadows creeping up the hill. Blank faces turn towards me; gaping holes imitating eyes and mouths.

Run.

Branches whip by, lashing skin and snatching at hair. Leaves crunch underfoot. Twigs snap. Behind me, feet slap against rock in pursuit, but no voices call out.

Faster.

Cold air burns my throat and a stitch wedges between my ribs.

A backward glance.

Pale bodies flit through the trees, closing the gap.

Nowhere to go but up.

Slabs of granite jut from the ground. I scramble over them, fingernails tearing on the rock. Pebbles skitter down the slope. Breath comes in ragged bursts. Lungs ache and calves throb.

The slope levels off, and I collapse, body shaking. A flat piece of granite marks the summit—too smooth to be natural. Sandstone pillars protrude from the rock. Veins of beige and ochre mar their surface.

Up close the pillars resolve into statues—men frozen in contorted positions. One has thrown an arm up for protection, another howls at the sky. The elements have worn away the details, but a sense of familiarity lingers.

I touch a worn face, and a lifetime of memories sear my fingertips: Norman England, poverty, foreign oppression... forgotten until this moment.

I stare at the statues—at me—at all the lives I've lived and lost.

Pale bodies emerge from the mist. They surround the summit,

pressing against each other.

"Please," I say. "Not again."

The circle tightens in silence. Row after row of blank faces appear until all I can see is bone-coloured flesh and the terrible holes where individuality has been ripped from them. I retreat into the statues, but there's nowhere to go.

A hand touches my shoulder. I turn to find a doppelganger's face morphing into mine. The dark eyes and rounded chin are a perfect replica. Even the stubble-shadow is identical.

Those nearest to the one who touched me begin to change as well. Their features shift, and my face ripples outwards across an impatient sea of inhumanity.

"Choose," they demand with my mouth. The word rolls across the plateau, echoing the earlier crack of gumtrees.

"No." Waning memories of Joce and the twins give me courage. Choosing would mean losing them forever.

"You must."

They may have stolen my face but subtle differences remain—a slight frown on this one, that one's chin tilting at a different angle. All my countless possibilities jostling for their turn.

"I want my old life back."

"Choose." A doppelganger lurches forward.

I dodge behind one of the statues and push.

Another surge of memories: bitter cold. Fur. Bloodstained snow. Traps.

The statue topples with a crack and crashes on the doppelganger.

"Send me back," I scream at the others.

"We will decide for you," they reply in lifeless unison.

Violence erupts among their ranks. Clusters form, grappling, fibrous limbs entwining. Their bodies melt together, forming a pool of heaving, ivory liquid.

A new shape—long limbs and grasping fingers—rises from the sticky morass.

"Get back," I warn it.

I stumble, disorientated by the competing memories. A half-formed hand grasps my ankle. Glutinous liquid seeps over my skin and into my pores. A single chime reverberates as destiny's touch shivers through my flesh, and I fling one hand out in protest before my body petrifies.

The last thing I see is the broken statue. Its features are now clearly recognisable, as is the anguish, and I know I'll lose the memory of Jocelyn and the twins forever.

My mind screams as the transition into the next life begins.

L ight.
Pain.
Division.

Afterword

The Sidpa Bardo was one of the pieces I wrote whilst attending Clarion South. It was—and remains, I think—an experimental piece that prioritises mood and setting over telling a complete story. Like most flash fiction, it presents a snippet of a larger story that allows the reader to fill in the backstory, or decide the ending, if they so choose.

This story was first published by Brimstone Press in March 2006 in Issue 10 of *Shadowed Realms*. It also received an Honourable Mention in *The Year's Best Fantasy & Horror (20th edition)* and was reprinted in *Australian Dark Fantasy & Horror Volume 2*, edited by Angela Challis and also published by Brimstone Press.

7 Kinds of Wrong

Don't care what nobody says, ma'am. Moments of charity are the 'ception, not the rule. It's the seven kinds of wrong that done run our lives.

See, that's why when you speak all polite and smiley, I know it ain't really a kindness. Uh-uh. Only the seventh wrong wears a kind face like yours.

Don't be all hypey-ventillating and pleading with your eyes. Ain't gonna help. I's here to teach you, and no lesson worth learning don't come hard.

Now the first wrong is the bad things we say 'bout each other, so you just open your mouth and I'll take care of it with this here knife.

No sense screaming, ma'am. We still got six more to go.

Afterword

"7 Kinds of Wrong" was published in the *Shadow Box* e-anthology released by Brimstone Press back in 2005. As I said earlier, the brief to authors was simple: invoke a sense of horror within 120 words.

Almost Human: A Memoir of the Thirteenth

*I*f you're going to read this, here is the first thing you need to under-stand: this memoir is not some belated attempt to explain my actions to humanity or the Order that has tugged on my leash for so long.

No.

These words are solely intended for me...or perhaps more accurately, that which I fear I will become. I suppose that makes no sense to you, gentle Reader. Bear with me and I dare say it might.

The point is this: my impartiality is crumbling.

I have made judgements, taken sides.

Some may call this growth, and perhaps there is some truth to that. Yet I cannot deny that I am diminished as well.

Of course, the thirteenth Archetype is meant to be an empty vessel, the bridge between the twelve that form the Ladder and the mortal plane where their wills vie for supremacy.

And so...there must be a reckoning.

How can there not be?

The Order recognised this risk long ago and has been preparing ever since. Yet their contingencies will prove inadequate. The weight of history guarantees it.

So, my time grows short, and what a delicious irony that is for one who has chaperoned humanity for over eight centuries.

If you recall nothing else, then remember this: reality is humanity's finest creation.

Ophiuchus, 2019.

INCURSION 317 – ISTANBUL, 2019

A stream of passengers rushes past to clear immigration at Kemal Ataturk Airport. Some wear face masks to protect themselves. Others are stooped over their phones, scrolling through the minutiae of their lives. Every one of them shares a common desire to be somewhere else as soon as humanly possible.

Lounging against a viewing window, I couldn't help but smile. Certainty is such a fragile construct. I mean, it doesn't take much for it all to evaporate, does it? Let's say a plane falls from the sky for no apparent reason. Or a protesting passenger is dragged away by officials in biohazard suits. What then?

Fear runs rampant. An entire airport is paralysed in an instant. And there's history in a nutshell: the never-ending cycle between progression and regression. If you're looking for reasons why I renounced my own kind, start there.

Sighing, I hefted my battered satchel over one shoulder and strolled towards Immigration. The queue was almost at a standstill. I didn't mind, to be honest. When your life is like skimming a stone across the pool of time, rubbing shoulders with the masses is important. Otherwise, how else do you ground yourself?

We all need anchors.

Especially me.

"Passport, please." The Immigration Officer's smile was fixed beneath her detached gaze. I gave her a warm smile and reached into my satchel. A jolt shot up my forearm as my fingers brushed against the swirling pocket that I had siphoned from the Ladder.

Agents *always* want to know what this feels like. The truth is I've never found a satisfactory description. The best I've come up with is banging your funny bone, except that tingling sensation that shoots up your forearm pulses in your fingertips like a second heartbeat. A heartbeat that possesses a primal desire to reshape things, to alter whatever it touches.

See? I told you no one ever gets it.

I withdrew my jangling hand to find it clutching a Turkish passport. The official flicked through the pages, glanced at my picture and then at me, and stamped the passport without a word.

Judging from my photo, I had a neatly trimmed beard and black hair swept back from a high forehead in this incarnation. A few strands of silver dusted my temples and the quirk of my lips that passed for a smile hinted at a sardonic view of the world.

All in all, a fair representation.

"Welcome home, Mr Zeite." The official didn't appear to notice my bemused look at the choice in surname. She was probably unfamiliar with German and hence the derivation from *zeitgeist* obviously escaped her.

As names go, it fit well enough.

The welcome party was waiting just outside Customs. They had dressed casually to avoid attracting undue attention, but the two agents watched the stream from *Arrivals* a little too intently. The man was built like a monolith, his arms and shoulders straining at the seams of his short-sleeved linen shirt. His female companion wore a light-blue blouse and striped slacks. Her dark hair was pulled back into a ponytail.

I kept my distance, curious to see how long it would take for them to identify me.

The man's stare deepened into a frown as minutes ticked by and the stream from Arrivals thinned to a trickle. In stark contrast, a smile tugged at the corners of the woman's mouth. She did a slow turn to scan the crowd.

I stepped behind a concrete pillar, unwilling to make things too easy. It was critical I understood what these two were capable of.

Failing to locate me with her mundane senses, the woman closed her eyes and drew in a series of centring breaths. I knew what came next. The Order calls it "pulling the thread".

The woman centred her awareness and then extended it beyond her own field. I've met precious few who had mastered the art over the centuries, and it was a rare talent in one so young. I watched in fascination as her consciousness spread out like roots from a tree. It brushed against people nearby, tugging on their fields to ensure they were indeed what they appeared to be. Her skill was rudimentary compared to mine, so it would be simple enough to avoid detection. Yet there was no point; I had learned what I wished to know.

The woman's questing eventually reached me. It fluttered across my field and recoiled, as if teetering on the edge of a deep well. Her eyes shot open, concentration broken. She reeled as her consciousness whiplashed into her body and her companion caught her elbow.

Turning on her heel, she faced me as I approached.

"Esmeray," she said, trying to seize back the initiative. "Field Liaison." She held out her hand, allowing me to see the double helix inked into the webbing between thumb and forefinger.

A swift recovery.

Up close, I noticed she had the most extraordinary hazel eyes, framed by thick lashes.

"This is Khavad," she continued. "We're honoured that you accepted our summons."

Khavad nodded and glanced between us, obviously sensing something of significance had occurred, but uncertain as to what it was. Eventually, he said, "We have a car waiting."

I briefly studied the space between the two agents. Their fields refused to touch, fluxing around each other in a careful dance. Despite the barrier between them, subtle tendrils occasionally lifted from Khavad, yearning towards Esmeray, yet never extending too far.

The dynamic was easy to interpret. The two of them were close. Khavad longed for her affection, although he was careful not to show it. Esmeray knew, of course, but since she didn't reciprocate his feelings, she pretended not to notice to maintain their professional relationship. An old pattern, one I'd seen countless times before.

"You're an adept," I said to Esmeray.

"Hardly. I just do my best to listen." She tilted her head in a gesture of humility. For a moment, I could picture her wearing earrings dripping with jade and amethyst in the style the Ottomans had once favoured. With a mental shrug, I shook off the image. Right place, wrong time.

"You hear better than most." I turned to Khavad. "I gather we're in a hurry. You better take me to the...event."

Khavad shook his head. "Reception first."

"Your commander wishes to see me?" That never boded well.

"It's *Station Chief*," Esmeray corrected. "The Bureau doesn't use that term anymore."

That's right. They had renamed the Order as part of "modernising" their operation.

"If you'll follow me?" Khavad gestured toward a side exit, his gaze sliding across my satchel and veering away as he narrowly avoided a bow.

"Let's keep it informal," I said. "Call me Zeite."

K havad chose the scenic route from the airport. We drove along the main thoroughfare with the ruined walls of ancient Constantinople on our left and the Sea of Marmara on our right. Enormous tankers ploughed through the water, keeping their distance from the shore, yet still managing to loom like thunderclouds gathering on the horizon. I liked the steamers better, even if they were slower.

Khavad turned left and drove up the hill into the Old City of Sultanahmet, dodging tourist buses and taxis.

"Are we going to snap a few shots of Hagia Sofia?" I asked with a smile.

Esmeray, who was sitting in the back of the BMW with me, didn't return my smile. "The streets are narrow here. We closed some to ensure we're not being followed."

"Are you expecting trouble?" I placed a hand on my satchel.

Esmeray shrugged, revealing the butt of her pistol in her shoulder holster. "A deep incursion requires hosts, yes?"

"We used to call them acolytes. I find the old term more evocative, don't you?"

Her expression became curious as she studied my face. "You are not as I expected. Our briefing mentioned you could be incisive, but I didn't expect to find you so..."

"...flippant?"

"Not the word I was searching for."

"Let's go with matter-of-fact then."

I turned away from her scrutiny, familiar with this line of questioning. Humans have always been obsessed with questions of free will, perhaps because at some deep subconscious level, they've always suspected they never possessed it in full measure.

Esmeray's field flared with spikes of indignation, which quickly subsided into irregular ripples that indicated confusion. I wanted to take her hand. I wanted to explain how I had been trapped in a war that could never be won, to make her understand the cost of locking away humanity's darker self in the Ladder. Yet how could I ever find the words to explain such things? Besides, the telling would only prove a distraction and I couldn't afford that in people I might need to rely upon.

"How much further to Reception?" I asked.

"Ten minutes," Khavad replied over his shoulder. "If the traffic is kind."

I ignored Esmeray and gazed out the deeply tinted window. We were crossing the Bosphorus on the Galata Bridge. Sunlight glittered across the waves as we drove towards the old merchant district.

The BMW pulled up outside a nondescript building a few minutes later. Perched on the slope overlooking the Bosphorus, it was a short walk from Taksim Square. To the untrained eye, it looked like any other small office building built in the '70s: a rectangular block no more than ten storeys high with a revolving front door.

That's what the mortal part of me saw.

As I stepped from the car, the part of me that was still an Archetype shuddered. Subterranean pipes beneath the building pumped salt water through a series of three interlocking triangles. Even in ancient times, salt had been used for purification. This particular configuration was designed to ward against the influence of the twelve Archetypes. Unfortunately, it wasn't particularly kind to me either.

I grabbed the car door for support. Reality was so rigid here I felt like I was standing in a brittle world filled with sharp edges. Any attempt to alter these surroundings would be akin to pressing against shards of glass. I forced the Archetype deeper into my mortal flesh.

"Here." Esmeray approached, holding a silver chain that was spotted with age. A large, amber pendant hung from the chain. "Our Tender provided this. It should help." Squinting, I could see the pieces of a finger bone trapped inside the amber. No doubt the remains of some ancient philosopher or saint.

"This reliquary will deaden my sensitivity," I said with a grimace.

"Exactly. You'll be safer inside the Station that way."

She was right, of course. Just standing in the shadow of the building was enough. It would turn ugly if I tried to pass through that revolving door with the three triangles intersecting immediately beneath the entrance.

I donned the reliquary with a scowl and the constant hum of Istanbul's vibrant reality receded. For want of a better explanation, it felt like someone had stuffed wool in my ears, blindfolded me, and then wrapped me in a Turkish carpet.

When did I become the enemy, I wondered?

Khavad guided us inside, his broad hand hovering behind my back. After a cursory ID check, we passed a security detail armed with automatic weapons. The elevator took us to the ninth floor. Exiting the lift, we turned right, passed another security check point, and entered a plush office with a stunning view of the Bosphorus.

Despite my dulled senses, the reality in this room reeked of an obsessive sense of order coupled with a fierce protectiveness. All of it oozed from the neat figure sitting behind an antique desk.

"I am Mehmet Vuran, Station Chief of Istanbul." His dark, close-cropped hair was greying at the temples, and his moustache seemed too thick for his lean face. Intense brown eyes studied me over a proud nose. I noticed that he didn't stand, nor did he offer me a seat.

"Well met," I replied, easing into the chair. "I assume there is a pressing reason for meeting at your stronghold?"

Mehmet blinked. "This is 2019. Do keep that in mind, Thirteenth." His gaze flicked to Khavad and Esmeray, who remained standing by the door. Khavad cleared his throat, but I cut across the inevitable report that was about to be given.

"To save us all time," I said, "let me confirm that I have cooperated with your agents. I have even accepted the indignity of this reliquary." I leaned back in my chair. "Naturally you're concerned by my presence here. However, we both know the situation has deteriorated to a point where you had no choice but to summon me. An incursion has opened in your city, and you need me to stitch it closed. You wish me to use discretion. I wish to be as efficient as possible. Hopefully both parties will be content with the outcome. That said, dealing with the primal forces of the Ladder is hardly an exact science, so I offer no guarantees."

I'd lost count of how many times I had delivered variations of this speech.

Mehmet frowned. "Thank you for your candour. *Naturally*, we are all mindful of your vast experience. However, you will appreciate that I wish to avoid ending up with a larger…mess than I started with."

"A larger mess?" I leaned forward. "Do you have any idea what happens when one of the Vices gains a foothold in this world? I arrived at Yeniseysk too late to stop Nemesis, the Lord of Vengeance, from touching the mortal realm. Would you like me to describe the size of the resulting mass grave on the outskirts of that town?"

To his credit, Mehmet didn't flinch. "I've read the Yeniseysk file. That is precisely why I hold grave concerns."

"Then you also understand the need for haste," I snapped. "So, why don't you stop talking to me about discretion and just tell me how bad it is."

Mehmet stroked his moustache, as if trying to wipe away something distasteful. "We have seven bleeds. All contained for the moment, although we have suffered casualties." He pointed at an aerial map of Istanbul on his wall. Seven yellow pins marked the bleed-throughs. They appeared to be random, except someone had charted the chronological sequence by connecting each pin with cotton thread.

A spiral spun out from the heart of Sultanahmet.

"Well, shit," I said with feeling.

"Exactly." Mehmet moved to the map and pointed at the first pin. "This is the site of the Million Stone, once the very centre of the Byzantine Empire. The incursion point is swarming with tourists. Now do you see why I insist on discretion?"

I studied the map. "You'll need to find a way to clear the area before I go in." A quick glance out the window confirmed only a few hours of daylight remained. "Night will help." I pointed at the most recent bleed. "Take me to this one. I need to establish which Archetype I'm dealing with."

"One more thing," Mehmet said. "The amulet remains on while you're in my city. No exceptions."

Staring into his eyes, I saw he wouldn't budge on this. I swore in a local dialect. Something to do with goats and Mehmet's ancestry.

It didn't change anything, but I felt better afterwards.

"**W**hy have we stopped here?" I peered through the tinted glass at a dishevelled block of flats on the far side of the Galata district. No sparkling views of the Bosphorus on offer here. Only battered cars and fraying posters covered in old graffiti. The street screamed neglect.

"I need you to see something." Esmeray exited the car.

"What's going on?"

Khavad turned to face me from the driver's seat. "Trust her. It's important." He left me sitting alone in the back seat like an idiot.

I joined them in front of a dilapidated foyer. "Mehmet hasn't sanctioned this stop, has he?"

Esmeray studied me, obviously weighing up a risk. With the reliquary still draped around my neck, I could only glean vague impressions from her field. It was enough to gather that strong emotions were churning beneath her calm exterior.

"It won't take long, but there is someone you must meet." Not waiting for a reply, she entered the building.

I glanced at Khavad. His expression had softened into something that might be mistaken for tenderness. Intrigued, I followed Esmeray into the building.

She took us up four flights of dusty stairs littered with empty foil packets of potato chips. The patterned wallpaper of interlocking hexagons was peeling away in large bubbles.

Even through my dampened senses I felt a wave of inertia pervading this apartment block. It felt...forgotten. Left behind by the rush to embrace progress. The old ways lingered here. Old customs were still honoured, and the bond of family remained paramount.

That was the way of great cities; the future was built upon the desiccated bones of the past.

Esmeray stopped at a green door at the next landing. All the others so far had been grey. She knocked quietly, waited, and then spoke too low for me to catch the words. Khavad and I waited at a respectful distance.

The door opened to reveal a tiny, wizened woman. Bent over by the accumulation of years, the top of her head just reached Esmeray's shoulder as they embraced. Her face was heavily lined so that her eyes appeared to twinkle from a deep crevasse. Khavad approached, a tentative smile on his broad face, and dropped to one knee. The old woman laughed at the courtesy, but she still struggled to kiss him on either cheek.

"Zeite, I would like you to meet Nene Sitti," Esmeray said, a slight catch in her voice. "She took me in when my parents were killed in a bomb blast."

Nene was a generic name for grandmother, so I guessed Sitti was not a blood relative.

"Please tell her that I am honoured." I could have said it in the dialect they were using, but Esmeray was the intermediary here and I didn't want to rob her of that role. Bowing low, I took Sitti's hand and kissed her papery, spotted skin. Sitti laughed and cupped my cheek as if I were some overly confident suitor. I smiled, uncertain how to respond. That simple act of acceptance had completely disarmed me. I was used to being greeted with wariness or suspicion, not an open heart.

A smile hovered at the corners of Esmeray's lips.

Sitti waved us in, leaning heavily on her cane as she shuffled into her apartment. It was small and had seen better years. A handful of children, all under four, were playing with mismatched pieces of Lego on the floor. Their clothes were obviously hand-me-downs, but they seemed content. Khavad took up position by a window, which faced an identical apartment block.

I chose to stand by the balcony, where a hesitant breeze toyed with the faded curtains. Esmeray and Sitti disappeared into the kitchen, only to reappear with a pewter platter that was mottled with age along with a matching kettle and cups. Much to the delight of the children, Sitti carried a plate of brightly coloured sweets: a stack of baklava sprinkled with crushed pistachio, blocks of Turkish delight dusted in powdered sugar, and candied almonds. Sitti handed the sweets to Khavad, who accepted them with a sheepish grin, before settling into a hard-backed chair. Her sigh of relief was just audible.

The children surrounded Khavad, demanding their favourite morsel in high-pitched voices. He made a show of measuring their size before deciding which piece to give each of them. I was surprised at how good he was with the youngsters.

Esmeray poured tea into small pewter cups and the strong aroma of apple chai filled the apartment. Sitti nodded to herself, as if remembering better days. I accepted the chai from Esmeray with a nod of thanks. Since there were no other chairs, I sat cross-legged on the floor. Esmeray sat at Sitti's feet and the old woman placed a gnarled hand on her shoulder.

Sitti mimed drinking and chuckled as I tentatively sipped the tea. It was very hot, almost scalding, so I swirled it around a few times and blew away the steam. The chai was spiced with a hint of cinnamon. I smiled at Sitti and said, "Delicious."

Esmeray translated, but I could tell from Sitti's nearly toothless grin that she understood.

Khavad offered me the tray of sweets. I popped a salmon-coloured block of Turkish delight into my mouth. The sweet taste of apricots flooded my palate. Sitti clapped her hands as wonder bloomed across my face.

Esmeray leaned forward. "I wanted you to see this."

"Why?"

"To remind you of what we fight for." She gestured towards the little ones. "Left on the street, these children would have faced two choices: either sell themselves or prey on others to survive. Instead, thanks to Nene Sitti, they have known love. They understand the value of belonging. And so, a new path opens before them."

"Like you," I ventured.

"Yes."

I glanced between Nene Sitti and her adopted granddaughter. Each a product of this city, yet so vastly different I could scarcely believe they were related in the only way that matters.

"Thank you for sharing so much of yourself. It is a rare gift." I bowed my head. "However, you're mistaken if you think I've forgotten what I'm protecting."

Esmeray tilted her head and quoted: *"And in 1199, the Thirteenth Archetype renounced his role so that humanity might be allowed to shape its destiny without the malfeasance of the Vices. With the help of the twelve Tenders who anchor him to this plane, the Thirteenth has dwelt among us ever since. And so, our Order was born, and the Renaissance followed in his footsteps."*

I shifted uncomfortably. It sounded rather pompous when put like that.

"When we find the incursion," Esmeray said, "I want you fighting for Nene Sitti and her children, not some pact made centuries ago. This is *my* city and *my* people. Do you understand?"

Her ferocity caught me by surprise.

"Yes. I believe I do."

Nene Sitti glanced between the two of us, a puzzled expression deepening her wrinkles.

I smiled, raised my cup and finished my apple chai.

Khavad cleared his throat. "Esme."

She rose to her feet without a word.

Setting my empty cup aside, I knelt before Sitti and took both of her hands. "Thank you," I said to distract her from the energy seeping from my fingertips into her walnut skin, while a lifetime of memories flowed the other way. It was difficult with the reliquary trying to shackle my field, but when I was done, I knew Sitti would sleep soundly tonight. She would wake in the morning to find her back no longer troubled her and she didn't need her cane. The effect wasn't permanent, but it would linger for a few days. It was the least she deserved.

"May Maia the Nurturer keep you." I gave her hands a final squeeze.

Khavad led me back downstairs while Esmeray hugged the children and said farewell to her Nene. I remained silent, mulling over what I had just experienced.

Every now and again, humanity reminded me that I did not know its soul completely, that I had not seen all it has to offer. Sitti was one such reminder. Her life contained more than the usual quota of grief, yet she had persevered with a humble spirit, set aside her own aspirations in service to others, and remained grateful throughout her long years.

Studying Esmeray as she joined me in the back seat, I knew that Sitti's love must be honoured in the face of whatever awaited us.

Khavad drove us back to Sultanahmet. Familiar with the layout of the city from Sitti's memories, I soon realized our destination was very close to the Kapali Çarşi, the ancient, covered bazaar.

"Mehmet mentioned casualties," I said. "How many are we talking?"

Esmeray sighed. "Seven dead. Four…we're not sure."

"I see." No wonder Mehmet dressed up his fear in outrage. "What does 'not sure' mean?"

"See for yourself," Khavad replied. "We're here."

The street was a minor offshoot in the old market district. Dilapidated buildings leaned over the alleyway, their wooden shutters all closed. A few blocks to our left, trams rattled along Yeniçeriler Road, dropping off visitors to the famous grand bazaar.

Khavad led us to a small plot boarded up with fresh timber slats. A detail was protecting the site; two uniformed guards stood at the locked entrance, another two in plain clothes patrolled further down the street. A sniper had taken up a position on the roof of an opposing building.

I raised my eyebrows. "Are you worried someone might break in or out?"

"Both." Khavad gave some swift commands and the gate was

unlocked. Both Esmeray and Khavad drew their guns.

I placed my hands on the timber boards. The damned reliquary resisted my efforts. Focusing, I extended my awareness beyond my field. The reality on the other side surged like a severed wire carrying a live current.

"This site is still active. Mehmet said it was contained."

"It is," Khavad replied. "Nothing leaves the perimeter."

I rapped my knuckles on the flimsy timber slats. "Jamming a door shut is not the same as locking it. Stay outside. I'll handle this."

Reaching into my satchel, I activated the pocket from the Ladder and summoned the tools of my trade: a small brazier with burning incense, a bracelet of tiny Himalayan bells, and bitter cocoa leaves. Each of these devices would stimulate my mortal senses and anchor me in this time and place.

"Zeite." Esmeray blocked my path. "We can help."

I nodded. "I'm sure you can. Still, I'd rather not risk Nene Sitti's wrath."

Esmeray's expression darkened. "That's not why I took you to meet her."

"I know that. However, there's no need to take unnecessary risks."

"That is what we trained for," Khavad said, although with less conviction than Esmeray.

"Just make sure I'm not disturbed."

Easing past Esmeray, I slipped through the wooden cladding and entered a small graveyard. This resting place was old. Very old. Crumbling statues balanced precariously on cracked plinths. Dry weeds poked through cracks in the pathways and curled around worn headstones. Ancient sorrows clung to the tombs, ground down by the anonymity of time.

I walked the perimeter, swinging the brazier, jingling my bells, chewing the leaves and humming from the centre of my diaphragm. *This is a human place,* I projected. *The last resting place of mortals. It does not belong to any Archetype. No foothold can be gained here.*

Reality seethed around me like a nest of angry snakes. The

normally static fields of headstones bubbled with potentiality. The ground thrummed with hidden force and long abandoned graves shifted unnervingly.

Each step towards the heart of the graveyard became increasingly difficult. The reliquary around my neck grew heavy and the amber became so hot I worried it might melt. Whatever caused this bleed was actively resisting my attempt to force it closed. The air thickened until I felt like I was wading across the bottom of the sea. The headstones shifted in and out of focus; one moment they appeared freshly hewn, the next they were crumbling, shapeless pieces of granite.

Spent rounds of ammunition littered the pathway. A spray of blood had spattered a gravestone. I rounded a small crypt and stopped. An agent lay slumped against a lion statue that guarded the entrance to a mausoleum. The lion had swallowed the man's head and torso so that only his legs remained visible.

Very slowly, I reached out and touched the agent's ankle. A thin pulse threaded through his veins. The lion's eyes swivelled towards me and blunt claws extended from one paw with a grinding sound. I caught its leg and said, "Stone. You are merely stone. Carved centuries ago, to honour those now long forgotten." I jammed my fingers into the pocket hidden within the satchel.

The paw trembled in my grip. It wanted to move. It wanted to rend and slash like the great beast it had been fashioned after. But stone has no business wanting anything, which finally revealed the Archetype I was dealing with.

"Old stone. Faithful stone. Remember the shape that you held during the winds and the rains. Remember how you posed, basking in the sun. Return to that shape. Be at peace." The human part of me said the words, but it was the Archetype within that channelled the potentiality from the pocket.

It was much harder than it should have been. Not only did the stone lion resist, the reliquary tried to thwart my efforts as well.

The lion shuddered and its jaws widened into the original roar that the statue remembered. The unconscious agent slipped from its mouth, blood seeping from a gash in his scalp. The lion raised its head towards the sky and lifted its paw. Potentiality wormed away from my grip, trying to escape my command that it be stilled. Focusing, I increased the flow from the Ladder. The ripples in the statue's field abruptly converged and struck back.

Unable to contain the two colliding forces, the statue shattered. The resulting explosion threw me backwards.

I lay still for a moment, allowing the shock to subside along with the blinding pain. A high-pitched whine buzzed through my ears and I tasted blood in my mouth. Climbing unsteadily to my feet, I wiped dust from my face. My palm came away smeared with blood.

An inanimate object cannot alter its energy field. It lacks the awareness to do so. This was no ordinary bleed-through.

Screw Mehmet and his demands. I lifted the cursed reliquary over my head and threw it on the ground. Whatever was happening here, it required my unfettered strength.

I rounded the crypt and was rewarded with my first uninterrupted view of the graveyard.

In the very centre of the small plots was an old mausoleum that had partly subsided in one corner, giving it an unbalanced, almost drunken look. A dead man lay on top of the roof. He appeared Turkish. Judging from his glittering gold watch, I guessed he'd been a local merchant of some kind. I edged closer, wary of more anomalies.

The dead man's skin had assumed the hue of alabaster. His right hand was bunched into a fist, while his left clutched an amulet around his throat.

Approaching warily, I touched his fist. Drawing on the pocket again, I commanded the flesh of his arm to return to its original state. Unlike the lion, there was no resistance this time. The alabaster faded to the man's natural olive complexion and I prised open his fingers.

He clutched a small, square piece of marble. Cut into one side was the unmistakable image of the Medusa, complete with her halo of angry snakes.

Metamorphoses, the Lady of Change, had chosen this symbol long, long ago. The Ancient Greeks had bestowed that name, but she had worn many others throughout the centuries: the

Magician, the Illusionist and Transformation, to name but a few.

The merchant's body was clearly the keystone holding open this breach. Tapping further into the pocket, I funnelled its energy into the dead merchant, demanding that his entire body revert to its original form. The field surrounding him flared. Tendrils of energy snaked across the ground and struck dozens of warped statues.

I had just enough time to fall into a crouch before they exploded into lethal fragments.

Dust and powdered stone filled the air. The sound of Metamorphoses' laughter reached me as the bleed closed, along with a parting image. From above, the cloud of dust resembled her face and the tendrils of energy were like a halo of snakes.

I coughed up blood and dust.

So much for not making a mess, I thought ruefully. A gash throbbed across my left cheek and blood trickled down my neck. The fact that Metamorphoses had anticipated my every move stung even more.

I withdrew my hand from my satchel and staggered through the billowing dust towards the sound of voices raised in alarm.

*T*he Ladder.

Could you have fallen so far that you have forgotten your place in it? It terrifies me to consider such a possibility. But if this memoir is to be a true account of my struggles, and yes, even my fears, then I must consider it.

So how to explain something that defies explanation? How does a tiny cog comprehend the purpose of the machine it is part of?

The Ladder exists on the plane of potentiality, where the limitations of time and space no longer apply. In the simplest sense, it is a representation of how the spark of existence becomes manifest in the mortal plane.

Let's avoid a tiresome debate about the religions of humanity and simply agree that all of them share some form of creation myth that explains how the world, and its various peoples, sprang into being. Study any culture and you'll find the same mythic figures present, garbed in allegory or fable, but recognisable nonetheless. Go on, I daresay you know some of them already. The Innocent and his counterpart the

Trickster. The Warrior and the Outlaw. The Nurturer and the Tyrant.

While there are twelve Archetypes, only six inspire human endeavour, always encouraging mortals to act on behalf of the greater good. These are the Archetypes of Virtue. However, each of the Virtues has an antithesis. Unlike the Virtues, the Archetypes of Vice stimulate only selfish needs and desires.

And so, the Virtues and Vices are locked together in a constant struggle for dominance of humanity. This is the twisted Ladder that inspires humanity to acts of great altruism and infamy, and everything in between.

Perhaps you have seen something like it before? Humanity discovered the double helix almost seventy years ago and now we know it's present in every human's DNA.

As the expression goes, "As Above, So Below".

"**H**e wants to talk to you." Esmeray offered her cell phone. Khavad stood behind her, his field jagged with anger as he scanned the rubble.

"And why would I possibly want that?" I wasn't in the mood for a dressing down.

"Please." She shook the phone for emphasis. "How can I explain this when I don't even know what happened?"

Guess she had a point. I accepted the phone with a grimace. "This is Zeite."

"What happened?" Mehmet demanded.

"What happened is your supposedly contained site was still active, that's what happened. What happened is I closed the bleed and recovered three of your agents."

"Khavad said you demolished the cemetery!"

I shot the agent a dirty look. He had the decency to look sheepish. "That's an exaggeration."

"The site is heritage listed," Mehmet replied, his voice rising. "How am I supposed to explain this?"

"Would you prefer to explain why statues were crushing people to death?"

"That is hardly helpful."

"Nor is this line of inquiry. Metamorphoses has found a foothold in your city. We need to dislodge her before it gets any worse."

Mehmet paused and I heard him draw in a long, slow breath. "What does she want?"

"Change. Tearing down the old. Throwing up something new. That's her thing."

"How was she able to manifest in the first place?"

"An acolyte," I replied. "No doubt he was promised a great many things, but he didn't live long enough to receive them."

"I see." Another pause. "What do you intend to do?"

"Face her. Stitch the incursion closed."

"I'm told you were injured. Are you sure you're strong enough to face one of the Vices?"

"Is there another option?"

"That's not an answer," Mehmet replied.

A fair point, given the circumstances. "It depends. She's already tapped into the dissident elements of your population."

Mehmet swore colourfully. I smiled at some of the more evocative imagery. Mastering his anger, he said, "Take a detail with you. Khavad and Esmeray are not to leave your side. If it's as bad as you say, we can't afford any mistakes."

I shook my head. Commanders always thought force was the answer. "Mehmet, what do you think Metamorphoses will do to them?"

"They know the risks," he replied. "Besides, you created the Fraternum to help you."

That last point was true. The Fraternum were the military arm of the Order. Their ancestors had been fighting by my side almost from the beginning.

"Very well," I said. "By the way, the reliquary slipped off during the commotion. It should be under the rubble somewhere." I disconnected before he could reply and handed the phone back to Esmeray. "Your boss says take me to the Million Stone."

She gave me a look that would have withered a cactus. "I'm not waiting outside again."

I opened my mouth to protest but she silenced me with an imperious finger. "If I'm going to be held accountable for destroying another national monument, I need to be absolutely sure it was unavoidable."

"Esmeray, facing down an Archetype is no place for a—"

"If you say *woman*, I swear to God I'll punch you in the face." She balled a fist. Khavad turned to watch, the ghost of a grin on his lips.

"I was going to say *mortal*," I replied, raising my hands in surrender.

Night had fallen when we parked half a block from the Million Stone. I was grateful for the darkness. Fewer tourists for a start, with their troublesome smart phones. No doubt the Bureau had engineered a "service interruption" for the nearest cell phone towers. Still, that didn't guarantee our activities would go unremarked.

Khavad and Esmeray escorted me to the ancient finger of stone while our detail of agents fanned out to form a loose perimeter. This site had once been the place where all distances along the old Roman highways were measured. The weathered stone hummed faintly under my touch. It had worn this shape for so long its field was almost completely inert.

A tram rattled by and distant laughter followed in its wake.

I glanced down the concourse to the west. The two Egyptian obelisks that attracted droves of tourists were normally illuminated by floodlights. Tonight, they were just vaguely menacing shadows. More strings pulled by Mehmet.

"Well?" Khavad shifted on his feet and glanced uneasily towards the bright lights on Divan Yolu Street. I caught a whiff of cooking meat from a distant kebab stand.

"Patience," I replied.

Khavad folded his arms across his broad chest. "We already inspected this site. Nothing here."

"Perhaps, perhaps not." Placing my hand inside my satchel, I pressed the tip of my index finger against the pocket and touched the Million Stone with my free hand. The field rippled without warning and a numbing jolt lanced up my arm. Lurching back, I watched in horror as large blisters erupted across my skin and swiftly hardened into scales that spread up my arm. Gripping the pocket with my entire fist, I concentrated, willing the reality of human flesh to return. After a brief struggle, the scales withered and fell away, like leaves in winter, revealing unmarked skin underneath.

"What the hell was that?" Esmeray's eyes were wide in her face.

"A warning," I growled.

Metamorphoses was toying with me.

A bout of dizziness struck, whining through my ears. The night receded in favour of a city I once knew; braziers replaced electric lights and the roads became cobbled streets filled with a heaving throng of people moving towards the chariot races at the Hippodrome. A roar swelled from a thousand voices. I merged with the crowd, my voice hoarse from cheering, thrilling at the sight of sand spraying from beneath flashing wheels. Horses screamed when they fell. Chariots disintegrated in a spray of timber and flying bodies as they collided with fallen mounts. Cries of dismay were met with shrieks of triumph as the opposing factions rode the fortunes of their favourites.

I closed my eyes, trying to block out the vision. Is that what Metamorphoses wanted? A return to the old ways, before modern medicine and science, when life was so precarious that every fleeting pleasure had to be cherished?

Perhaps.

Ever mercurial, she was a force that lived only in the moment and cared nothing for the needs of tomorrow.

The emotions of the Hippodrome tried to draw me back. I resisted, shaking with the effort.

"Zeite?"

The shaking became more insistent.

"Zeite!"

I blinked, blundering through ancient ghosts, trying to find my way back to the *Now*.

Esmeray gripped me by the shoulders. "Are you all right?"

Anchors. Without them, we're all adrift.

"I'm…fine. Just remembering. Different times. Different ways of living."

"The incursion point." Esmeray squeezed for emphasis. "Do you know where it is?"

147

I touched the tip of my index finger against her temple. "Why it's right here, Esmeray. That's where they always begin."

She drew back, uncertain at whatever she saw in my expression. "Not what I meant." Prickles of fear lifted from the edge of her field like the hackles of a cat. It was her distress more than anything else that finally grounded me in the present.

"I'm sorry."

A shiver ran through me. I turned towards the enduring magnificence that is Hagia Sophia and pointed to the left of it. "The incursion is underground. Somewhere over there."

"The Basilica Cistern," Khavad said to Esmeray. "Been closed for renovations for weeks."

"Or so we were told." Esmeray spoke quickly into her mic and the security detail tightened ranks. Each agent was clad in jeans and bulky jackets to hide their weapons.

We hurried over to the main entrance to the cistern, less than a block away.

"We go down first," Khavad said. "Once we've cleared the area of any hosts, Esmeray and Zeite will follow."

"No." I shook my head. "Go down there without me and you'll never be the same. Have you forgotten the graveyard?"

The men traded uneasy looks.

"The Chief said to protect you," Khavad argued.

"And you should," I agreed. "In this instance, that means staying close. You, Esmeray, and you two, stay with me." I picked two of the security detail at random. "Station two men at the entrance to ensure we're not ambushed. The other two need to cover the exit on Alemdar Street."

"This is not what I agreed with the Chief," Khavad protested. "He said—"

I held my hand up for silence. "Station Chief Mehmet is thinking in conventional terms. Whatever is waiting down there is anything but conventional."

Khavad glanced at Esmeray, who nodded reluctantly. "Very well." Khavad dispatched two agents to guard the far exit.

I rolled my shoulders to loosen the tension knotting my spine. Metamorphoses and her acolytes were waiting for us. She had carefully engineered this outcome, and I could think of no way to surprise her.

"If someone would like to break in," I said in a casual tone, "we can finish this."

Khavad's men made short work of the lock and the alarm rigged to the tourist entrance. The main fuse box had already been wrecked. Khavad and one of the agents led the way down, their flashlights slicing through the darkness. Esmeray took up a position behind my right shoulder, while the remaining agent flanked me on the other side.

A wide set of steps took us deep underground. It was cooler down here and very still. Istanbul's vibrant pulse faded as we descended to the original level of the ancient city. Water glinted in the beams of the torches and slowly, almost reluctantly, magnificent pillars emerged from the gloom. The tourist walkway threaded between two rows of columns that stretched into the darkness, only a foot above the waterline.

"Zeite?" Khavad's whisper thrummed with tension. The beams of the torches cut off unnaturally a dozen feet from our position, as if they'd struck a black velvet curtain.

"Wait," I ordered.

We halted amidst the worn pillars, my senses straining to pierce the ancient veil that blanketed this place. The cistern had once been a vital arterial of Constantinople. Time had reduced it to a withered vein, yet water still trickled into it and the sheer press of humanity over the centuries lent the reality of this place a density that few places in the world could rival.

Metamorphoses had chosen her location with care.

The satchel was a heavy weight against my hip. I connected with the pocket and teased out four strands. They glowed silver, pure potentiality that would be visible to even mortal eyes.

"What are you doing?" Esmeray asked behind me.

"Linking us together." I wrapped a strand around each of the four mortals and bound them to me. So long as we remained connected, they would continue to abide in the reality they knew and understood.

Or so I hoped.

"Follow the walkway."

Khavad nodded and inched forward. The beam of his torch caught tiny ripples in the water beneath the raised platform. An occasional pale fish darted through the inky water, startled by the sudden light.

We were being lured in, one reluctant step at a time. Yet it was the only way to close the incursion.

The first change was subtle. Where the darkness had been so deep it almost possessed a texture, the shadows took on a faintly green hue. The temperature dropped until our breath misted. As if that were a signal, fog rolled in across the water, unfurling between the ancient columns like sails.

An arrow hissed past my leg, narrowly missing Esmeray. Khavad dropped into a crouch and fired three quick rounds. Someone cried out, followed by a heavy splash.

A second arrow from the opposite side of the cistern caught Khavad in the upper arm. He grunted, then cursed as his weapon dropped into the water. The two agents returned fire as Esmeray dragged me to the ground, shielding me with her body. The sound of gunfire was deafening.

The fog thickened, obscuring all visibility. No more arrows whispered through the darkness. Esmeray eventually let me up and I dissolved the shaft in Khavad's arm, leaving the head embedded until it could be safely removed.

We shuffled forward. Our flashlights created strange shadows in the fog. The silence gathered, taunting us with what might lie just beyond our sight.

Tendrils of water crept up the pillars, winding sinuously around the old stone. They reminded me of vines, and as that thought occurred to me, the water became thick with fibrous ropes that sprouted white flowers.

"What's happening?" Khavad swept his torch with his good hand.

"Transformation," I replied. "Stay close. Touch nothing."

Glittering serpents rose from the water and bared crystal fangs at us, only to drop away and reappear in new positions. One surfaced next to the walkway and struck at the agent on my left.

It bounced off the bubble of reality that I had summoned. The agent fired a round before I could stop him. The bullet lodged in the snake's head and it assumed a gunmetal hue. The next round bounced off with a ringing peal that echoed through the cistern. The serpent struck again, lodging metal fangs in the agent's leg, and dragged him into the water. He didn't even have time to scream. Water serpents swarmed over him, turning an arterial red.

The thread connecting me to the unfortunate agent snapped with a painful recoil.

"Amir!" The second agent rushed forward to aid his comrade. I caught the thread that connected us and dragged the agent back from the water.

"We must help him," the man panted, wild-eyed. "He's not dead. He's—"

"Gone," I cut in. "You can't save him. Holster your gun. You too, Esmeray. This isn't the place for them."

Ophiuchus.

My ancient name shivered through the fog and rippled across the water.

Come, my wayward brother.

A breeze whispered through the mist, teasing out impossible shapes. A replica of the agent's face appeared on the right, his mouth open in silent horror. A miniature version of the Blue Mosque faced Hagia Sophia. A chasm widened between the two iconic buildings until they toppled over, crashing into each other.

Stone groaned as it shifted. The mist parted, a damp, grey curtain suddenly drawn aside. One of the pillars twisted towards us. Carved into the base of the column was the stylised face of the Medusa. Marble eyelids blinked and a glistening tongue rasped against cruel lips. The carved asps radiating from her scalp pulled free of the pillar with audible cracks.

Come.

She drew in a deep, grinding breath. The satchel jerked towards her, pulling me off balance. I stumbled and crashed into Khavad, who groaned in pain. Esmeray checked my slide towards the Medusa. The remaining agent caught my elbow and helped me up.

Come. This rebellion of yours must end. The ladder teeters without you to hold it.

"No," I replied. "Humanity deserves the chance to write its own destiny, free of your influence."

The Medusa smiled, revealing blackened teeth.

And never have they been closer to extinction. Have you truly become so blind?

I scrambled back from the Medusa and clutched the satchel to my chest. A serpent rose from the water. Unlike the ones before, it glittered silver with potentiality.

I twisted away from the strike, reinforcing the field of reality around me by drawing on the memories of the three mortals anchoring me to modern Istanbul. It should have been enough. Too late I realised that Metamorphoses had focused her incursion into this single point. The snake's fangs sank into the back of my hand.

Venom raced up my arm and scales reappeared in its wake. My right hand became twisted and clawed as I watched in horror.

My taloned fingers closed around the agent's windpipe.

"Zeite! What are you doing?" Esmeray's eyes were wide with terror.

The pulse of the crowd from the Hippodrome beat a tempo through me. They wanted sport. They wanted blood. What was one more victim in the endless tide of humanity?

I squeezed and the man's fear flooded into me as he fought to break my grip.

Drawing heavily on Esmeray and Khavad's memories, I resisted the compulsion to tear out the man's throat. The poison seared my veins and my grip tightened.

The agent gave up trying to break free. He closed his eyes instead, committing his soul to the Spark or whatever god he believed in.

It was the submission that saved him.

His willingness to sacrifice his life reminded me of Nene Sitti. A well of compassion opened inside me. Drawing upon this unexpected source of strength, I forced my grip open. The agent fell to his knees, gasping for breath.

The Medusa inhaled again. I staggered as I fought the pull on my satchel. The Archetype within me strained against the flesh that housed it. It felt like my tendons were ripping apart and I groaned with pain.

Metamorphoses drew the pocket of the Ladder towards her.

"You mustn't let her touch me," I said through gritted teeth. "If she draws me back into the Ladder, the Vices will sweep across the world unchecked. Everything will be plunged into chaos and darkness."

Esmeray looped an arm around my shoulder and locked her hands. After a brief hesitation, Khavad did the same.

"Tell us what to do," she said

The Medusa drew in another breath. I was dragged across the wet stone despite their best efforts.

"The two of you need to anchor me in this reality. Think of mundane things. Bus timetables. Your favourite brand of coffee. Supermarket shelves. Anything."

I turned to the remaining agent. "Find the acolyte that's holding this incursion open. They must be down here somewhere." I struggled to summon my chimes and salt. "Douse the body in salt, walk around it ringing these, then set the body on fire."

He accepted my tools with shaking hands, a wild and uncertain look in his eye. "I'll do my best."

"Get it done." I cut the thread that bound us. "Go!" He dashed off into the fog, the sound of tiny bells following him.

The Medusa sucked more air through her marble lips. The satchel slithered across the ground and dragged me with it. "Focus," I yelled at Esmeray and Khavad. "Close your eyes. Think of recipes or shopping lists. Now!"

I wrestled my satchel to the ground and pinned it with my knees. The Medusa was only a dozen feet away. I might resist her pull for another two, maybe three breaths, but that was all.

Esmeray and Khavad braced me, their eyes shut and faces clenched as they strived to ignore the madness surrounding them.

I desperately searched for another way out of this, but with the pocket being drawn ever closer to Metamorphoses, my main weapon was useless. Only the two mortals could anchor me. I thought of Sitti again, of her sacrifices. Had they all been made, unknowingly, for this moment? I pushed the idea away in disgust.

The satchel skidded further across the floor. I was almost out of time.

Twisting, I placed my hands on Esmeray and Khavad's foreheads. "I'm sorry," I whispered.

You must understand that I draw my existence from the collective agreement that you mortals call reality. The collective unconscious is my blood, it's my muscle and sinew, it's the marrow of what I am.

And yet...I wish to be one of you.

An individual in my own right. Not simply some remote, dispassionate curator.

So, I drew their memories, their lives, their individuality, into me. A flood of sensations and images rushed past. I only caught glimpses flashing through the conduit that I had created; unfamiliar faces smiling and laughing at a wedding; standing in a shady park and watching the sun setting over the Bosphorus; crying in Sitti's lap as she stroked my hair.

These memories and many more settled into the core of my being.

I clung to the Istanbul of today through Esmeray and Khavad. Trams rattled overhead. Tourists browsed brightly lit shops filled with carpets and coloured glass lamps. Cell phones connected via invisible lines of data. Countless thousands laughed and wept, lived and died, and yearned for something *more* in between.

There was no room for myth here.

No place for glittering serpents that rose from water or statues that moved with a will of their own.

Most people in this city agreed that such things could not exist. And I channelled that denial at the Medusa.

Metamorphoses' lips curled back in a snarl. The watery serpents writhed furiously, lashing their tails in frothy fury. The fog crackled with a dangerous charge, dissolving and reforming into a million different shapes. Yet I remained untouched. Through Esmeray and Khavad, I tapped into the consciousness of Istanbul.

The majority in this city worshipped certainty and progress, not half-forgotten legends.

The Medusa shrieked as her face cracked. Her asps splintered into shards of stone that fell into the water. The lips fractured and her eyes rolled back. In moments, the entire manifestation crumbled, and the cistern returned to our reality.

Badly shaken, I regained my feet and shouldered my satchel. The scales on my arm sank back into my flesh, leaving only faint scars. Yet I sensed a residue of her poison remained.

The surviving agent flashed his torch from the far corner of the cistern. A fire crackled above the water, so I assumed he had dispatched the acolyte. Esmeray and Khavad remained still, however, caught in mid-crouch, hands hanging loosely by their sides. I bowed my head, unable to bear the blank look on their faces.

I had no choice.

Please believe that.

I pressed my forehead against the cold glass of the observation window. Mehmet was talking at me, as usual. At least half a dozen people had squeezed into the observation room: security, high-ranking officials from the Bureau, report-takers. I ignored them all.

My gaze was fixed on Esmeray.

She lay on a hospital gurney, her glossy black hair draped over a pillow. The orderlies had drawn up the sheet to preserve her modesty, not that it was necessary. Not anymore.

She would eat or drink if sustenance was pressed upon her. She would close her eyes if the lights were turned off and open them again when the room was illuminated. Her pulse was a steady fifty-six beats per minute, and according to the doctors, she remained in perfect health.

Khavad lay on a gurney next to her, in a similar, almost unresponsive state.

My gaze dropped to the floor. The truth was I had stolen her. Khavad, too. Sacrificed them to keep the Archetypes contained. Yet in those last desperate moments, it was self-preservation that had motivated me. The taste of shame was a new and bitter flavour I had never encountered before.

"Are you even listening to me?" Mehmet forced his way into my field of vision. The Station Chief radiated barely contained fury.

"What happened?" Mehmet demanded. "How did they fall into this coma? When will they wake?"

Meeting Mehmet's angry stare, I said, "Long ago, I renounced my place. Do you know why? Do any of you know why?"

I paused, knowing that my response was being recorded for future analysis. The fate of the collaborator is to always be met with suspicion and distrust, is it not?

Pointing at Esmeray, I said, "This is what happens when the Vices are allowed to touch the mortal world." I glanced around the observation room. "You lose yourselves. Utterly and irretrievably. You like to think that whatever compass guides you in life will navigate their storm, but you are wrong. Esmeray and Khavad stood before the gates of oblivion and hauled me back. That's what happened."

Mehmet digested this in silence. Eventually he cleared his throat. "Has the incursion been closed?"

"For now."

Mehmet frowned. "Will it open again?"

I didn't bother answering that question. Metamorphoses had placed her mark upon me. I had no idea what that meant yet. Although while it remained, the incursion was not entirely closed.

Pushing past Mehmet, I entered the hospital room. Esmeray stared blankly at the ceiling. A terrible, aching heaviness settled within the part of me that was almost human. She did not deserve this. Neither of them did.

I placed a kiss on her forehead, brushed a strand of hair aside, and let the grief fill me. When I could stand no more, I quietly left.

Esmeray would want me to visit Sitti, yet I doubt I can face the old woman. No explanation I could offer would make sense. No apology would ease her grief.

I needed time.

Time to find a way to undo what I had done. Or failing that, time to find a way to live with it.

Afterword

This novelette is original to this collection.

The character of Zeite has been with me for quite a few years, and he has been quite insistent about having his story properly told. I soon realised it was much grander in scope than the piece you've just read, especially once I started researching his backstory and those of the twelve Archetypes.

Fortunately, his memoir continues in the next story, and concludes in the final one of this collection.

Almost Human:
Untethered

*S*ince Metamorphoses invoked my true name in the underground
cistern in Istanbul, the memory of what I had once been has been
circling ever closer.

*If you are reading this memoir, then I must assume the Vices have
stripped me of my memories and pressed me back into service of the
Ladder. If that is truly the case, then this memoir is the only record of
what I have come to understand.*

Please permit me a brief tangent.

*When the Babylonians gazed upon the Ophiuchus constellation,
they saw a serpent god in the night sky. The ancient Greeks came to
a similar conclusion, believing my stars were placed in the heavens in
honour of Asclepius, the god of medicine whose symbol was a rod with
a serpent coiled around it.*

My point?

*The snake from ancient mythology is the twisting, double helix of the
Ladder, which locks the Archetypes of Virtue into an eternal struggle for
supremacy with the Archetypes of Vice. So, it falls to me, the only Archetype
free of a pre-ordained struggle, to temper the ills that befall humanity.*

*To you, my future self, I say only this: do not be content with
simply channelling the primal urges from the Ladder into the mortal
plane. You must be both healer and warrior, always striving to dilute
the worst compulsions sent by the Vices. Without a steady hand at
the tiller, humanity will never set sail from the shores of its excesses,
dooming mortal and Archetype alike to an endless, pointless conflict.*

Ophiuchus, 2020.

INCURSION 318 – BOZHENTSI,
CENTRAL BULGARIA, JANUARY 2020

Snow fell gently outside the cottage, muffling all sound. No birds called. No cows lowed in the fields. Even the distant rumble of traffic had stilled. I felt cocooned from the world, wrapped in a silent, solitary moment that I knew couldn't possibly last.

After Istanbul and the inevitable interrogations that followed, I craved solitude. To justify my departure, I told the Order that I needed to unravel the nature of the poison Metamorphoses had infected me with. This was true, up to a point. Hidden behind this façade of honesty was a more difficult truth: every time I closed my eyes, I saw Esmeray's face. Her field is flat and inert, like a weathered slab of stone, and her gaze is fixed on some distant place that I can't reach.

I had done this to her. I had sacrificed her, and her partner Khavad, to save myself.

Unable to bear my cowardice, I fled to Bozhentsi, a tiny village in central Bulgaria.

The empty cottage I had chosen was little more than a hovel. Winter's cold fingers pried at the cracks in the crumbling mortar that held the ancient stones together. The builders had only seen the need for one small, square window. Happy to shut out the world, I had closed the curtains against the gathering dark. Smoke drifted up from the hearth in the middle of the cottage and eventually found a way out through the rudimentary chimney. There was almost no furniture to speak of; only a scattering of furs on the rough wooden floor and a solitary sideboard that might have been constructed from timbers pilfered from the ark.

A crude iron tripod crouched over the flames. Stew bubbled in a blackened pot that hung from the tripod, which I found strangely soothing. Using the hem of my grey, three-quarter length coat, I lifted the pot off the tripod and placed it on the floor. Rummaging through the shelves, I found a scratched wooden bowl and matching spoon.

I was just settling down to eat when someone knocked.

Bozhentsi was all but empty in late January when the full weight of winter blanketed the countryside. The only tavern in the village was closed and most cottages were boarded up. So how did someone reach my doorstep without me sensing them in advance?

Rising cautiously to my feet, I skirted a pair of empty vodka bottles, and retrieved my battered leather satchel lying in the corner. Only then did I extend my awareness beyond the walls of the cottage. My visitor was female, impatient and icily determined. Her field was also hazy, becoming more elusive the harder I tried to read it.

This was new.

I considered my options. Escaping into the snowbound night was not particularly appealing. Ignoring this visitor was unlikely to work, given she was undoubtedly from the Order and had gone to some trouble to track me down.

My gaze settled on the steaming bowl of stew. Food that I had cooked. With vegetables that I had purchased. After floundering through the snow to barter with my nearest neighbour.

Why should I leave? This was meant to be my sanctuary.

The knock became more insistent.

"Zeite, open the door. It's not getting any warmer out here."

The tone was familiar. The voice was not.

"Go away." Hardly sophisticated, I'll grant you, but brevity has its benefits.

"It's urgent!"

"It's always fucking urgent," I snapped. "Find someone else."

"We've already lost two teams."

"Not my problem." I knew I was being churlish but more important matters demanded my attention, like stew and unravelling the existential nature of identity.

The door shuddered in its frame from a heavy blow. "Stop being an ass! We've lost contact with a Tender."

I stilled.

That couldn't be true. The twelve Tenders were responsible for guarding the capstones that anchored me to the mortal plane.

Without them, I couldn't take physical form, just like the rest of the Archetypes. So, if something had happened to a Tender, I should have sensed it.

I slid my hand into my satchel and connected with the swirling pocket of potentiality that I had drained from the Ladder. Picturing a three-dimensional web, I expanded the visualisation to encompass twelve points radiating outwards. The closer the Tender, the thicker the thread. The nearest one was less than thirty kilometres away, yet I couldn't discern anything about them other than their proximity.

Something was definitely amiss.

Sighing, I stomped over to the door, lifted the heavy latch, and yanked it open. Deep snowdrifts had gathered outside the porch. The agent was swaddled in a white ski jacket with grey fur trim lining the hood. Her skin was pale, apart from a light smattering of freckles across the bridge of her nose and cheeks. Hard blue eyes studied me.

She was not alone.

At least two more agents—all dressed identically—had taken up positions around the cottage. One had bunkered down in a drift near the wood hut. Another was positioned in a nearby stand of trees. Both carried assault rifles.

"That fire looks inviting," the agent said with an arch of her eyebrows.

Wordlessly, I stepped aside. She hurried inside and squatted in front of the hearth, removing her gloves and hood. Wisps of auburn hair escaped a tight ponytail. Her face was lean, almost elfin. I closed the door with a sinking sense of despair.

"Eating alone?" she asked with a nod at the bowl.

"Company is overrated," I growled.

She shrugged, and I couldn't tell whether she disagreed or not.

"Got a name?" I asked.

"Delaine."

"How many in your squad?"

"Three." Delaine rubbed her pale hands together. "They've set up a perimeter to ensure we're not disturbed."

"Too late for that." I picked up my bowl and sat on a deerskin.

Delaine flashed a grin over the fire and crossed her legs on the hard floor. "I read the report on Istanbul. Some members of the Fraternum think your resolve is wavering. Do they have a point?"

This woman seemed to have an unnatural talent for asking uncomfortable questions. I couldn't decide whether I was warming to her or not. "Did you see the last team I worked with?"

"I did." She nudged a log further into the flames. "Didn't sound like you had much of a choice."

"Tell that to their loved ones," I replied.

Delaine shrugged. "We do whatever it takes. Every agent understands that."

I had no desire to rehash my mistakes with this woman. "What do you want?"

"An answer to my question would be a good start." She fixed me with a level stare. "Because if your conviction *is* wavering, I need to know right now."

That was a step too far. My rebellion against the Archetypes had spanned more than eight centuries and countless humans had fallen in those running skirmishes. Over time, I had grudgingly learned to accept that not everyone could be saved. Esmeray and Khavad were different: their loss had been my choice. And if I was willing to make that choice, was I any better than the Vices?

"What gives you the right to ask me that?"

Delaine gestured to the empty vodka bottles lying on the floor. "Well, first off, it looks a lot like you're hosting a pity party for one. Second, I've got friends in those teams that went dark. People I trained with. People who believe in the work we do."

Despite her brusque manner, the field around Delaine's chest was jagged with anxiety. She was more anxious than she was letting on. "And you've got someone inside the installation," I guessed.

"Huh." She gave me a searching look. "My father is Head of Operations at Dryanovski Monastery. He reported a power outage and system failures before they went offline. An emergency response team of four were dispatched. When they went dark, a heavily armed squad of twelve were sent to investigate. Command hasn't heard from the second team in over nine hours."

"And that's all you know?" I set the untasted stew aside.

"There's one more thing." Delaine withdrew a pouch from her pocket. "This was found at the extraction point for the second team. What do you make of it?" She untied the pouch and an onyx disc dropped into her palm. Etched into the surface was a symbol I recognised: a small circle surrounded by a larger one, with the twelve symbols of the Zodiac—the ancient signs of the Archetypes—punctuating the outer circle. Thin grooves connected each symbol to the inner circle, which contained a serpent entwined around a staff.

This seal was my gateway into the mortal plane.

My fingers trembled as I accepted the stone.

Potentiality whooshed through the cottage, more felt than heard, as if we were deep underwater. The walls warped and the flames in the hearth twisted into a spiral that strained towards the roof beams. The stone slid from my numb hand and fell, with me following close behind...

...the ground slammed into my back and air exploded from my lungs. I gasped, wheezing for breath.

The cottage was gone, replaced by a glittering canopy of stars overhead. I lay spread-eagled on the ground. Lifting my head, I found my limbs were tied to iron stakes that had been driven into a large slab of rock. A perfect circle surrounded me, like the circle enclosing da Vinci's Vitruvian Man. *Large braziers had been positioned at intervals perhaps twenty strides away. By their unsteady light I made out people sitting cross-legged in a large circle around me. Their simple woollen robes were rough and cinched with plain leather belts. Straining, I could just make out the double helix symbol embossed on each buckle. With their heads bowed, I couldn't make out their faces, although the variety of skin tones implied a gathering of the races of humanity. Each person bore a shallow cut in one hand, from which they squeezed a trickle of blood onto crystal figurines cradled in their laps.*

With a jolt of surprise, I realised this was the summoning ceremony that had allowed me to cross into the mortal realm for the first time. Each figurine was a capstone, a receptacle for siphoning the compulsions of the twelve Archetypes to ensure I was free of their influence when I inhabited the body of the thirteenth Tender. This was my birth, my first taste of humanity.

"Impossible," I whispered through numb lips. This all happened more than eight centuries ago. How could I be back here?

"Impossible?" a voice repeated. "How can that be true when it has already happened?"

A compact man with dark hair, olive skin and oddly tilted eyes appeared behind one of the robed Tenders. The Tender's figurine depicted a stern-faced man with one hand resting on the pommel of his sword, the other arm pointing in an unmistakable gesture of command: the capstone for Tyrannos, the Tyrant.

The stranger stepped between the Tenders, heedless of the boundaries of the seal he was crossing. He was richly dressed, garbed in a robe of royal blue adorned with thirteen polished black buttons that ran from neck to groin. A belt of woven gold encircled his slim waist.

The inner circle surrounding me flared at his approach, a shimmering wall of potentiality that twisted up into the sky. This seal was, in effect, one end of a tunnel. The other end led to the primal realm, and even though this was surely only a memory, I could still feel the pull of the Ladder.

The intruder stopped just beyond the edge of the inner circle.

"Who are you?" I demanded.

He studied me with eyes that were dark and full of disdain. "I am what you should have been. A loyal servant of the Archetypes."

"That certainly sounds like some of them," I replied. "No need for a name, just a position description."

The stranger smiled. "Ah, your infamous nonchalance. Do hold onto it for as long as you can, Thirteenth. This personality you've cultivated will soon be stripped away."

"This is a delusion." I tugged at my bonds. Annoyingly, they felt quite real.

"No. This is a foretelling wrapped in a memory."

He strode over to the Tender holding the Tyrant's capstone.

"You have held the Archetypes at bay longer than any thought possible. Yet inequality and conflict persist. It's time to accept your approach has failed."

Metamorphoses had said something similar in Istanbul. This upstart didn't deserve a better answer than I gave her. "Humanity will evolve. Given enough time, they'll outgrow the constraints of the Archetypes. It's the only way to break the cycle."

"And when will that be?"

"When they're ready."

"Hardly convincing." The servant placed his hand on top of the Tender's head. "Your rebellion is over. The Ladder will be restored, although I don't think you'll be forgiven." He drew a blade from his sleeve and tilted the Tender's head back. The cowl fell away to reveal the lined face of a woman with grey hair.

"Stop!"

"You set this in motion, Thirteenth." The servant sliced the Tender's throat open. Blood gushed down her chest and splashed over the capstone. The figurine split in two and a piece of me tore open. My heels and skull drummed against the rock as a convulsion wracked my body.

I fell, upwards this time, into a different body and time.

"Zeite?" A hand shook my shoulder. "Zeite!"

Delaine's concerned face swam into focus. My head throbbed and my throat was parched.

"What happened?" I croaked.

"You collapsed." Her gaze darted towards my outstretched hand. "When you touched that stone."

Propping up on one elbow, I let her pull me into a sitting position. She was stronger than she looked.

"I'll help you retake the monastery. But enough with the questions, understood?" I had let Esmeray get too close. I couldn't afford to repeat that mistake with Delaine.

Her worried expression softened. "Is fainting a habit with you? Sorry, but I need to know."

"I did *not* faint. It was…a…vision."

She arched an eyebrow. "If you say so." Thumbing her mic, she said, "G2G. Repeat: good to go. Decamp in five."

Groaning, I regained my feet. Why were agents always so exhausting?

"You never explained how you were able to sneak up on me." Not the best way to start a conversation, although the appearance of four agents without warning still irked me.

Delaine and I sat in the back seat of a white Range Rover fitted with snow chains. A grey, unmarked Hummer followed us as we drove through the dark, snow-shrouded landscape.

"Our gear is bonded with sodium chloride at a molecular level." Delaine grinned at me. "Don't ask me how it works. The design was inspired by something you said."

They had fused their clothes with salt. No wonder I hadn't sensed their presence earlier. "What did I say?"

Delaine tilted her head as she tried to remember. "Something like, 'Every intention leaves a ripple on the face of reality, but salt deadens the effect'."

I stared out the window and made a mental note to take more care with my phrasing in future. We passed through a stand of pine trees with drifts of snow piled against their trunks. Our convoy had avoided larger roads in favour of bumpy country lanes and we hadn't encountered any other vehicles. Hardly surprising given it was the early hours of the morning.

"How much longer?"

Delaine leaned towards me to see out the front windscreen. "This is our stop."

The track ended in a large clearing that might have been a picnic area in better weather. A few rough tables poked through the thick blanket of snow. We passed a second Hummer parked at the mouth of the clearing and stopped in front of a large white van with a number of aerials on the roof.

"Oh goody," I muttered. "Briefing time."

"This will be swift," Delaine promised. "The Regional Station Chief is not one for ceremony."

We trudged across the soft snow. The freezing air burned in my throat. I liked the sensation. Made me feel sharp.

The back doors of the van swung open and we were ushered inside. It was cramped inside with a set of shelves housing a short-wave radio, a satellite phone, and a few computer screens.

A rack had been bolted to the other side of the van and it held an impressive array of guns. I spied a handful of Heckler & Koch G36s assault rifles.

"Dobro utro," said a heavy-set, bearded man in Bulgarian. He was squeezed behind a small table and had one of the thickest necks I'd ever seen.

Deciding it was *not* a good morning, I replied, "Good evening," in Bulgarian instead.

"English, please," he replied. "For Delaine to understand." He gestured for us to join him at the table.

Delaine made the introductions. "Zeite, this is Commander Vasil Grigorov, Balkans' Regional Station Chief."

"An honour to meet legend," Vasil said with a heavy accent.

Drawing my frayed coat tight, I swung my battered leather satchel into my lap. "Well met," I replied.

A wary look flitted across the broad planes of Vasil's face. "That is pocket, yes?"

I patted the satchel. "Da."

"Good, good." Vasil unrolled a map, pinned it to the table, and tapped a location with a thick forefinger. "So, to business. Dryanovski Manastir is here. Is built in deep valley. Only one road next to Yantra River." He traced the river on the map. "Manastir is surrounded by limestone cliffs. One way in, one way out."

I studied the aerial map. The monastery's cluster of buildings was positioned at the foot of a natural cul-de-sac with the river bordering one side. Apart from an aerial bombardment, it should have been an easy place to defend.

"How many inside the installation?" I asked.

"The manastir houses Tender, her disciples, twenty guards, and support staff."

"Any signs of activity?"

Vasil nodded, which meant "no" in Bulgarian. "Power is still out. Drone surveillance shows nothing. No bodies, no movement. And no one talking inside."

"So, no demands or threats," I mused. "And you've lost contact with both teams that went in to investigate. So that's an additional sixteen personnel on top of the forty or so already stationed there?"

"Correct," Delaine replied. "We're assuming they're being held hostage."

I leaned back in my folding chair. "So, whoever seized the installation has plenty of equipment and human shields. Plus, they'll be expecting us to try again."

"Expecting *you*." Vasil pointed a stubby finger at me.

I nodded. "You have a plan, I take it."

Vasil gave me a broad smile. "Have *good* plan. We send detachment down main road to make perimeter. If can't take installation, we contain situation. Make sense, yes?"

"That's normal protocol," I agreed.

"Hostiles focus on perimeter. At same time, we drop small team on cliff here." Vasil tapped the map.

"Won't they hear our approach?"

"We have a stealth chopper," Delaine replied. "Quieter than a cricket's fart."

The Order was pulling out all stops with this incursion. "Fine. Let's assume we reach the cliff without being detected. Then what? Looks like an icy descent."

Vasil tapped the side of his flat nose. "Secret shaft in cliff. Used during Ottoman occupation. Reinforced now. Climb down shaft and through back door."

Not bad, although it relied upon a lot of things going right. "Are you sure this shaft is clear?"

"We believe so," Delaine replied.

"And the Tender's installation is underground."

Delaine nodded. "The original monastery was razed by the Ottomans more than once. It was rebuilt in the 1800s and that's when the bunker was excavated."

"Let's see the schematics then."

Vasil unrolled a set of blueprints. The underground complex was relatively modest: barracks for the guards, an octagonal mess hall, a few offices, private chambers for the Tender and her disciples, and a secure vault for the capstone. The bottom of our shaft connected with one of the administrative offices. If any hostages were still alive, that room was probably too small to contain them.

Vasil's field quivered with a subtle ripple of apprehension. I shot him a look. "You're not coming with us?"

He shifted uncomfortably. "I make perimeter. And Plan B." He spread his hands apologetically.

That wasn't a surprise: Station Chiefs tended to command from the rear. I studied the big man's field, noting the jagged edges that curled away from me. "Ah, Plan B. Yes, I suppose someone needs to give the order to bomb the complex if we fail."

The chair creaked as Vasil shifted his bulk. "Please understand. Bureau cannot lose capstone. This never happen in eight hundred years."

"It won't come to that." I frowned. "So, who is riding shotgun?"

Delaine lifted her chin. "That would be my squad."

"Only four?"

"The chopper can only carry six, which includes the pilot." Delaine gave me a questioning look. "Besides, didn't you once say force is not always the answer?"

These quotes of mine were becoming a problem.

"Get rest," Vasil said, waving us out. "Helicopter in one hour."

I suppose we should discuss the Order.

They call themselves the Bureau now, although in reality, not much has changed since the first Tenders ushered me into the mortal realm. Taking their cue from the militant orders that existed at that time, the Order was divided into three main branches, which persist even to this day: the Sophists, the Officium, and the Fraternum.

The Sophists are centred around the twelve installations scattered across the globe that serve as repositories for the capstones. Each Tender is charged with protecting their capstone, and to select a successor from their disciples, when their mortal span comes to an end. I'm told much of their time is spent in study, analysing the way their assigned Archetype influences the human mind.

The Officium are the administrative arm of the Order. Both accountants and diplomats, they are responsible for balancing ledgers, managing investments, and handling local authorities. I'm told some governments are aware of the Order and their activities, but many are not. Given the fleeting nature of most regimes, it's not something I've paid much attention to.

If the Sophists are the spirit of the Order, and the Officium are its beating financial heart, then the Fraternum are its fists and feet. To them falls the task of guarding the Order from threats, whether mortal or otherwise. From knights to commanders to agents, it has been members of the Fraternum who stood by my side when confronting the worst incursions. I may have lost count of how many have fallen over the centuries, yet their resolve and courage are etched into my vitalis, the essence of who I have become.

The Order's motto is "Honor est in ministerio": In service is honour.

Makes me cringe every time.

I approached Delaine as she inspected the magazine of her sidearm in the light of her headlamp. Flakes of snow drifted through the beam and settled over us like a whispered benediction. Otherwise the night was still.

"What did you think of Vasil's briefing?"

Delaine holstered her pistol and folded her arms across her chest. Only Harkins, Delaine's sandy-haired second-in-command, paused in his preparations to listen. He was tall and lean, like a marathon runner, yet unloaded large boxes of equipment from the Hummer without any sign of effort. Snowflakes glimmered in his closely cropped beard.

"To the point," Delaine replied. "Why do you ask?"

"Well, I'm compiling a list of unanswered questions. Care to add any?" That earned a snort of amusement from Harkins.

The corners of Delaine's eyes crinkled when she smiled. "Plenty, but I'm not sure we have time to play this game."

"Indulge me in just one then. How does a secure, underground installation fall with only a power alarm triggered?"

"Good question," Delaine conceded.

"Inside job," Harkins said over his shoulder.

We both turned to look at him and he shrugged. "Pretty obvious."

I nodded. "Perhaps you should be running this op."

Harkins laughed and returned to rummaging through the equipment he had unloaded.

"Looking to replace me already?" Delaine asked in mock outrage.

The tops of the pine trees stirred. She glanced up at the night sky and then at her watch. I saw it wasn't quite two in the morning. "Chopper's here."

I caught Delaine's arm. "This is no mundane op. Something bigger is at play." I briefly considered telling her about my vision but decided against it. Like she said, we didn't have time to play other people's games.

"We've spent a long time preparing for a mission like this, Zeite." Delaine carefully extracted her arm.

Damn humans.

Why did they always think that being "prepared" was enough? History was littered with examples where that fallacy had proven their undoing.

The helicopter settled in the middle of the clearing in a flurry of powdered snow. Delaine was right: the engine was remarkably quiet. The squad shrugged on their backpacks, shouldered their rifles and hurried over, hunching to avoid the spinning rotor blades.

I didn't like the smell of this. Not one bit.

The attack on the monastery had come too soon after the incursion in Istanbul. And the vision of the seal and my entry into the mortal plane had unsettled me more than I'd care to admit. I only had a few pieces to a puzzle that felt much bigger than just Dryanovski Monastery.

Delaine gave me a *get-your-ass-over-here* look.

Life has a way of winnowing out choices. Either I boarded the chopper, or I refused and proved my doubters correct.

I booted a chunk of snow into the pine trees. Just once it might be nice to hold the initiative.

For such a quiet machine, the ride was rough. Every gust of air sent my stomach lurching and I quickly came to the conclusion it was best to stare at something inside the cabin, rather than tracking the shadowed landscape below.

Delaine's squad appeared to be divided on how to treat me. Harkins kept his hands busy, triple checking his equipment in a way that spoke of long practice. Kennett was a broad, muscled woman with skin the colour of whipped caramel. She'd shaved the sides of her head but allowed the rest to grow, so it was bound in tight black braids and held together by a pair of elastic bands. Every time I glanced in her direction I was met with a frown and compressed lips. Ranieri, on the other hand, sought my gaze, although he made it a challenge, as if staring down the barrel of a gun. He was average in height and build, with sallow features and dark, unkempt hair. He spent most of the flight polishing an impressive collection of knives. No doubt a nervous habit, but one filled with menace. Out of all of Delaine's squad, his field was undoubtedly the darkest.

Delaine offered me a stick of gum. I nodded my thanks. The sour taste in my mouth retreated before a burst of peppermint.

Delaine touched the side of her helmet and spoke into her mic. They had provided me with a fancy helmet with an inbuilt headset too, but the conversation must have been on a private channel. A few seconds later, Delaine's voice came through. "Drop zone in five. Make sure your straps are tight. It's windy down there."

The squad unbuckled from their harnesses and checked their gear a final time. I watched Harkins—who was sitting directly opposite me—and worked out how to cinch the parachute straps around my upper thighs until I was afraid to go any higher.

"G2G?" Delaine asked me over the channel.

I gave her the thumbs up.

"OK, folks," Delaine said. "Radio silence once we jump. Watch the crosswind. Keep your chutes tight. Overshoot the cliff and you're target practice."

Ranieri threw Delaine a casual salute and slid the door open. Freezing air swirled through the cabin. The chopper had slowed— not quite hovering—to ensure we all landed in the same vicinity. Harkins was first to jump, his expression calm yet focused. Kennett and Ranieri followed in quick succession. I stared at the yawning rectangle of darkness. How many of these agents were going to walk away from the monastery?

All of them, I decided.

Bracing my feet on the edge of the door, I fell forward, keeping my arms and legs spread as wide as possible. Icy air whipped at my coat and my eyes teared up. Idly, I wondered if this was what death was like; alone, untethered and hurtling into the unknown.

...four...five...six...

No lights below. The moon shrouded by clouds. In the distance, a glimpse of starlight glinting on a strip of river.

...seven...eight...nine...

Steep cliffs jutting from uneasy pools of darkness.

...ten...eleven...twelve!

I yanked on my ripcord and the chute snapped open. The straps ripped into my armpits and rode up my thighs. It felt like an enormous hand had reached down from the heavens and plucked me from the air.

Twisting in my harness, I scanned the ground below. Two chutes sliced through the night beneath my feet. Straining, I saw a third—had to be Harkins—collapse inwards as he landed.

A sudden gust of wind pushed me towards the valley and the monastery a long way below. I banked hard, lurching to the left and the cliff top. The ground rushed toward me, like a blow that you see coming and can't avoid. I flared my chute desperately. A jolt shuddered through my body as my descent slowed.

My reunion with the earth was not gentle. I tumbled and my helmet bounced off rock. Branches clawed at me as I rolled to a stop. The fabric of the chute settled over me, dowsing the night sky.

I lay still, accepting the pain that burned along my nerves. The edge of the cliff was perilously close. Someone landed behind me, only a quick stutter of light footsteps betraying their presence. Had to be Delaine.

I remained where I was and pictured myself hale and whole. Once the image was fully formed, I connected with the pocket of the Ladder and willed my body to return to its former state. My skin prickled as bruises and scrapes healed, all except the arm that had been poisoned by Metamorphoses.

"Seems quiet," Harkins murmured, his face distorted by night vision goggles.

The three of us lay at the edge of the cliff, studying the monastery below. A cluster of buildings was centred around the small church. It was hard to make out much beneath the thick layer of snow, although I could picture where the original stables and dormitory had once stood, along with the foundations of what had once been a fortified wall. There had been no sign of movement amongst the buildings, even though further down the valley, Vasil and his men were making a racket as they set up a roadblock with heavy floodlights.

"No heat signatures," Delaine whispered. She motioned for us to pull back.

Ranieri and Kennett had been busy while we scouted. Three shiny new ring bolts had been drilled into a large slab of rock. Ranieri tested one with the heel of his boot. It didn't budge. "Secure, boss," Ranieri reported.

Harkins was first to rappel down the side of the cliff. He pushed off from the outcrops with practised ease, controlling his descent in loping bounds. Kennett followed while we covered them from the edge of the cliff.

The monastery remained unnervingly quiet. Harkins disappeared into the mouth of a cave about fifteen metres down. Kennett followed. Three sharp tugs on the rope indicated they were ready for the rest of us.

"Ranieri, then Zeite," Delaine whispered.

Ranieri clipped into the line and leaned out over the side, both hands clasping the black rope. He scuttled down the rock face like a spider.

"Here, take these." Delaine passed me a pair of gloves. "Ever done this before?" she whispered.

"Once or twice," I murmured. "Good to see the gear has improved."

I clipped in and began my descent. The rock was rough and crumbling in places. I took care to plant my feet wide on either side of the rope and kicked off lightly.

The cave mouth soon yawned beneath my feet. I eased down the rope and Harkins pulled me in. A rank smell of ammonia filled the darkness. Stepping gingerly across the uneven floor, I realised it was covered in a layer of black, decomposing guano.

"Bats," I murmured in disgust.

"Yep." Harkins squatted on his haunches to avoid cracking his head.

Delaine swarmed down the rope. "No chatter from here on. There's no way of telling how far sound travels."

Harkins led us into the cave in single file. Delaine switched her head lamp on using the lowest setting and the others followed suit. Faint beams revealed moisture glistening on the rock face. The cave widened as we moved deeper inside.

Eventually Harkins halted and dropped to his haunches to peer at something on the ground. I couldn't make out what it was with Kennett and Delaine blocking the way.

Harkins grunted and metal groaned in response.

"Wait." Delaine unshouldered her pack and rifled through its contents. She unstoppered a container and the biting smell of acid filled the air. "Try now."

Harkins bent down and I caught the hiss of breath as he strained. Something gave way with a metallic groan that was loud in the stillness. Harkins staggered to one side. Looking over Kennett's shoulder, I saw Delaine peering into a dark hole. A rusty rung was just visible at the lip of the shaft. Harkins placed a corroded metal disc the size of a trashcan lid against the cave wall.

"Open sesame," Delaine whispered.

"Wait." I edged past Kennett and touched the stained metal. Sections had badly corroded and some of the rungs would not bear our weight. I shoved my left hand into my satchel and connected with the swirling pocket of potentiality. Picturing the shaft when it was first constructed, I nudged the damaged sections back to their original state. It was a small manipulation of reality in the scheme of things, yet the skin of my right forearm itched, and I felt the poison stir.

Delaine leaned over the shaft. A few of the rungs gleamed in her headlamp. "Impressive." She didn't seem to notice as I surreptitiously rubbed my forearm.

"Ranieri, Harkins and Kennett go first. Zeite and I will wait two minutes, then follow. Don't enter the complex without us."

"Understood," Harkins murmured.

Ranieri loosened the knives in his sheaths, cinched the G36 to his chest and began the descent. Harkins was quick to follow.

Kennett gave me a hard look. "Watch your step."

The metal shaft dropped a dozen metres through solid rock. Moisture glistened in dark veins that seeped from joins and slicked the rungs. The descent ended in a short, roughly hewn tunnel that was sealed by a steel door. A small keypad was the only obvious means of opening it. Harkins and the others patiently waited for us to join them.

Delaine moved towards the keypad. "Wait," I whispered. "Let me see if I can sense anything on the other side."

"OK," Delaine whispered, "lights out." With the lamps off, we were plunged into utter darkness.

I shuffled forward and rested my hand against the cold steel. A sense of inertia permeated its field, suggesting it had not been opened in a long time. Straining further, I probed the reality on the far side of the wall. The room was modest—just as Vasil's schematics had promised—and seasoned with a variety of emotions, efficiency and worry chief amongst them. I caught a fleeting sense of discipline, but it dissipated before I could glean anything further.

"Well?" Delaine breathed.

"Small office. Feels strange—" Something was off, although I couldn't put it into words. "Old places usually have a strong patina. Layers of experiences and emotions that infuse the flavour of a place. This site feels like it's been scrubbed clean."

Delaine shifted in the dark. "What does that mean?"

"I'm not sure."

"Fine. Ranieri, take point. Harkins, cover him. Silencers only." The two men screwed the silencers onto their sidearms by touch.

Delaine tapped out a nine-digit code on the keypad. A tiny, inert light flashed green and the door clicked. Harkins edged it open to reveal a thin layer of plasterboard. Ranieri shouldered through it and dropped into a crouch, his gun levelled. Harkins followed, aiming over Ranieri's shoulder.

"Don't move," Ranieri said in a low voice. The two men fanned out, their weapons trained on someone I couldn't see. Delaine stepped into the room, followed by Kennett.

The main lights were out and only a thin strip of emergency lighting along the skirting boards illuminated the office. A pair of filing cabinets flanked our hidden entrance. Delaine's team had stepped around an unoccupied desk with a blank computer screen.

"What is this? Who are you?" asked a man dressed in a blue business shirt and black trousers. He had thinning red hair and a distinctive smattering of freckles across his cheeks. Catching sight of Delaine, his eyes widened. "Del? Is that you?"

Delaine lowered her Glock. "Dad! Thank god! What happened here?"

He ignored the question and studied me. "Who are your friends?"

A sense of *wrongness* prickled against my awareness. I shifted perception and studied the field surrounding Delaine's father. Tight bands of control, visible as angry red lines, spiralled down from the crown of his head all the way to the end of each limb.

"This is my team and this is—"

"The Thirteenth." Delaine's father pulled a revolver from his pocket and aimed it at my chest.

"What are you doing?" Delaine cried.

I threw one hand up as I connected with the pocket and commanded him to be still. The bands of control pulsed in response. Delaine's father trembled, caught between the compulsion to shoot me and my countermand.

"Zeite? What the fuck is going on?" Delaine took a step towards us, her gaze darting between her father and me.

"He's being...controlled...by Tyrannos," I said through clenched teeth. The itch beneath the skin of my right forearm became a burn as the poison from Metamorphoses ignited. Blisters formed beneath my skin.

"Dad? Put the gun down," Delaine urged. "He's here to help us take back the monastery."

"No," her father replied in a strained voice. "He's why we lost it."

"Let's talk this out," Delaine pleaded.

"No!"

"Boss?" Harkins shot Delaine a questioning look. She reluctantly nodded and stepped in front of her father.

"You can't shoot him, Dad."

Ranieri slid behind Delaine's father and caught him in a sleeper hold. Harkins was a fraction slower, twisting the revolver from his grip.

I released my grip on Delaine's father and he struggled to break free, spitting and cursing. Delaine pleaded with him to stop, to no avail. The man was beyond reason. Eventually he slumped unconscious, his brain starved of oxygen. Ranieri eased him to the floor, rolled him over and secured his hands with zip ties.

Delaine spun around to face me. "Explain," she demanded, her face a tight mask.

I rubbed my burning arm. Damn Metamorphoses. I cleared my throat. "Your father is under the control of Tyrannos, the Archetype who has inspired every dictator and despot known to history. We must assume every person on site is too."

"What are you saying? Our people are hostiles now?" Harkins turned to Delaine. "We can't shoot them."

Delaine glanced at her father and then at the door to the office. "Make sure that door is locked."

Harkins obeyed, a look of frustration on his bearded face.

"Let me play this out." Delaine fixed me with a piercing look. "This installation is one of our most secure sites. It was specifically designed to resist an incursion, with both arcane and mundane defences. Yet somehow, Tyrannos has manifested in the very monastery that contains his capstone. Is that what you're telling me?"

179

"Afraid so." I sat on the edge of the desk. "I expect they cut the power first. Probably took out your secondary and tertiary back-up systems as well. Once the salt pumps shut down, no purification barrier to deal with." I could feel the salt that had settled to the bottom of pipes beneath us.

"Your emergency response team arrives," I continued. "They're lured inside, disarmed, and the Tyrant's lackeys take control of them as well. A few hours later, your second team arrives. No doubt they were more careful, but as the incursion deepens, so does the Tyrant's influence. They obviously put up a fight, as we know at least one of the team made it back to the extraction point with that disc you handed me."

Delaine gnawed on her bottom lip. "So now we have two problems. One, how do we keep our heads straight and stay on mission? Two, how do we get past our people without slaughtering them?"

They all turned to me.

I resisted the urge to sigh.

"Remove your helmets."

Delaine was the first to comply. "What's the play?"

I gave her a grim smile. "We keep Tyrannos out of your head."

Manipulating the field of a person is exponentially more complex than tinkering with inanimate objects. Without sufficient care, it can have unintended, even disastrous, effects.

Concentrating, I teased three separate strands from the pocket of the Ladder. Each glimmered silver with potentiality. The first I infused with independence, the second clarity, and the third defiance. Weaving the strands together, I created a single cord. The independence hardened and turned the colour of steel. The clarity became translucent, whilst barbs lifted from the strand of defiance. I tied the cord into a tight circle around Delaine's forehead and then drew it downwards, moulding it around the field that surrounded her skull.

I was shaking when I stepped back to admire my handiwork. A net of glimmering, barbed threads covered her head. The Tyrant would find no purchase in her mind.

Taking a long, slow breath, I repeated the process with

Harkins, then Ranieri. The fire in my right arm grew steadily. Underneath my sleeve, more blisters formed and cracked open. Scales suppurated along my forearm, deadening the sensitivity of my fingers.

With each alteration of reality, I too was being altered. Into what, I couldn't be sure. Yet some distant, objective part of me, could only marvel at the subtle genius of Metamorphoses. The rest of me cursed her with all the passion I could muster.

By the time I reached Kennett, sweat slicked my chest and back. I swayed with the effort of remaining upright. Kennett shot Delaine a worried look. Ignoring both of them, I set the netting in place and dragged it down. Halfway through the process, my maimed hand spasmed. The protective netting collided with Kennett's field, barbs puncturing her consciousness. She stiffened and her eyes rolled up into her head. A moment later, she crumpled to the floor.

"What happened?" Delaine dropped to one knee to check on Kennett. Perspiration beaded across her forehead, which was unusually pale.

I released my hold on the pocket and sucked in air. "My fault," I gasped.

"Will she be OK?" Harkins asked. Ranieri watched on with a scowl.

I nodded. "Mother of a headache when she wakes."

"How long?" Delaine demanded.

I leaned against the leg of the desk. "Hours. Maybe a day."

"Shit." Delaine quickly assessed the situation. "Harkins, drag her back to the bottom of the shaft. Then pull the door closed."

"You sure, boss?" Harkins glanced at Ranieri. "If the Chief calls in an airstrike…"

"Can't leave her here," Delaine growled, "and we're not aborting."

"And your Dad?" Harkins asked carefully.

Delaine turned to me. "Can you keep him under?"

I shook my head. "Not without unravelling the compulsion."

"And that would alert Tyrannos to our presence," Delaine guessed.

"Yep."

"Fuck it!" She paced around the desk, wrestling with an impossible choice. "If he wakes before Kennett..." She didn't need to finish the sentence. In his current state, he was a liability we couldn't afford. Delaine crouched next to her father and touched his cheek. "Sorry, Dad. I'll fix this."

When she straightened, her mouth was set in a grim, determined line. "Ranieri, find a gag. And I want his feet bound as well." She pivoted and stabbed a finger at me. "What about problem two?"

A tired smile spread across my face. "Well, I have some thoughts on that."

Harkins unlocked the door and let it swing open to reveal a dimly lit corridor. As with the office, the overhead lights were out. Only thin strips of emergency light glimmered along the skirting boards. A few doors were visible before the corridor bent away to the right.

Delaine's team quickly searched each room. One contained a bunch of servers that were all offline. Red LED lights blinked in warning with no one to attend to them. A second room contained stacks of files in neatly ordered rows. Thankfully all four rooms were unoccupied.

Harkins and Ranieri led us down the hallway, their weapons lowered. Delaine followed a few paces behind, adamant that I keep on her shoulder. The complex was unnaturally still and the rigid sense of control I had sensed earlier increased with each step.

Ranieri reached a right angle in the corridor. Dropping into a crouch, he removed a small mirror from his pocket, extended the telescopic arm attached to it, and angled it so he could peek down the new corridor. After a tense moment, he made a circular motion with his free hand and flashed his fingers three times.

Large space ahead. At least fifteen hostiles.

Delaine moved aside so I could join the two agents. Harkins gave me an expectant look. I connected with the pocket and nodded. He stepped into full view of the adjoining room and fired a brief burst into the ceiling. The noise was deafening in the confines of the narrow passage.

Taking advantage of the distraction, Ranieri tossed a tear gas canister down the hallway.

Harkins spun out of the way just as a volley of return fire peppered the wall behind where he'd been standing.

I had modified the gas canister, infusing the usual mix of pyridine and cyanocarbons with a combination of nitrous oxide, xenon and the oil of a noxious plant only found in the Amazon basin. The resulting mix would induce unconsciousness in an adult human in less than fourteen seconds.

Concentrating, I accelerated the spread of the gas so that it engulfed the troops stationed in the mess hall and any that had been drawn towards the sound of gunfire. The sound of running footsteps faltered. A few more rounds were fired in our direction, followed by coughing and the thud of bodies.

The gas billowed into our corridor, but I held it at bay. Even this modest manipulation of reality caused my scales to itch, and the burning sensation beneath my skin rose past my elbow. I shied away from considering what might happen once it reached my shoulder.

Delaine made us wait for a full count of one hundred for the gas to take effect. "Switch to exotics." She removed the magazine from her G36 and loaded a new one marked with white tape. Ranieri and Harkins followed suit.

I frowned. The new ammunition set my teeth on edge.

"Hollow points with an iron tip and a mix of salt and water blessed by a Tender. Extra insurance in case of any weird shit."

Hard to argue with that, so I kept my peace.

Even though the gas was thinning as it dissipated throughout the complex, I surrounded us in a bubble of clean air. The mess hall was a large, octagonal space with a servery on one side. People had collapsed at the long trestle tables. Others had slumped to the floor. All of them were armed, even the cooks.

"Neatly done, Zeite," Delaine murmured.

Two other corridors connected to the mess hall. Based on the schematics Vasil had shared, the Tender's quarters should be on the far side. Ranieri and Harkins adopted flanking positions as we moved across the open space.

I paused to briefly examine one of the soldiers who had passed out. As expected, the Tyrant's bands of coercion encircled his skull. Otherwise he seemed unharmed. If we could locate the keystone holding this incursion open, the compulsion would fade.

"Zeite, how long will our friends stay under?" Delaine nudged one of the fallen soldiers with her boot.

"Not sure. Probably best we keep moving."

"My thoughts exactly." Delaine gave Harkins and Ranieri the signal to proceed.

We entered the new corridor, which was wider and more luxurious than the one with offices and the server room. No doors or intersecting corridors, just a deep blue carpet and intermittent paintings that were too deep in shadow to make out. Two soldiers lay sprawled in the hallway, still under the influence of the gas.

"How far to the vault?" Ranieri murmured.

"This corridor ends in a suite," Delaine replied. "The Tender's private quarters are on the far side, along with the vault."

"Home straight," I murmured. No one returned my half-hearted smile.

The corridor ended in a pair of closed iron doors. I rested my hand on the black metal. All felt still on the far side, although I was reluctant to draw upon the power of the pocket. I gave the doors a gentle shove and they swung open on silent hinges.

Almost a dozen bodies lay sprawled on the plush carpet. Unlike the troops in the mess hall, the victims were dressed in simple linen robes with silver belts that cinched their waists. Each had suffered a gunshot wound to the back of the head, apart from one that had collapsed just before the double doors. He lay face down, one hand thrown towards the exit and a pair of bullet holes in his back.

"The disciples," I murmured.

"No sign of the Tender though," Delaine noted.

I counted the bodies. "Eleven."

"Where's the twelfth?" Delaine asked.

"Like I said, inside job," muttered Harkins.

"More like a fucking execution." Ranieri glanced at Delaine. "Gloves off, boss?"

Delaine nodded, her expression grim.

We moved through the chamber, slipping between overturned chairs and edging around congealing pools of blood. The echoes of pleas for mercy clung to the walls and the stench of terror had soiled the carpet.

A short passageway connected the chamber to the Tender's round foyer. Unlike the previous rooms that had been shaped from concrete, the walls here were hewn from rock. A large, ornate desk occupied pride of place, along with an ancient Turkish rug depicting the double helix and the names of each Archetype in Arabic. Alcoves had been hollowed out from the rock and each contained a marble statue.

I spied a wizened old woman, bent over with age, and didn't need to read the brass plaque to know that this was Sophos, known to some as the Sage. Facing her was Metamorphoses with her perpetual snarl and halo of snakes. Wisdom and Transformation, locked together in an eternal contest on the fifth rung of the Ladder.

Tyrannos stood in the alcove next to Metamorphoses. Like my vision back at the cottage, he was depicted as a stern-faced man, with one hand resting on the hilt of his sword and the other hand pointing into the distance. Facing Tyrannos was Maia, the Nurturer. A scarf covered her head, which was bowed in humility, and the palms of her hands were turned outwards in a universal gesture of benevolence.

I moved into the centre of the suite, staring at the depiction of each rung of the Ladder. This was a human interpretation of the Archetypes, a distillation of mythology and philosophy and history into a set of exquisitely detailed statues. And while the interpretation was tempered by a mortal's perspective, these statues still possessed a potency that could not be denied.

Drawn to the statue of Tyrannos, I studied the harsh lines of his face. How many times had Tyrannos roused some petty warlord to conquer their neighbours by instilling the belief that it was their divine right to rule? How many lives had been lost in the ensuing conflicts? How many civilisations had been destroyed just to satiate the desire for dominance and absolute authority?

Out of all the Archetypes, I detested his urges the most. None of those self-proclaimed tyrants ever lasted. Their fiefdoms and empires always fell in time, swept away by the next wave of conquerors. Control was the worst of illusions, as fleeting as it was addictive.

As if in response to my loathing, the statue slowly twisted its pointing arm until its palm faced the ceiling.

"Something's happening," I said in a low, warning voice.

Delaine's squad lowered their weapons, alert to any threat.

"Can you be more specific?" Delaine hissed.

The statue uncurled its three clenched fingers to reveal a small, onyx disc hidden in its palm. It was identical to the one Delaine had shown me in the cottage.

I stared at the disc. This was too obvious to be a trap.

Delaine edged closer and stopped abruptly when she saw what had captivated my attention. "Don't touch it."

"I wasn't planning on it."

After a moment, she said, "Leave it. We have to find the Tender."

"That would be unwise." I turned to face Maia, my thoughts churning as I tried to interpret the statue's gesture. Milky tears dripped from her lowered face and spattered on the floor. A chill settled in the pit of my stomach.

"Holy shit," Harkins cried.

Delaine and I spun around to face the corridor leading back to the mess hall. The fallen disciples burst into the foyer. Their eyes were black like onyx, and despite their various injuries, their expressions were identical to the Tyrant's statue. Some carried knives, while others swung their heavy metal belts.

Harkins had taken rear guard as we examined the foyer, and he released a burst of fire into the disciples. Craters bloomed in their flesh where the hollow points struck. The first rank went down, writhing in agony as the potent mix of salt and holy water vied with the Tyrant's control.

The next wave leapt over their fallen companions and split

apart. The first group swarmed over Harkins, bringing him to ground even as his G36 erupted with another round of fire. A knife flashed in the air and plunged downward.

Delaine dropped into a crouch and fired, felling a pair of disciples charging towards us. As they collapsed, I caught sight of the onyx discs wedged in their mouths. Ranieri shifted position to open up a direct line of fire and picked off the disciples attacking Harkins with brutal efficiency.

Delaine fired another controlled burst. More robed bodies tumbled to the ground and thrashed on the stone floor. Ranieri felled the last one and replaced his ammunition clip, swearing continuously under his breath. Delaine shot me a wild look, as if somehow I was responsible for raising the dead. She rushed over to Harkins and shoved aside the body of a disciple.

"Thanks, boss." Harkins coughed up a wad of blood.

Delaine helped him to a sitting position. A knife jutted from just beneath Harkins' clavicle. "Is it bad?"

Harkins gave her a bloody grin. "Stings a bit."

"You'll have to sit this one out."

"No chance."

Delaine glanced at the double doors. "Someone needs to guard this entrance."

I walked over to Harkins and knelt next to him. "Let me see." Delaine moved out of the way and I gently probed the wound. "You're lucky, Harkins. The blade missed your lung."

"Not feeling particularly lucky," he replied with a weak smile.

"Can you patch him up?" Delaine asked.

I sat back on my heels. "It'll take time. A lot of internal bleeding to stem."

Delaine nodded. We both knew the mission took priority.

"Boss, we got movement." Ranieri peered down the gloomy corridor that led back towards the mess hall.

Bullets tore through the Tender's desk. Ranieri rolled out of the line of fire, taking cover behind the stone wall that flanked the entrance to the foyer. I yanked Delaine out of the way as another round shattered a flagstone near our feet.

"I'll hold them," I yelled to Delaine over the thunderous

sound of gunfire. "Smash the disc in the statue's hand." It had to be amplifying Tyrannos' incursion.

Thrusting my fist into my satchel, I called upon the full power of the pocket. Reality shimmered as the Archetype within me surfaced. Half a dozen mindless troops were running towards us, while the remaining occupants of the installation were stirring. As expected, all of them had succumbed to the Tyrant's control.

This mission would become a bloodbath if I couldn't stop them.

I raised my free hand and willed the air in the corridor to thicken into the consistency of pitch. The soldiers slowed to a crawl, their movements laboured. Some managed to fire at me, the bullets slowed but not halted by the altered reality. With a twist of my wrist, I sent them arcing harmlessly into the ceiling.

"Go," I growled at Delaine. The effort of holding the troops had awoken the burning sensation in my scales. Blisters blossomed along my shoulder and spread across my chest. The acid of the poison spread up my neck and my vision dimmed momentarily.

Delaine scrambled over to Tyrannos' statue and slammed the butt of her rifle into its outstretched hand. The marble arm broke and shattered upon the flagstones, sending the onyx disc skittering across the floor.

More figures appeared at the far end of the corridor, intensifying the strain of holding them at bay. Ranieri took aim with his G36, a look of agonised indecision writ across his dark features.

"Wait," I ordered. "I've got this." Another volley of bullets sped towards us and I flicked them aside. The poison surged, boiling at the back of my eyes.

Delaine slammed the disc with her rifle and it spun away. "It won't break," she cried.

"Use…hollow points," I panted. My mortal body couldn't take this strain for much longer. I was on the verge of passing out.

Delaine took aim and fired at the disc. The stone split apart with a loud report and the approaching soldiers sagged, sinking to the ground as they lapsed back into unconsciousness. Releasing my hold on the reality of the corridor, I collapsed onto the bloodstained rug.

"Clear?" Delaine called to Ranieri.

Ranieri took a careful look down the corridor. "Clear."

Delaine rushed to my side. "Are you alright?" She froze, a lock of shock spreading across her face. "Zeite, what happened to your eyes?"

"What do you mean?" Fear twisted in my gut.

"Your eyes. They're yellow. And the pupils have contracted like…"

"Like a snake's," I said, finishing her sentence. Perhaps it was my imagination, but I thought I caught the faint sound of laughter coming from Metamorphoses' statue. Why didn't I figure this out sooner?

"It's temporary," I said with as much confidence as I could muster. Wearily, I climbed to my feet. "Harkins, I need you to hold this entrance. Don't let anything past you. Whatever it takes."

"Understood."

I turned to Delaine and Ranieri. "When we reach the vault, don't follow me inside. You're not trained for what might happen if the seal is activated."

Delaine shook her head. "The Fraternum stands with you, shoulder to shoulder. That's how it's always been."

"We don't have time to argue," I snapped.

"Then don't." Delaine replaced her ammunition clip and motioned Ranieri towards the Tender's private quarters. Lacking the energy to argue any further, I followed as they circled the splintered desk and entered the master bedroom. The sheets were a tangled mess and a trail of blood spatter ended at a sliding panel in the wall, which had been left ajar.

The vault containing the capstone was on the far side.

Delaine and Ranieri trained their weapons on the entrance. I took a moment to marshal the tatters of my composure. My entire arm was covered in scales and much of the upper part of my chest. Metamorphoses seemed determined that I relinquish this body or be remade in her image.

Ranieri nudged the panel open. The vault was a circular chamber of reinforced concrete laced with iron mesh and salt.

For me, passing through the entrance would be like sliding naked past barbed wire. Yet despite those protections, there was no doubt the incursion was emanating from the far side.

Steeling myself, I lurched into the vault. The sensation was akin to squeezing between two giant vegetable peelers.

The servant from my vision in Bozhentsi stood in the centre of the chamber. He was dressed in the linen robe of a disciple and held a knife to the throat of an elderly woman who wore identical robes, except her belt was gold. The Tender held the Tyrant's capstone to her chest. The statuette's outflung hand was pointed towards us and the weight of Tyrannos' compulsion settled over me.

Submit.

Surrender and know peace.

The mortal part of me trembled beneath the weight of his command while the Archetype shrugged it aside.

The servant smiled. "Apologies for such a rude welcome, Thirteenth. However, I had to be sure it was you. Please, why don't you ask your friends to join us?" His gaze latched onto Delaine and Ranieri, who had just entered the vault.

Another wave of potentiality pulsed through the figurine. The Tender gasped in pain and I realised with a jolt that she was the keystone holding open this incursion, not her former disciple. The Tyrant's compulsion flared outwards, wrapping around Delaine and Ranieri.

The angry red bands of coercion contracted until they encountered the silver netting I had woven. The competing energies crackled and sparked. Delaine and Ranieri collapsed to their knees, palms pressed into their eye sockets in a vain attempt to block out the blinding feedback.

The struggle was fierce but brief. Delaine was first to stagger back to her feet, followed by Ranieri. She levelled her G36 and said, "Not this time, you little turd."

The servant pulled the Tender to her feet, using her body as a shield. "Very impressive. Weapons on the ground. *Now!* Otherwise your precious Tender gets a new mouth." A thin line of blood trickled down the woman's neck where the blade pressed against her throat.

"Ashraf, please," the Tender whispered. "You can't trust Tyrannos. He'll never give you what you want. All he knows is how to take."

"Quiet, you arrogant bitch," Ashraf snarled. "I've listened to you long enough. Drop your weapons. I won't ask again."

Delaine shot me a sideways look and I nodded. She placed her rifle and sidearm carefully on the floor. Ranieri followed suit, his expression murderous.

"Slide them over," Ashraf ordered. Delaine and Ranieri complied.

Ashraf's dark gaze flicked back to me. "You don't look so well, Thirteenth. Perhaps Metamorphoses claimed a bigger piece of you than we thought." His gaze darted between Delaine and Ranieri. Taking a fistful of the Tender's hair, he pulled her head back. "I'll give you a chance to demonstrate your nobility. Your life for hers."

I lifted my hands in surrender. "All right, Ashraf. I'll pay your price."

"Zeite," Delaine hissed in warning.

I took a step toward Ashraf and the terrified Tender. "What are you hoping to accomplish, if that's not too much to ask?"

"You don't fool me walking around in that stolen skin," Ashraf replied. "You're not one of us. You never will be. Lord Tyrannos showed me what you really are. And humanity deserves better."

My cracked lips curved into a weary smile. "By better, I assume you mean yourself."

"Exactly." Ashraf slashed the Tender's throat. Blood gushed down her chest and splattered over the capstone, just as it had in my vision. Delaine lunged forward with her knife extended. Ranieri drew two throwing knives and cast them at Ashraf in a single fluid motion.

Ashraf was quicker.

He dropped to his knees and pressed his hands against the bloody capstone.

Lines of blood radiated from the figurine, illuminating the double helix and snake in the inner circle, followed by the outer circle and the symbols of the Zodiac. Delaine froze and Ranieri's knives quivered in the air a foot from their target. Once the seal was activated, reality was suspended between the inner and outer circle.

The unfettered presence of the Ladder tugged on me as the mortal and primal planes were connected. The Ladder pulled at my vitalis, trying to tear my essence from my mortal shell. Only the capstones prevented me from being drawn back.

Ashraf rose from the capstone. Potentiality infused his body, visible as the ancient signs of the Archetypes etched in silver sliding beneath his skin. "'To every thing there is a season: a time to be born, and a time to die'," Ashraf quoted. He retrieved his bloody knife and carefully walked along one of the lines that connected the inner circle to the outer.

I didn't struggle. Having activated the seal, Ashraf commanded the reality inside this space. I was helpless. And if my body died here, inside the seal, there was a good chance I would be drawn back into the Ladder even if the twelve capstones remained intact.

Ashraf raised his knife, his eyes hard and triumphant. "I will become what you should have been."

Stop.

The command reverberated through the seal. Ashraf faltered, then spun to face the Tender's corpse. Tyrannos' keystone was at the centre of the seal, and it had not been properly closed, which meant...

The Tender's lifeless body lurched into a sitting position.

It is not your place to strike him down, she said with cold, unyielding authority.

"But we agreed," Ashraf cried. "He needs to be brought to heel, you said."

And so he shall.

Coils of coercion lifted from the Tender's body and snaked towards Ashraf. He flinched as they wrapped around his skull and constricted. Ashraf dropped his knife and pressed his hands against his temples.

I struggled against the seal, fearing what might happen once Tyrannos assumed full control of his servant. With the blood of a

Tender powering the seal, reality refused to do my bidding.

A final scream of denial split Ashraf's throat before he fell silent. His chest heaved, as if he'd just surfaced from underwater after holding his breath too long. When he finally lifted his head, the man who had murdered his fellow disciples and the woman he'd sworn to serve, was gone. Dark, pitiless eyes stared back at me. The field surrounding Ashraf's body had become a dead zone, a void that couldn't be read or manipulated.

The former disciple retrieved the capstone from where it lay in a pool of blood. He turned and faced me.

Ophiuchus, your rebellion is over. The remaining Tenders will fall. Their capstones will be sundered. And with their destruction, your hold on this plane will be broken.

Once-Ashraf lifted the capstone above his head. I strained against the binding of the seal, but without the power of the pocket to draw upon, it was hopeless.

"You will return to us and you will be remade." He flung his arms downward. The crystal capstone struck the concrete floor and shattered.

My field ripped open down one side and flapped about, as one of the twelve bindings that tethered me to this plane snapped. It felt like someone had just torn out a kidney. Blocking out the pain as best I could, I gathered the shredded pieces of myself together, like a warrior trying to hold their intestines in.

Pure potentiality burst from the capstone and detonated inside the seal. The unbridled energy coursed along the twelve lines connecting the inner and outer circles of the seal. With no way to escape the outer boundary, the potentiality rebounded, converging upon its focal point. Ashraf's body lit up from within. His skin became translucent, veins and arteries clearly visible. As his body faltered, so too did the binding.

Summoning my remaining strength, I crashed through the barrier of the seal. Stumbling, I caught Delaine around the waist and spun, hurling her bodily through the door of the vault. Ashraf had become incandescent and the ferocity of the energies building inside him beat against my back. I managed two steps towards Ranieri before Ashraf's field splintered. Blinding light speared through the vault, followed by a concussion wave that picked me up and tossed me through the air. My hip struck the doorframe to the vault and I spun in a wild arc. For a fleeting instant, I wondered if death waited at the end of this drop.

The floor rose up to meet me and it was not a gentle reunion.

Delaine's singed face slowly came into focus. A nasty burn marred one side of her head and a weeping gash ran parallel with her hairline. I wanted to close her wounds, but my maimed hand and I were not on speaking terms yet.

She leaned over me, mouthing words. A painful, high-pitched whine buzzed through my eardrums.

"Can I not have a moment's peace?" My words were thick with blood. Must have bitten my tongue.

Delaine gave me a half-smile. "…you weren't coming back."

The buzzing subsided, only to be replaced by a throbbing at the back of my skull. I grasped Delaine's elbow. She helped me into a sitting position and I promptly deposited the meagre contents of my stomach on the floor.

"Sorry." I'm not good with embarrassment.

"Seen worse at the pub," she replied with a faint smile.

Harkins leaned against the bedpost, his face pale and covered in a sheen of sweat. I suspected he looked better than I did.

With Delaine's help, I managed to stand, more or less. The Tender's bedroom took a little longer to steady. Boiling oil seemed to slosh about in my hip.

"Ranieri?"

Delaine bit her bottom lip and her eyes filled with tears she refused to shed.

"Show me."

We limped to the doorway of the vault. The reinforced concrete walls were badly scorched. The weapons had melted into lumps of metal and all that remained of Ranieri and the Tender were charred bones and ash. Nothing whatsoever remained of Ashraf.

"I'm sorry," I whispered. "I wasn't quick enough. I should have—"

"Hush. I'd be dead if it weren't for you."

We stood at the threshold for a moment, honouring the fallen. I kept thinking that I had promised they would all survive. Once, not so long ago, I had kept my oaths. Now it seemed the more a promise mattered to me, the less chance I had of keeping it. Was that an aspect of mortality as well? If so, it truly sucked.

Unable to bear the sight any longer, I limped over to the Tender's bed and sank onto the mattress with a groan.

Delaine joined me. "I have questions."

"From the very first moment we met."

She made a sound that caught in the back of her throat. It could have been a laugh or a sob. "Why didn't he kill you? Ashraf, I mean."

I wiped a trickle of blood running from my nose. "Oh, he wanted to. It's just that Tyrannos had a larger design."

"Explain." Delaine's eyes were bright with pain and confusion. Harkins sank to the floor, his back propped against the bed.

"Ashraf believed he could assume my place as the Thirteenth by killing me inside the seal. Only that's not how it works."

"OK. And?"

"And Tyrannos knew that if Ashraf had killed my body, the Sophists could reincarnate me because the twelve capstones tether my vitalis to this plane. Now that we've lost one capstone, I cannot reincarnate safely."

"Oh. Can't we just replace it?"

I sighed. "Not without infusing all of the capstones at the same time. They're all linked."

Delaine absorbed this in silence.

"It won't end here," I warned. "Metamorphoses, Hephaestus, all the Vices will seek to destroy the remaining capstones. If enough are destroyed, I'll be drawn back into the Ladder."

"They've made you mortal," Delaine said, a look of apprehension spreading across her face.

"In a sense," I agreed.

"What happens if you're forced back into the Ladder?" Harkins asked.

Tyrannos had made me a promise: *You will be remade.*

Delaine read the expression on my face. "That bad, huh?" She changed tack. "So, what do we do now?"

"Well, you should radio Vasil, so he doesn't bring this place down on our heads. And make sure he brings a medic. Then you should check on your dad and send someone to fetch Kennett. I don't think she likes me very much, especially after the headache that's coming her way."

Her gaze narrowed. "What are you planning?"

I laughed and instantly regretted it as a series of injuries made themselves known. "I see you haven't lost your talent for posing difficult questions."

"And you haven't lost your talent for deflection."

Touché. I decided they had earned the right to something approaching a straight answer. "It's become clear that I've been playing a losing hand for some time. So, my options are either fold or draw a new set of cards. Either way, it's time I approached the house."

"What does that even mean?" she asked with a frown.

I shrugged off my coat and rolled up my sleeve to reveal my withered hand and the scales covering my skin. "It means my humanity is receding every time I draw upon the pocket. I need to find a way out of this dilemma before I run out of choices." I waved her away. "Now go before they decide to bomb the shit out of us."

Delaine gave me a final searching look before slipping under Harkins' arm to help him up. As I watched them leave, I realised I could no longer rely upon the Fraternum. They had taken far too many casualties defending me. Besides, no amount of force could win this war.

No, my final journey must be completed alone.

In the end, I suppose that's true for all of us.

Afterword

This novelette is original to this collection.

The thing about heroes and heroines, I find, is that they're far more interesting when they are imperfect. Zeite, I hope, comes across as one such character.

I'm sure you've read about plenty of immortal characters who become bored with the world (vampires, anyone?). So, I quite liked the idea of exploring a character who came into our world with a fierce, almost fanatical, sense of purpose that is slowly ground down by time and inertia.

What would such an entity be like? Would they still believe in their mission, yet be too world-weary to expect it to be accomplished? How would they reconcile themselves to such an existence, especially with each new generation of bright-eyed, idealistic humans nipping at their heels?

Yeah, I'd be grumpy too.

Almost Human: At Rest

Night gathers. Do you see it stealing amongst the trees and lurking beneath the eaves? I cannot keep it at bay, and dawn is a remote, elusive thing, no longer guaranteed. Is this mortality? Carefully unwrapping each day like a precious gift?

I need more time.

Time to rectify my mistakes, or failing that, to at least understand how they were fashioned.

I had always perceived the Ladder as a dichotomy, a struggle for dominance between the Virtues and the Vices played out upon the stage of the mortal world. Yet now I see their compulsions are a complex byplay between the needs of individuality and those of community. Why did it take becoming almost human for me to realise the Ladder is far more nuanced than I had ever thought?

As Above, So Below.

Two parts of an inseparable whole.

I was once Ophiuchus, the thirteenth Archetype, the bridge between the primal and mortal planes. Now, I am something less and something more. I'm fairly certain it's an improvement.

Traveller, I wish you well upon the road that lies ahead. May you find the strength to complete the journey to who you wish to be, as this is the only destination that matters.

Ophiuchus, 2020.

KINABATANGAN, BORNEO, APRIL 2020

My guide shot me another surreptitious look under his baseball cap as he adjusted the tiller of the outboard. We had been powering down the Kinabatangan River for over an hour now, and his curiosity had only grown as we ventured deeper into the jungle.

To be fair, I was an unlikely looking tourist: my entire right arm was wrapped in bandages beneath my loose linen shirt and I wore gloves despite the humidity. Aviator sunglasses covered my eyes and I had drawn my fedora low over my forehead.

"EcoLodge back that way," my guide said in English over the growl of the engine. He threw a thumb over his shoulder for emphasis.

"I know," I replied in Malay.

His eyes widened and he switched to his native tongue. "You speak Malay?"

"Well enough."

"Huh. My name's Rayyan. People call me Ray."

"An honour to meet you, Ray." He didn't seem to mind that I didn't offer a name in return. Ray's wiry limbs jutted from the sleeves of a faded Chicago Bulls T-shirt and matching basketball shorts. Despite an air of worldliness, I estimated Ray couldn't be over twenty-five.

The river narrowed as we continued upstream and the jungle pressed against the banks on either side. I caught a glimpse of a pair of proboscis monkeys leaping through the trees before they disappeared in a rusty-brown blur.

"How much further, tuan?" Ray nudged a plastic container filled with fuel with his foot. "No gas stations out here, only crocodiles."

"Not much further." I lifted my battered leather satchel into my lap and adjusted the backpack wedged between my feet. After the disaster at Dryanovski Monastery, I had slipped away from the Order and flown into Sandakan just ahead of the border closures caused by the pandemic. No doubt a search was underway, but I needed advice, and being accompanied by a dozen agents would only hinder my pilgrimage.

"Just jungle along this stretch of the river," Ray persisted. "No sightseeing."

"Over there." I pointed to a narrow opening almost hidden between two mangroves.

"You sure, tuan? Not much up there except snakes and mosquitoes." Ray dropped the throttle to an idle that held the boat's position against the current.

"I'm sure. And you won't have to wait for me." Reaching into my satchel, I pictured five thousand ringgit and withdrew the crisp notes.

Ray studied me suspiciously. "That's too much."

"No, it's not. Your time is precious, as is my privacy." I leaned forward. "If anyone comes asking after me, tell them you dropped me off at the Rainforest Lodge. Then take a holiday. Somewhere remote, where people can't find you. That's what the money is for."

Ray pulled the baseball cap off his head and ran his fingers through his messy black hair. "You'll die if I leave you here. It's easy to get lost in the jungle and you have no equipment or food."

"True, although I have this." Unzipping my backpack, I flourished the satellite phone I'd 'borrowed' from Delaine.

Ray shrugged. "Won't help if a rescue team can't reach you in time."

"True. Although I do understand the risks." I gave him a reassuring smile and offered the ringgits again.

After a brief hesitation, Ray shrugged again and accepted the notes. He upped the throttle and nosed between the mangroves and a thicket of reeds that guarded the mouth of the tributary. Fallen tree limbs and sunken roots thudded against the aluminium hull. The water here was noticeably browner, hiding whatever might be lurking beneath the surface. Midges lifted off the surface in shifting clouds, disturbed by the bow wave from the boat.

Having lost the light breeze from the river, the humidity settled over us like a wet blanket. My bandages were soon damp from sweat and my scalp prickled under the fedora. The tributary continued to narrow as the forest canopy closed overhead. The light became dappled, a spotted, skittish creature that slinked in and out of view.

Eventually the hull scraped against a rock beneath the surface and Ray let the throttle fall idle. "Sorry, tuan. This is as far as I can take you."

"Thank you, Ray. Over there is fine." I pointed to a section of the bank that had collapsed into the water. Ray poled us into position with a spare oar. Taking care to centre my weight in the boat, I stepped onto the shore. My boots sank into the mud all the way to the ankle. Grabbing a nearby branch, I pulled myself up onto higher ground.

Ray watched me with obvious concern. "I'll wait at the river mouth for two hours, tuan. Just in case you change your mind."

His concern for an odd foreigner was touching and it unexpectedly lifted my spirits. "You're a good man, Ray. I wish you well." I threw him a wave and trudged into the wetlands of the Kinabatang wildlife sanctuary.

Once I was far enough away from the river and any prying eyes, I removed my fedora, folded my sunglasses and deposited them both on the muddy ground. My gloves and sweat-drenched shirt followed, along with the now-superfluous bandages. I rolled the cuffs of my cargo pants to just above the knee.

It was a relief to be rid of the clothing in the stifling heat. I examined the scales running up my arm and across half of my chest. In the dappled light, they seemed to shimmer with hints of jade and aubergine. Even the stubby, scaled fingers of my withered right hand looked less monstrous.

I drew in a long, deep breath. The humid air was rich with the scent of damp soil, decomposing leaf matter and the delicate fragrance of the white flowers blooming on liana vines. The smell was so rich I could taste it at the back of my throat. I briefly wondered whether Metamorphoses' poison was affecting my sense of smell, before discarding the thought.

Closing my eyes, I turned in a slow circle. This part of the jungle was virtually untouched by human hands. Without the usual patina of human emotions and aspirations, the reality of this place felt...*uncluttered*. Nature ran rampant in the wetlands, a series of mutually dependent life cycles that aggregated into a broader ecosystem. There was an elegance to the complexity of it all that I could only admire.

I did not fool myself into believing I could hide here, however. The world had a way of intruding, no matter how hard I tried to withdraw from it. I had learned that lesson in Bozhentsi and it was still painfully fresh in my mind. Better to confront your fate than let it spring upon your unawares.

There was no obvious path through the trees. Not that I had expected one; the temple I sought could not be found on any map. I lifted the strap of my satchel over my head so that it ran diagonally across my chest and shouldered my backpack.

"The first step is always the hardest," I murmured.

Pushing a low-lying branch aside, I stepped through a gap between two trees. The mud squelched between my toes and flying insects buzzed past. Drawing upon the pocket hidden in my satchel, I set up a small field to repel these winged marauders.

Occasional gaps opened in the jungle—small spaces where a tree had fallen and shafts of sunlight pierced the canopy. At these junctures, I would stop and choose whichever direction took me towards higher, firmer ground. The foliage slowly changed as I gained elevation. The mangroves and reeds fell away, replaced by palms, banyan trees and banana leaves. The humidity remained oppressive and sweat beaded across my forehead. I could have cocooned myself from the heat as well, but that felt like cheating. Other pilgrims had reached the temple without such luxuries and it was fitting that I should follow in their footsteps.

The boundary of the temple emerged from the overgrowth without warning. I had just climbed over a fallen fig tree to find the jagged foundations of a stone wall. The crumbling stonework barely reached my knees and was covered in moss and leaf litter. The wall disappeared into the jungle in both directions.

Shifting perception, I studied the space in front of me: reality had been folded back upon itself, twisted in an ingenious fashion to form something akin to a Möbius strip. I frowned as I studied the anomaly. This was far more subtle than a forbidding or a conventional barrier.

As far as I could tell, anyone who stepped over the wall would be diverted back the way they had come without even realising it. The anomaly also masked whatever lay on the far side. From my current position, the jungle appeared to continue as far as I could see. Peering closer, I realised the fold was diverting the light, effectively reflecting the overgrowth I had already passed through. I had never encountered anything like this before.

"Brilliant," I murmured. After eight centuries on the mortal plane, any original experience was a delight to be savoured.

How then to proceed?

If I tried to step over the wall, I was almost certain I would end up back at the tributary from where I'd started, tired and no doubt confused. Plus, there was no way to guarantee I would even remember reaching this boundary.

I considered forcing my way through and immediately discarded the idea. A true pilgrim would not be able to do this. Besides, I was loath to damage such a skilful manipulation of reality. Looking in both directions along the wall provided no clues.

I licked my lips. Over a week had passed since I'd slipped away from Dryanovski Monastery. The Vices would be moving against the installations that housed my remaining capstones. And the Order wouldn't be able to stop them, even though they had been forewarned by Delaine and Harkins. So I couldn't afford to wait outside these walls like the village idiot.

"I wish to speak with Sophos," I said, hoping the words would penetrate the boundary.

Reluctantly, I sat on the trunk of the fallen fig, folded my legs beneath me and waited. Doing nothing has never been my forte. A fact Sophos knew only too well.

Night had almost fallen before I received a response.

A space in the fold of reality opened without warning. Through it stepped a local man dressed in a beige shirt and matching trousers. He wore a faded green sampin, or sarong, around his waist, and battered sandals. His most striking piece of attire was the piece of lapis lazuli hanging from the woven silver chain around his neck. The stone was oval in shape and almost the length of my thumb. A stylised eye had been etched into its surface and a tight spiral formed the pupil. It drew my gaze with unexpected force.

I lifted my eyes to the man facing me with an effort. His skin was a rich, nutty brown, tanned from years in the sun, and he appeared to be in his early forties. If he was surprised by my strange, scaled appearance, he gave no sign of it.

He bowed and said in Malay, "Many seek wisdom, although few can remain still long enough to receive its blessing."

I smiled and bowed in return.

"You wish to speak with Sophos?" he asked.

"I do. She may have been expecting me for…some time."

The man laughed, revealing brilliant white teeth. "You have a talent for irony. Thank you for that unexpected gift."

My smile became uncertain. "You're welcome. Are you one of her priests?"

"Oh no. We don't have such things here." He waved the suggestion aside as if it was faintly embarrassing. "I am merely a traveller with an open heart, like everyone else who wanders this way. Here: you will need this." He withdrew a second necklace from his pocket and offered it to me.

The lapis lazuli hanging from the chain was smooth and warm in my hand. I avoided gazing into the pupil. The spiral was another representation of the Ladder, as old as the astrological serpent. As for the eye, it had long been associated with peace, harmony and wisdom in this part of the world. An apt symbol for Sophos.

"Come, I will take you." The man stepped back over the low wall surrounding the temple and promptly disappeared. I pulled the necklace over my head and followed.

The fold in reality parted around me and pressed together seamlessly in my wake. There was a momentary, yet disconcerting, sense of inversion. I staggered for balance, feeling like my feet were no longer beneath me. When the sensation passed, I found the jungle had retreated to reveal a broad rice paddy field. On the far side of the field was a steep, conical hill. Swiftlets darted amongst its rocky outcrops, flitting from their nests to snare insects in the deepening twilight. The sun was setting over the hill's left flank, throwing the eastern face into shadow. I spotted the dark mouth of a cave nestled amongst the creases of the hill's skirts.

"Can you see the temple?" the man asked. "It took me many attempts."

I stared up at the hill and resisted the temptation to draw upon the Archetype within me. At first, I couldn't see any signs of human architecture. The harder I tried, the less likely it seemed. Bushes jutted from the rock and vines obscured the cliffs. The swiftlets were a constant distraction, darting about and constantly drawing the eye. Remembering my lesson at the wall, I relaxed, taking in the entire hill rather than focusing on specific sections.

I stood that way for some time, ignoring everything around me, even my guide. The light faded as the sun dipped toward the horizon. Eventually the swiftlets retreated to their nests. Shadows crept across the paddy field, turning the stalks into a phalanx of spears aimed at the sky. All the while, a stillness grew inside me, like an undisturbed pool that catches and reflects the starlight.

Perhaps it was the changing light.

Perhaps it was the churning of my thoughts finally coming to rest.

Perhaps it was both. Or neither.

Whatever the case, the temple emerged slowly, almost shyly, into view. What I had assumed were crevices in the rock face proved to be too regularly spaced to be natural. There were six on either side of the cave mouth, positioned about ten feet off the ground and tapering into a point high above. The alcoves had weathered differently over the centuries, lending them an irregularity that fooled the eye. Similarly, the figures that stood on each dais were masked by vines and tenacious trees whose roots wormed into the cracks of these crumbling representations of the Archetypes.

"I see it," I breathed.

"That is good," my guide replied. Waving me along, he walked through the paddy field, following a path of raised pavers. I followed at a respectful distance, noting the worn astrological symbols that had been carved into the stones. This path was not only functional, but symbolic.

We had almost crossed the field when an agonising pain tore down my left hamstring. I gasped and fell onto my side, clutching my stricken leg. It felt like the muscle had been ripped from the bone.

The Archetype within me rose to the surface and dampened the pain. Focusing, I visualised the web that kept me anchored to this plane. Just as I had feared, another strand had been severed: the capstone for Hephaestus the Misfit had been destroyed. No doubt more would soon follow.

My guide turned, his expression lost in shadow. "You have arrived late indeed, Thirteenth. Are you able to continue?"

The agony eventually receded, leaving a numbness in my leg. I felt drained and less...substantial. Regaining my feet with a grimace, I said, "I'll manage."

He nodded and continued through the stalks of the paddy field. Emerging on the far side, he led me to the foot of the hill. "Please pay your respects to the Archetypes before entering the temple. It has been an honour to assist you along your path." He bowed deeply and I responded in kind.

Smiling, the man turned and walked back the way we had come.

I stared up at the steep hill crowding out the night sky. When I first entered the mortal plane, I'd possessed a burning clarity of purpose. I had been adamant that if humanity was given the opportunity to develop without interference, they would blossom. So, I helped fashion the Order, fanning those early, hopeful sparks until they became a fire that spread across the continents. Yet, despite my intervention, individual Archetypes were still venerated in pockets throughout the world. Standing before this temple to Sophos, which undoubtedly predated my arrival, I couldn't help but wonder if I had presumed too much.

After all, the Archetypes had infused human storytelling and mythology for thousands of years. They were, in every sense of the word, woven into the fabric of this reality. While I might have succeeded in snipping some unruly threads, they would always be present, influencing humanity.

It was a humbling admission. And perhaps one I had resisted for too long.

I veered to the left of the cave mouth and faced the first alcove, which was shaped like a teardrop. The statue it contained had eroded over the centuries, becoming a misshapen lump covered in vines and stained with bird droppings. Drawing upon a thin trickle of potentiality from the pocket in my satchel, I shifted perception, viewing the statue as it had appeared when first crafted. It had once been a small child, its face turned to look back over one shoulder, clearly lost and afraid. Touching my forehead, lips and heart, I said, "I offer my respect to Hestia, keeper of the hearth in whose embrace we find home."

Moving to the next alcove, I noticed subtle signs of care: a small bouquet of jungle flowers, a handful of burned-out incense sticks, and a lily floating in a shallow wooden bowl of water. In contrast to the Orphan's statue, this sculpture had once depicted a wizened old woman, hunched over and looking down upon the pilgrim with a piercing gaze. Repeating my earlier gestures, I said "I offer my respect to Sophos, the Sage, keeper of the paths of wisdom."

Working down the rungs of the Ladder, I paid my respects to Maia, the Nurturer, Kratos, the Warrior, and Astraea, the Innocent. Reaching the final alcove, I gazed up at the empty space that had been left for the Spark, the unnamed creator who had manifested all the planes of existence. Shrubs jutted from crevices and vines hung in abundance, all but concealing the cavity. The nests of the swiftlets were thickest here, and they must have sensed my presence, for the sound of rustling feathers drifted down from above in the still night air.

I bowed low before the Spark and wondered whether the human beliefs were true: did their souls return to the creator, or were they collected by the Spark's dark counterpart instead? It was a mystery I could not solve. The bottom rung of the Ladder was a paradox—an inflection point, if you like—that was forbidden to the Archetypes, including myself.

Walking back to the cave mouth, I suppressed the doubts that had been bubbling up inside me. I could not indulge in second-guessing when facing the Archetypes of Vice, even if they were only effigies.

Stopping at the first alcove, I altered perception again. The twisted, malformed shape of Hephaestus gradually emerged from the rock. A large hunchback dominated his dwarven frame, and he held a hammer and a pair of tongs. The expression on his face was both pained and cunning. "I offer my respect to Hephaestus, the Misfit, patron of outcasts and ingenuity," I said with as much sincerity as I could muster.

Moving to the fifth rung of the ladder, I faced the statue of Metamorphoses. Her halo of snakes had long since eroded, and swiftlet droppings stained the sweep of her once-regal robes. Silently, I applauded the birds' efforts.

"To Metamorphoses, the Lady of Transformation, I offer my respect…and a gift of her own making." Using the hardened nail of my withered hand, I dug out a scale from my maimed chest and tossed it at her feet. Blood trickled from my torn flesh, and despite the pain, I revelled in this small act of defiance.

Hurrying now, I worked my way down the rungs of the ladder, acknowledging Tyrannos the Tyrant, Nemesis the Lord of Vengeance, and Eris the Lady of Conflict.

I came to a stop at the final recess. The rock here was barren. Nothing grew anywhere within the inverted teardrop that had once housed the statue of Annihilis. If anything, the hollowed crevice resembled a scar, as if some ancient landslide had permanently gouged the hill.

Steeling myself, I gazed upon the original statue: the cloaked figure was enormous, towering over me so that it appeared larger than the cliff it had been carved from. Mercifully a cowl hid most of its face, and a large, almost bestial hand held a staff that ended in wicked blades that curved in opposing directions.

I bowed low and said, "I offer my respect to Annihilis, the Ending of All Things."

A blanket of chill air settled over me and I suppressed a shiver. Was that an acknowledgement or a benediction? Or perhaps something more sinister?

I backed away from the statue, thoroughly relieved to have dispensed with the formalities.

To my astonishment, the sun was already rising as I returned to the cave mouth. Somehow, facing the twelve Archetypes had taken most of the night.

The ammonia stench of bat guano wafted from the entrance. Taking a final breath of fresh air, I stepped inside.

Large stones set into the ground had been worn smooth by the tread of countless feet. The layers of reality in this place were rich and thick, and spiced with a dizzying array of peoples and thought. Overlaying it all was a prevailing sense of calm, almost meditative in flavour.

I followed the pathway deeper into the cave. The ceiling drew further away with each step. Moisture seeped from the ceiling, dripping occasionally onto the hard-packed earth on either side of the walkway. Bats shuffled overhead, thousands roosting in the comforting darkness. There was no welcoming party. Not that I had expected one. No doubt this shuffle through the darkness was intended to be symbolic.

The path curved in a wide arc around an enormous, natural column of rock. Even in the almost absolute darkness, the twisting mass resembled a gigantic tree whose uppermost branches supported the roof of the cave far above. The path coiled around the trunk, dropping deeper and deeper into the earth with each turn. The temperature fell as I descended, and the humidity leached away. It soon became clear that the path was a spiral that ended in the deepest roots of the cave.

A glow of light finally appeared as I neared the bottom. Five figures waited for me in a gap between two thick roots of rock. The foremost figure lifted its lantern, which I was a little surprised to discover was electric.

"Welcome to the temple of Sophos. We are honoured by your presence." The speaker was a woman with plaited black hair and the round, tapering eyes of the mountain folk from the Himalayas. Despite her smooth skin, I estimated she was in her late fifties. Her companions were women of varying ages and nationalities, although each wore a high-necked dress with long sleeves, a tapered waist and flowing skirts. The colour of the fabric shifted in the lantern light, mostly silver with hints of emerald and salmon. I noted the spiral eye of Sophos had been stitched into the collar at their throats.

"Thank you," I replied. "It has been a long journey. And perhaps more difficult than it needed to be."

The woman smiled and her eyes crinkled in amusement. "That is as it should be. My name is Bilhana. If you'll follow, we'll take you to our Sage."

Bilhana turned and passed through the gap in the roots. Her companions parted and lifted their lanterns, illuminating a path for me. They averted their eyes as I passed, although I could sense their disquiet at my scaled appearance.

A short tunnel ended in a wide antechamber carved from the rock. Four wrought iron candelabras filled the space with flickering candlelight. Thick, luxurious rugs covered the hard floor, all featuring the eye of Sophos. A wide variety of tapestries from different cultures adorned the walls.

I walked over to examine a particularly old hanging. The original background had been black, but had now faded to a murky grey. Delicate Sanskrit lettering framed the tapestry, and in the centre, the seal linking the primal and mortal planes had been reproduced. The twelve symbols of the Archetypes at the edge of the outer circle had been picked out using a spectrum of colours, whilst the inner circle contained a silver serpent coiling around a staff. I suspected this tapestry commemorated my arrival just over eight hundred years ago.

"Looks familiar," I said with a wry smile.

"I thought it might," Bilhana replied. Her colleagues settled onto rich cushions that lay scattered across the room.

"This way." Bilhana drew one of the larger tapestries aside to reveal a hidden entrance. I ducked beneath the low lintel and took a few cautious steps in the gloom, before emerging into a

second, smaller chamber with a high, vaulted ceiling. A statue of
the Sage dominated this inner sanctum. She was hunched over,
hands resting upon bent knees, and staring at a thin, improbable
shaft of sunlight just in front of me. A second shaft lit the space
between the statue's feet. A small child—no older than five or
six—sat cross-legged before the statue. Her black hair was cut
in a neat bob and she wore the same outfit as Bilhana. The child
cupped a wooden puzzle box in her hands, and I watched as
she twisted a protruding piece and pushed it inwards, before
turning it over to view the result.

"This is Sachita," Bilhana said.

I dropped to my haunches. "Hello, Sachita. What a beautiful
name." In Nepalese it meant *consciousness*.

Sachita looked up, stared deeply into my eyes, and then tilted
her head as she took in my scales. Her complexion and the shape
of her eyes were identical to Bilhana's. "Your granddaughter?" I
murmured.

"Yes," Bilhana replied. "Please excuse her for not returning
your greeting. She is mute, except for when communing with
the Sage."

"Ah. A conduit." Sachita's presence in the temple suddenly
made sense.

"Please give me a moment to prepare the communion." Bilhana
bent over Sachita and whispered in her ear. Sachita put her puzzle
down with a hint of reluctance and nodded solemnly. The child
stood, rolled her head and moved through a series of yoga poses
that would loosen her limbs. Meanwhile, Bilhana unlocked a trunk
partially hidden behind the statue and removed a bowl, a flask, a
mortar and pestle, and a pungent bag of herbs.

Finishing her exercises, Sachita sat in the shaft of sunlight at
the feet of the statue and adopted the lotus pose. I glanced up at
the ceiling, trying to ascertain how sunlight could reach us down
here.

"Mirrors," Bilhana said over her shoulder to answer my
unspoken question. "Carefully positioned to capture the sunlight an hour after dawn. We must hurry before it begins to
wane." She measured out a portion of the herbs and crushed

them with the pestle. An astringent smell filled the air—one I couldn't place. Bilhana unstoppered the flask and poured a pale, golden liquid into a thimble before tipping it into the mortar. She repeated the process twice more and continued grinding the herbs. Eventually satisfied, she scraped the eggplant-coloured paste out of the mortar and into the wooden bowl.

Bilhana crouched in front of her granddaughter and sketched the eye of Sophos on Sachita's forehead with the paste. She then drew a teardrop under each eye and spread the remaining paste over Sachita's protruding tongue. The girl didn't complain throughout the ritual.

"Please." Bilhana gestured to the shaft of sunlight in front of me. I stepped forward and sank into a matching lotus pose facing Sachita. Already the girl's head had begun to loll, and her fingers twitched. Bilhana retreated to a corner of the sanctum. Sachita's lips trembled and her fingers fluttered, as if responding to ethereal currents.

A knot of nervousness drew tight in the pit of my stomach. After the debacle with Tyrannos in Bulgaria, I had not allowed myself to dwell upon how Sophos might receive me. If she chose to turn me away, I had no idea what to do next. Two of my capstones had already fallen. There would be no reincarnation when this body failed, and if too many more capstones were destroyed, my vitalis would be ripped from this shell.

Sachita's voice, when she spoke, was rich and melodious, with a hint of gravel that was far beyond her years. "So vast," she said in Nepalese.

"Like the sky," she continued in Hindi, "only falling."

Her hands floated in the air, wafting on currents even I couldn't perceive. Individual strands of her hair lifted, floating about her face like a sea anemone. Her eyes closed and the eye of Sophos on her forehead shimmered with potentiality.

"Look at all the pretty connections," Sachita murmured, this time in Urdu. "So beautiful." Her head lolled, and for a moment, I feared she might pass out. A tipping point had been reached, for she straightened and her hands stilled, coming to rest on her knees. Her head lifted, although her eyes remained closed. A presence had settled over the inner sanctum, one I knew well.

The air prickled, dense with the awareness of Sophos centred upon this tiny speck of earth. Sweat broke out across my skin and even oozed between my scales. Sachita exhaled through her nose and drew her shoulders back. The spiral that formed the pupil of Sophos rotated, slowly turning clockwise.

"Disappointment overflows within her," Sachita said in Malay in her too-old voice. "Sadness pierces her at seeing how low you have fallen. Frustration too, for your pride. Don't you see the connections? So delicate, an unbreakable gossamer web, woven through all of us. Even you, *Ophiuchus*."

"I beg your forgiveness, Sophos," I replied in a hoarse voice. "Whatever mistakes I am guilty of, they were made in pursuit of my conscience."

Sachita's body swayed and the tips of her fingers drummed upon one knee. "Sand spills from a broken hourglass," the girl said, in English this time. "Count the grains if you must."

I accepted the rebuke. Sophos was right: I did not have time to debate my past actions. The end was inevitable. What mattered was how I met it. "I seek your counsel, Sophos. Not for myself, but for those I have wronged."

Sachita swayed and the spiral on her forehead swirled. I dropped my gaze before it mesmerised me.

"I sacrificed two people from the Fraternum to escape Metamorphoses, although as you can see, she marked me nonetheless. I stole their identities—their vitalis—to anchor me in this plane. It was wrong. I wish to understand how it can be undone."

Sachita stilled and the shaft of sunlight crackled around me. The girl cocked her head as she communed with Sophos, now rocking from side to side on her buttocks. The exchange took far longer than the previous ones. I feared the reply might be beyond Sachita's ability to interpret. Bilhana shifted on her feet in the periphery of my vision, obviously concerned as well.

Eventually Sachita said, "The body heals if we wish to be well." The girl paused. "She wonders, why give the snake its fangs?"

I frowned, trying to make sense of that. Was she suggesting

the poison was only effective because I had allowed it to be? How could that be true? Unless my guilt over Esmeray and Khavad's fate had been powering Metamorphoses' transformation. I sat back in astonishment. *The body heals if it wishes to be well.* Did some repressed part of me believe I deserved to be maimed?

Sachita cupped her hands together in her lap and her small body trembled. I could only imagine the strain of maintaining this connection. "Every leaf in a forest is precious. Though it may wither and fall, it is not lost, for the earth gathers it in and so the forest remembers. Turn the seasons. Coax forth new growth, for are you not the memory of the forest?"

"Thank you, Sophos. I think...I understand."

Sachita's trembling increased and she shook her head. "'Ware the tempest. Tearing off branches. Rending trees." She flung her hands up into the air.

I stiffened. "What tempest? What do you mean?"

"A madness. A delirium. An end to all seasons." She twisted in distress at whatever Sophos showed her. The shafts of sunlight flickered and waned. Sophos' presence faded and Sachita slumped, like a discarded marionette. The inner sanctum was pitched into total darkness. Bilhana flicked on her lantern and hurried over to her granddaughter. Sachita remained in her lotus pose, chin touching her thin chest, her breathing deep and regular.

I cleared my throat. "Is she all right?"

"Yes, just exhausted." Bilhana unfolded the girl's legs and lay her gently on the ground, tucking an errant strand of black hair behind one ear. "And what of you, Ophiuchus? Have your questions been answered?" She turned, a tight expression pulling at the corners of her mouth.

"Some," I replied, "although new ones are queuing up to take their place."

Bilhana accompanied me on the slow climb back to the surface, although she refrained from asking any questions as I considered the implications of my exchange with Sophos.

We stopped just inside the mouth of the cave. After the cool depths, it felt like I was about to step into a wall of heat, and I regretted leaving my sunglasses back at the river. I turned to Bilhana. "Thank you for receiving me so swiftly. I know some pilgrims have waited years to be admitted."

"Sophos told us to expect you and we knew your need was great," Bilhana replied with a gracious nod. She gestured towards the paddy field and the jungle beyond. "Besides, we're not as isolated as you might think. Rumours of the troubles stirring across the world reach us even here. Where will you go now?"

"Ankara," I replied without hesitation. "I need to set my affairs in order before this *tempest* finds me."

Bilhana nodded. "You'll need to get to Sandakan, then. There's a hidden trail that will take you to the main road. Can you ride a motorbike?"

I grinned. "Better than a donkey."

The corners of Bilhana's mouth twitched with the ghost of a smile. "I will have it fuelled and brought around. I wish you well, Ophiuchus. May the gratitude of all the peoples of this plane light your way." She bowed solemnly and I returned the courtesy. Bilhana withdrew into the cave and a familiar knot of anxiety tightened in the pit of my stomach. This visit had always been a stopover, yet I had felt safe here. Soon the world, and all its incessant demands, would come flooding back.

I unzipped my backpack and retrieved the satellite phone. Powering it up, I was relieved to find the battery still held a decent charge. I thumbed through the menu and dialled the number I wanted. I had no idea what time it was in the Balkans and I didn't care.

After a few moments, the call connected to a cell phone on the far side of the world. It took seven rings before it was answered.

"Hello?" The voice on the line was sleepy.

"Delaine, it's Zeite."

"Zeite?" Her tone sharpened immediately. "Who is this?"

"I just told you."

"Zeite? Is that really you?"

"Yes, it's really me. Isn't this meant to be a secure line or something?"

"Where the fuck have you been? Do you have any idea of the shitstorm you dropped me in after Dryanovski? And yes, this is an encrypted line, so how did you get this number?"

"I stole your sat-phone," I replied, deciding to answer the last question as it was the easiest.

"You stole…my sat-phone. *That's* your answer. Jee-zus! Do you have any idea what's been happening in your absence? COVID-19 has killed thousands and the only thing spreading faster than the virus is panic. The US and her allies are escalating a trade war with China and countries are closing their borders. And if that wasn't enough to contend with, the installation housing Hephaestus' capstone has gone dark, along with another of our sites in Syria."

"You're yelling," I said.

"*Of course* I'm fucking yelling! The world is going to shit and it's our job to prevent that."

"True." I gave her a moment to find her equilibrium.

"Where are you?" she asked in a level tone.

"Borneo."

"Borneo? What the fuck is in Borneo?"

"A temple belonging to Sophos. I needed some advice."

Delaine hesitated. "You spoke with Sophos. What…um… what did the Sage say?"

"I'll tell you on the flight back."

"The flight back?"

"I need you to collect me at Sandakan airport. Yes, I know international borders are closed, so I'll meet you at a freight warehouse. No doubt one of the Order's corporate entities will own one."

"Oh, sure. No problem. So what, now I'm an Uber driver?"

"No, you're a member of the Fraternum. So quit your bitching, down a coffee and get over here ASAP." That pulled her up short.

"I'm sorry. This is all just…very sudden. You've been MIA for weeks and I'm the last one who had contact with you. Can you imagine what I've been through?"

As it happened, I could. The Order didn't mind the odd interrogation. "Look, I get it: Dryanovski went sideways. Once the Tyrant's capstone was destroyed, I realised I was running out of runway fast. So, I went to Sophos. We're in the endgame, Delaine. I need your help."

She let out a sigh. "Understood. What else do you need, apart from a chauffeur service during unprecedented travel bans?"

"Two more things. Firstly, keep this quiet. Involve as few of the Fraternum as possible. Secondly, I want to know where Esmeray Burakgazi and Khavad Demirci are located. You read the report on the incursion in Istanbul, so you know they're the agents who saved me. Our destination is wherever they're located."

"You need to see patients in comas."

"I need you to trust me on this. Decide now, otherwise I'll make other arrangements."

My guide—who had first ushered me into the temple—emerged from the depths of the cave. He waved as he pushed a yellow Kawasaki motocross bike towards me. A broad grin split his face as he caught sight of my surprised expression.

"Well?" I demanded.

"I'm neck deep in shit anyway."

I could picture her shaking her head. "Fair assessment. Get to Sandakan as soon as you can. Oh, and find a way to let Vasil—or whoever is in command—know that investigating any sites that go dark is a bad idea. Hephaestus has conjured something nasty, so conventional weapons aren't going to cut it. Am I clear?"

"Zeite, what the hell is going on?"

"Just find Esmeray and Khavad. I'll explain once Sandakan is in the rear-view mirror." I disconnected the call.

"Isn't she a beauty?" My guide patted the Kawasaki's seat.

I took in the wide, knobby tyres and heavy-duty suspension of the motorbike. "She's gorgeous." I swung my satchel behind my back and cinched the straps on my backpack to hold both in place.

"The trail is over there." He pointed past the alcoves that housed the Archetypes of Virtue to a small gap between the trees. "It's not much more than a goat track. Eventually you'll reach a wooden bridge that crosses the river. Stay on the path and turn right when you reach a T-junction. From there, it's about twenty kilometres to the main road."

"What about the barrier surrounding the temple?"

"Only works one way." He gestured to the Kawasaki. "Do you need me to demonstrate?"

I grabbed one end of the handlebar, swung a leg over the seat and started the ignition. "I'll be fine."

My guide nodded, noted the eager expression on my face, and wisely stepped back.

I revved the accelerator, dropped the clutch, and sped off in a spray of dirt.

To be honest, I did not think I would find time for another entry in this memoir. With events moving so quickly, it seemed unlikely. However, apparently even Archetypes are forced to twiddle their thumbs at airports.

For the record, I hate waiting. Especially when time is no longer an ally. Although on this occasion, I will admit the wait did provide an opportunity to consider what to do with these thoughts...

The Boeing C-17 Globemaster touched down on the runway with a squeal of heavy-duty rubber. It was a huge plane favoured by the US military, although the markings on the white fuselage indicated it belonged to a corporate conglomerate known as *12 Apostles Inc*. This was one of the corporate fronts established and operated by the Officium.

I watched the heavy cargo plane taxi from my hiding spot on the wrong side of the hurricane fence. Fortunately, security was lax, and it only required a minor adjustment of reality to weaken the wire fencing surrounding the airstrip.

The Globemaster decelerated and began a slow, sweeping turn at the end of the runway. No doubt Customs would be waiting at the hangar to inspect their cargo. Frankly, I didn't have time for all that bureaucratic bullshit. I released the clutch and the Kawasaki surged forward. I had used some of my wait to build a small ramp from discarded timber packing slats and a few well-placed stones. Hitting the ramp at speed, I opened up the throttle. My front wheel popped up just as I launched into the air. The weakened wire fence toppled over, and I landed on the tarmac with only a minor wobble. Kicking up through the gears, I sped towards the Globemaster.

The alarm sounded sooner than I had expected. Warning lights flashed along the runway strip and a siren wailed from speakers at the terminal. I hunched over the Kawasaki and raced towards the plane. The Globemaster finished its turn and I caught a glimpse of the pilots pointing at me. I threw a glance towards the terminal and spotted distant figures spilling out of the building.

Airport security would be on their way presently.

I swung out of the path of the Globemaster and raced under one wing. The plane had come to a stop and I was relieved to find the rear gantry was already opening. A handful of vehicles emerged from the terminal, their lights flashing. I gauged the distance between us and estimated how long it would take before we could achieve take-off velocity. Security would reach us before then.

I thrust my hand into the satchel and focused on the approaching vehicles. Picturing a tremendous, explosive pressure, I altered the reality beneath each of the SUVs. The tyres exploded in a cloud of vaporised rubber and the vehicles careered out of control, sparks arcing from their bare metal rims.

My skin prickled at the sudden use of potentiality and my vision dimmed momentarily. I nearly dumped the bike before I recovered. The gantry was almost down. Revving the Kawasaki, I bunny-hopped over the lip and raced into the belly of the Globemaster.

Delaine was operating the ramp. Despite the urgency, I was surprised to find she was dressed in cargo pants and a pale blue Rip Curl T-shirt. I ditched the bike and yelled, "Let's go!" Harkins emerged from between two secured crates, a grin splitting his bearded face. It dissipated when he took in the extent of the scales covering my arm and shoulder. Delaine hit a button and the ramp began to close.

"What the hell, Zeite?" Delaine rushed over, her face tight

with concern. "Are you *trying* to cause a diplomatic incident?"

"Just get this plane in the air," I replied. "I don't have time for formalities." I jammed the bike between two crates.

Delaine took in the scales covering my skin. "It's spreading, isn't it?"

"Every time I draw upon the Ladder."

Delaine pursed her lips and shot a sharp look at Harkins, who was dressed in shorts and an offensively bright pink Hawaiian shirt. "Wheels up, ASAP. Check with the Captain to ensure we have enough fuel to reach Ankara."

"On it, boss. Nice ride, Zeite." Harkins gave me a double thumbs up and disappeared towards the front of the plane.

"Ankara," I repeated. "Is that where Esmeray and Khavad are?"

"Not quite. Let's get strapped in before take-off." Delaine led me past wrapped pallets that had been secured to the floor and the curving walls of the Globemaster. She took a set of steep stairs to reach the upper deck.

Kennett was peering through one of the windows. She turned as she heard our footsteps on the metal stairs and threw a thumb over her broad shoulder. "Airport security seems pissed. I'm guessing that's your handiwork." Like the others, she was dressed in civvies: a black ACDC T-shirt and light camo pants that complimented her caramel skin.

I shrugged. "Lost my passport."

"Mm-hmm." Kennett took in my scaled appearance and arched a laconic eyebrow. "Good to know I'm not the only one who suffers migraines when you're around."

"Nice to see you as well," I replied with a wink.

Delaine smoothly intervened. "Zeite, you remember my father, Cormac."

Cormac was leaner than last time we met. His thinning auburn hair was dishevelled, giving the impression he'd been running his fingers through it. A pair of black glasses perched on his nose and his creased white shirt and black trousers suggested he'd just left the office. He clutched a bottle of sanitiser in one hand and a packet of disposable face masks in the other.

"Head of Operations for the Officium," I said. "How could I forget?"

Cormac turned a delicate shade of red. "Please excuse my behaviour the last time we met. I was not...myself."

"You weren't the only one."

Cormac nodded in obvious relief. "I don't suppose...you know." He half-heartedly offered the sanitiser and masks.

"That's kind of you, but I've seen my share of plagues. You won't have to worry about COVID in my presence."

"Of course." Cormac stowed them in a compartment under his seat.

The Globemaster shuddered as its engines whined. Harkins hurried back into the cabin. "Better strap in. We're about to take off, although the Captain isn't happy about it."

We settled into seats on opposing sides of the cabin and secured our belts.

"Do we have enough fuel?" Delaine asked.

Harkins nodded. "The Cap is confident. He's just spinning some line about a biohazard breach to Sandakan air control. Not sure they'll buy it, but we'll be airborne before they can stop us."

"Good enough," Delaine replied.

I turned to Cormac. "I presume we have you to thank for all of this."

"More or less," he said with a self-deprecating shrug. "Fortunately, this aircraft was already in Jakarta. Commissioning the Learjet for the four of us to reach it took a little more wrangling, especially since I couldn't tell the Officium what it was for. But after what you did for us at the monastery, well, it's the least I could do."

The Globemaster gathered speed.

"Prepare for take-off," the Captain said in a terse voice over the intercom.

I leaned back against the cushioned headrest and placed my battered leather satchel in my lap. The plane rumbled down the runway. I caught the wail of an alarm over the strain of the engines before it fell away behind us. The Globemaster parted ways with the ground, its four massive engines powering us into the air.

I leaned as far forward as my straps would allow and addressed Delaine. "Tell me about Ankara."

Delaine glanced at her father. "Agents Burakgazi and Demirci are in a long-term care unit at an installation outside of Ankara. Security is tight, although Dad—I mean, Cormac—was able to access their medical records. Zeite, you should know they've remained unresponsive to all stimuli since their admission."

I waved her concern aside. "That's because their minds aren't in this reality."

Delaine frowned. "What—?"

I cut off any further questions. "This installation... Is it hidden near the old underground cities in Cappadocia?"

"Why yes, it is." Cormac thumbed his glasses up his nose. "Have you been there before?"

"Once, a long time ago. I left a staff there, although it's a secret known to very few. Over time, the site became a repository for other reliquaries. I assume that's still the case."

Cormac nodded. "It is, although the Sophists manage the site, and they refuse to supply the Officium with an inventory. That's beginning to make more sense after what you've just told us."

Delaine frowned. "I couldn't give a toss about their need for secrecy. If they're caring for injured members of the Fraternum, then I expect the welcome mat to be rolled out." Harkins folded his arms across his chest, a thoughtful expression on his bearded face. Kennett twisted one of her tightly knit braids between her fingers.

Cormac shrugged. "I can understand their reluctance. The Order needs somewhere to store items that should remain lost to history. Can you imagine the international attention if an eighth-century Celtic torc with ancient Greek symbols suddenly turned up for sale in the Grand Bazaar in Istanbul?"

"Point taken." Turning to Delaine, I asked, "Has anyone investigated the temple in Jordan that housed the capstone for Hephaestus? It was destroyed a day and a half ago."

"We sent in a team to investigate," Delaine replied. "That was before your warning," she said hurriedly, seeing the expression on my face. "The site was untouched. No damage whatsoever, except to electricals. All the computers were fried and back-ups were wiped. Even uploads to the cloud had failed. At first, we thought it was an EMP attack."

"What about the Tender and his disciples?" I asked.

"Well, that's where it gets weird. Physically, they were unharmed, except they all suffered from amnesia. It was the same with the staff from the Fraternum and Officium. Cognitive tests are still being conducted, but they appear to have no memory of what happened. Even stranger, they don't seem to recall the Order. It's like our entire organisation has been wiped from their collective memory."

A madness. A delirium. An end to all seasons.

"And I suppose that's what happened to our outpost in Syria."

"After your warning, we sent in a drone," Delaine said. "I haven't seen all the footage, but I'm told our people were just wandering around aimlessly, like lost children."

I leaned back in my seat. Whatever Hephaestus had conjured was moving north, and eradicating all traces of the Order along the way. I didn't doubt for a moment it was headed for the same destination as us.

"We need ground transport as soon as we touch down in Ankara. Once we reach the site, we'll need to separate into two teams. Here's what I want you to do." Their expressions clouded over as I outlined my plan.

It was a bit after midnight when the Globemaster touched down at Esenboğa Uluslararası Havalimanı international airport. We had been kept in a holding pattern for almost forty-five minutes while the Captain negotiated with Turkish air traffic control. In the end, the corporate influence of 12 Apostles Inc won out and we were granted permission to land on an outer airstrip.

A pair of silver Jeep Grand Cherokees were waiting for us once we came to a stop in the freight hangar. Cormac had called in some favours at the local branch of the Officium to "expedite" the usual Customs process. We were in the Jeeps and moving before the Captain and his co-pilot had completed their post-flight checks.

Given the hour, traffic was mercifully light, and we joined the O-20 ring road heading south in good time. Delaine, Cormac and Kennett had taken the lead Jeep. That left me with Harkins, who had opted to drive. Delaine was travelling about ten kilometres over the speed limit, which wasn't fast enough for my liking, but restrained enough to avoid the attention of the local authorities.

"It's about a four-hour drive to Cappadocia," Harkins said in a conversational tone. "So, you have plenty of time to tell me how you really see this playing out."

I glanced at Harkins. He remained focused on the road, outwardly calm. His field was flat and tightly bunched, all of his emotions tightly battened down: a veteran on the eve of battle. "Didn't we have that discussion on the plane?"

Harkins glanced at me. "Not so much. You just told us what you wanted us to do." He changed lanes, following Delaine's Jeep as she prepared to turn off the ring road. "I've seen my fair share of fights, Zeite. I recognise that expression you're wearing."

Harkins was a man who doled out words like they were drops of water in the desert. This was the most effusive I'd ever seen him. "And what expression would that be?"

"The one people adopt when they step into the ring convinced they can't win."

Delaine's Jeep peeled off the O-20 and took the road towards Kırıkkale. Harkins followed, his movements smooth and efficient.

"Failure can be forgiven," I replied in a neutral tone. "Remaining idle cannot."

"Hmph. Delaine said you're like a politician: always answering the question you wanted, not the one you were asked."

I laughed and Harkins shot me a surprised look. His expression softened—marginally—and he sniffed, amused despite my evasions. "So Zeite, have I earned one straight answer yet?"

I chewed my lip in silence and stared out at the twinkling lights that peppered the dark landscape outside. "Nothing lasts forever, Harkins. Not here, in the mortal plane, anyway. But that doesn't mean human lives aren't precious. So, I'm done with the Fraternum taking bullets for me. Once I get to Esmeray and Khavad, I want you to evacuate the installation. That includes you and your team. Something bad is heading our way, and it's for me alone to deal with."

"And what if you can't?" Harkins asked so quietly I almost missed it over the hum of the engine.

"Well, then it will fall to you—and the rest of humanity—to not remain idle."

Delaine turned off the bitumen road in favour of a dusty, nondescript track that entered a narrow valley. The sun had only just crested the horizon, and it picked out veins of rose and ochre in the upper reaches of the cliffs. No signposts pointed the way. I had expected razor wire fencing and armed guards at checkpoints, but there were no visible signs of security. Clearly this installation relied upon secrecy as its chief form of defence.

The Jeeps eventually came to a stop in a natural cul-de-sac. Outside, the air was chilly, especially after the heat and humidity of Borneo. Thankfully, I had found a loose shirt, a fleece jacket and some ill-fitting boots while on the Globemaster.

Kennett opened the boot of the lead Jeep and handed out the G36 rifles the Fraternum preferred to use in the field. Delaine and Harkins accepted the familiar weapons gratefully, although Cormac declined.

"Where did these come from?" I asked, tucking my hands under my armpits to keep them warm.

"My buddy is the Supply Master in Ankara," Kennett replied. "These are on loan, so don't lose 'em."

I shook my head. "They'll be useless, unless you have that exotic ammo. Even then, I can't be certain."

Kennett grinned. "I might've missed the firefight at the monastery, but I heard all about those dead disciples coming after you." She handed out clips of ammunition with a white band. "Stick to semiautomatic. We've only got two clips each." Delaine and Harkins switched their clips with brisk efficiency.

"The entrance should be at the end of this valley," Cormac said, peering uncertainly at the steep valley walls.

"The entrance to the underground cities were hidden to provide refuge to the early Christians during their persecution,"

I said. "We'll find it if we look closely enough." We spread out, picking our way carefully over the dusty ground to take a closer look at the folds and niches in the valley walls.

I turned and glanced back the way I had come. A distant smudge was visible on the horizon. Narrowing my eyes, I strained to make it out. Delaine noticed and followed my gaze. "Probably a dust storm. Not uncommon in this region."

I disagreed but kept my misgivings to myself.

"Over here." Kennett had disappeared behind a fallen boulder. We converged upon her position to discover a narrow passage hidden behind the large rock. The shaft dropped below ground level and was quickly swallowed by darkness.

Kennett, Harkins and Delaine fitted compact lights to the barrels of their assault rifles and led us underground. The shaft continued for twenty odd paces before bending left and ending in a small chamber. It was noticeably warmer underground, and the roof was low enough to force Harkins to duck a few times.

A quick scan of the chamber revealed exits on our left and right. Both new tunnels were blocked by worn steel doors fitted into the rock. I tapped Delaine on the shoulder and pointed to a discreet camera set in the ceiling.

Addressing the camera, Delaine said, "My name is Delaine Kearney and I'm a member of the Fraternum. This is the current incarnation of the Thirteenth, along with members of my squad, and my father, who is part of the Officium. I know our visit has not been scheduled, but we're here on Bureau business. It is imperative that you grant us access to this facility."

We waited a full minute for a response, growing increasingly restless.

Cormac was the first to lose patience. "There's no point pretending you can't hear us. We know this is a manned facility. You Sophists are answerable to the Thirteenth just as much as the rest of us."

"Identification sequence." The artificial voice emerged from a speaker hidden somewhere in the ceiling.

Delaine replied, "Foxtrot-Alpha, seven, nine, seven, three."

"Invalid," the voice replied. "Status: Detain." A mini portcullis dropped from the ceiling of the tunnel, locking us in the chamber.

Delaine struck the metal bars with the palm of her hand. "My clearance must have been revoked."

"Well, we asked politely." I walked over to the steel door on the left and thrust my left hand into my satchel. There was little point trying to weaken the door when the surrounding stone was relatively soft. No doubt they had braced the door frame with concrete, but I was in no mood to be patient. Focusing, I pictured the stone surrounding the door dissolving, drew potentiality from the pocket, and willed it into reality. The rock softened into a grey slurry that ran down the steel frame. The now familiar prickling of poison ran up along the side of my neck and down towards my navel. Ignoring the sensation, I kicked the door and it fell backwards with a loud clang.

Alarms would be sounding in a command centre somewhere below us. Matching ones had probably been triggered in the regional station in Ankara. Agents would be mobilising to converge upon our position, which would only serve to put more people in harm's way. To avoid that, we needed to complete our mission here as quickly as possible. I repeated the process with the second door and grimly ignored the poison boiling beneath my skin.

Harkins kicked the second door in and scanned the far side of the tunnel. "Clear," he called.

I hadn't released my hold on the pocket yet. Picturing my memoir, I imagined all the entries I had recorded—all the hard-won lessons—set out clearly on consecutive pages and bound in a hardback of rich, deep green leather. On the cover I pictured the seal of Ophiuchus, the staff and encircling serpent embossed in silver, surrounded by an inner and outer circle and the twelve ancient signs of the Archetypes. Willing this tome into reality, I withdrew it from my satchel. It was thicker than I had expected and included a locked clasp.

Offering the memoir to Cormac, I said, "When you reach the archives where the reliquaries are kept, I want to you to hide this somewhere where it won't be found."

Cormac accepted the memoir reverently. "I will, although if

you don't mind me asking…what is it?"

"An account of my doings. If I succeed in freeing Esmeray and Khavad, and you judge her to be of sound mind, give it to her."

Delaine's eyes narrowed. "Why not give it to her yourself, Zeite?"

"Always with the questions." I shook my head. "Get to the archive. Go!" I pointed towards the open shaft on the right.

Delaine hesitated. "Harkins and Kennett can—"

"No," I snapped. "You got me here. For that, I'll always be grateful. Now stick to the plan. Find whatever reliquaries you can, dump them in this chamber and get out. Hopefully you'll buy me enough time to reach Esmeray and Khavad. I don't want to see you unless you find my staff. Now go." I gave her a shove towards the archive.

Delaine still hesitated.

"We have our mission," Harkins said to Delaine. "Let him complete his." He gave me a short nod to show he understood. Solid fellow, that one.

Kennett adjusted her grip on her rifle as her gaze shifted between Delaine and me. Cormac clutched my memoir to his chest with a look of stunned reverence.

It was unlikely I'd see any of them again. I committed this moment to memory, treasuring the fact that they cared.

"Thank you. And take care of one another." As farewells go, it was woeful. Embarrassed, I gave them the briefest of nods, and hurried down the corridor, resisting the urge to look back.

Redemption was only a few more levels below.

The site soon gave up its pretence of being an ancient haven for people hiding from religious persecution. The hand-chiselled stone gave way to concrete floors. Reinforced steel beams jutted from the ceiling at regular intervals, and a clear polymer had been sprayed over the stone, presumably to prevent further erosion.

Automatic lights switched on as I moved down a corridor that looked more like a hospital ward with every step. No guards rushed out to meet me, for which I was grateful. Metamorphoses' poison still simmered beneath my skin. I knew that blisters, and eventually scales, would soon follow. Every manipulation of reality was transforming me into some beast drawn from the depths of mythology. Perhaps Sophos was right and at some level I was allowing this to happen. While that might be true, it didn't explain how to prevent the process, or better yet, how to reverse it.

The corridor ended in another tight chamber. This one contained a spiral ramp, which I hurried down. I noted the camera tracking my progress and wondered who was watching and what they made of my incursion. Did they see the Thirteenth, the founder of their Order, or some scaled monstrosity losing its hold on humanity?

Numerous tunnels branched off the ramp, although none were signed. Clamping down on my frustration, I closed my eyes and sifted through the reality of this refuge. The uppermost layers were infused with the deep and contemplative thoughts of the Sophists. Cormac had been correct in his description: this site had the feel of an archive, a place to store relics that had no place in the modern world. The fact that this included Esmeray and Khavad angered me. Buried beneath that anger was a deep sense of shame.

I concentrated on Esmeray, recalling the shape and texture of her field, and her talent for sifting through the threads of reality. It was a rare talent, and once I had rekindled it from memory, it was easy to detect. She was on the next level beneath me: a further full turn down the spiral ramp, then onto a branch that ran off to the left. I hurried, pursued by a mounting sense of urgency.

The sound of distant gunfire echoed from above. Was that Delaine's squad? Had they encountered resistance? Or had the Tempest finally caught up with us?

I hesitated, torn between having almost reached my goal and the desire to protect Delaine and her team. A few cells down, Esmeray and Khavad lay helpless, caught in an alternate reality I had trapped them in. Delaine and the others were not helpless: they had made a choice to help me rectify that wrong. In the end, I had to honour their decision.

Rushing down the corridor, I nearly collided with a nurse who emerged from one of the cells. She cried out in surprise and dropped her clipboard. I glimpsed a patient lying prone on a gurney over her shoulder, an IV drip connected to their arm.

"We're under attack," I said as I rushed past. "Evacuate as many as you can."

She gaped in response, obviously stunned by my strange and unexpected appearance, let alone the urgency of my message. No time to explain.

A man appeared at the far end of the corridor. He unholstered his sidearm and took aim. "On your knees," he growled.

I lifted both hands above my head. "I am the Thirteenth. It is imperative that I reach Agents Burakgazi and Demirci." I pointed one finger upwards. "You must know this installation is under attack. Everyone needs to evacuate. Now!"

The man cocked his head, listening to his earpiece. I didn't have time to be designated as 'Detain' again. "Let me prove who I am." Moving slowly, I knelt on the floor and my left hand drifted to the satchel resting against my hip.

"Show me your hands!" The security guard tightened his grip on his weapon.

"I have identification." Giving him a reassuring smile, I opened the mouth of the satchel wide. The guard was exposed to an uninterrupted view of the pure potentiality that I had siphoned from the Ladder. I cannot begin to guess what images flooded his mind. Completely overwhelmed, his arms dropped to his sides and the gun clattered onto the floor.

I stood and hurried past a handful of openings before turning left into one of the larger cells. Esmeray lay on a gurney, her eyes closed and a blanket drawn up to the top of her chest. Her arms lay slack by her sides. An IV line had been inserted into one forearm, while an oximeter had been clamped on the finger of her other hand. Khavad lay prone in a second gurney in an identical position. A set of monitors tracked their pulse, blood pressure and oxygen saturation levels. All the readings were unchanged from when I had last seen them in Istanbul.

Another burst of gunfire echoed from above. Definitely closer this time. I found it hard to imagine Delaine would shoot at other members of the Order, so that could only mean one thing.

I removed the oximeters and IV lines from Esmeray and Khavad. They both seemed so peaceful. Would they really thank me for dragging them back into the chaos of this world? I shook off the doubt and lay my unmaimed hand on Esmeray's forehead.

They had saved me. The least I could do was return the favour.

I closed my eyes, took a steadying breath, and fractured my awareness.

Part of me remained in a converted cell deep beneath the earth. The other part let go of this reality and stepped into...

...a broad, stone corridor.

A sudden bout of giddiness brought me to my knees. The floor tiles were worn and cracked, although a handful at the edges still bore their original design—a star of midnight blue surrounded by pale blue flowers on a white background.

The murmur of many voices drifted down from a set of steps. At the top of the landing stood an imposing pair of doors. I straightened and mounted the first step. The buzz of voices swelled. Another step and the chatter grew louder again. With each step, the clamour grew until I was forced to cover my ears. The sound of countless voices—all in need— ricocheted around my skull.

Reaching the double doors, I gave them a shove with both hands.

"What are you doing?" the nurse demanded. "What's going on?" Her accusing gaze darted between me and her patients.

I blinked. It was the nurse I had rushed past. Evidently, she had found the courage to confront me.

"I'm the Thirteenth," I said in a voice hoarse with strain. Fragmenting my vitalis was extremely taxing. "These agents fell defending me. I'm here to bring them back." Ominous silence had replaced the gunfire. "Please, you must evacuate everyone you can."

She glanced back down the corridor. Potentiality suddenly detonated two levels above. I felt the *whoompf* of it barrelling through the tunnels. Lunging, I caught the nurse by the elbow and dragged her out of the way as the concussion wave rolled past.

She pulled away from me. "What was that?"

"A reliquary was just destroyed," I replied. "You have to get out. Now!" Any doubt over whether the Tempest had arrived had been dispelled.

"But—"

"I'll take care of these two. Just go," I yelled.

The doors swung open to reveal a chamber the size of a large mead hall. The ceiling was low, with heavy timber beams dividing the peeling plaster. On my left, shafts of sunlight pierced the gloom from crescent windows set high along the wall. I caught the clatter of hooves on cobblestones and realised we were below ground.

Heavy wooden trestle tables had been set up in three parallel rows. Over a hundred ragged children were in varying stages of consuming meals on tin plates. The food was modest: a hunk of bread with a watery soup splashed over the top of beans and carrots and a small dollop of mashed cauliflower.

The children fell silent as the doors groaned on their hinges. Spoons hovered, halfway to mouths, eyes wide in thin faces. Not one had reached adolescence yet. I glanced down at myself, afraid my scales would terrify the children, only to discover that I was dressed in a black suit, with a silver waistcoat and a matching tie cinched high up against my throat.

The contrast between their dirty, mismatched clothing and my finery could not have been more acute. A woman in a shapeless dress of faded grey cotton marched towards me. She wore a pale blue hijab, and a look of thunderous anger was spreading across her face. It took a moment before I realised it was Esmeray.

Glancing past her, I spied Khavad at the servery. His wavy black hair had grown to shoulder length and was tied back at the nape of his neck. He had rolled up the sleeves of his tunic to the elbows and wore loose, flowing pants of deep blue. Putting his ladle down, he walked around the queue of waiting children and picked up a nasty-looking cudgel that had been leaning against the wall.

"Esmeray," I said in delight. "At last."

She stopped a few feet away and studied me. "I do not know

this Esmeray. My name is Sitti," she replied.

Another reliquary detonated above, followed by a third. Each surge in potentiality buffeted the poor nurse, who eventually fled in terror. I looked down at Esmeray. She twitched beneath my palm, faint frown lines marring the smooth skin of her forehead. Khavad tensed on his gurney, straining against bonds of his own making.

While I may have found them, the reality they had escaped into still maintained a fearsome hold upon them. In hindsight, it was hardly surprising that Esmeray had adopted the identity of Nene Sitti: she revered her adopted grandmother and had clearly inherited Sitti's desire to nurture and protect the homeless. Separating Esmeray from Sitti's identity would take time and patience, both of which were in perilously short supply. However, ripping her from this world where she cared for abandoned children—as she had once done—could cause lasting trauma.

I hesitated. It had not occurred to me that they might be happier in a reality of their choosing, yet now it seemed blindingly obvious.

Slow, deliberate footsteps echoed down the corridor. The thick patina of reality that coated this ancient sanctuary bubbled like paint under a heat gun. Long forgotten deeds and cherished memories rose to the surface and withered before the approaching presence.

The Tempest had arrived.

I looked down at Esmeray. She would be safe if all memories of the Order, the Ladder, and the Thirteenth, were wiped from her mind. But then she would no longer be the person I cherished. Nor would she be able to live the life that she had chosen.

I could pretend that I was acting on behalf of Esmeray and Khavad, but really, the truth was I craved absolution. Was this, then—finally—what it meant to be human: to crave acceptance, regardless of one's failings and mistakes? If so, it was a realisation that I found both humbling and liberating.

I touched Esmeray's cheek and then stepped into the corridor

to face the end of my seasons.

"Rent is not due for another five days," Esmeray said, her tone simmering with outrage. "These poor children only experience the grace of a meal once a day. Can't you leave them in peace? You'll have your money once we've collected the donations."

I lifted my hands in surrender. "I'm not here for money. I merely seek your forgiveness…and to return you to where you belong. Both of you," I said, shooting a look at Khavad.

Esmeray planted her hands on her hips. "My place is here, with these poor children. As to any apologies you might owe, offer them to Allah. The mosque is that way." She pointed towards the double doors behind me.

Khavad rounded the last trestle table and came to a stop, the cudgel resting upon his broad shoulder. The nearest children retreated, sliding off their seats and stepping back, their eyes never leaving me, the intruder.

"You're not welcome here," Khavad said in a flat voice. "Please spare the children any unpleasantness. They have witnessed enough." The head of the cudgel thudded into the meat of his palm for emphasis.

"I'm sorry," I replied, "but there is a world outside this hall that needs you."

Esmeray spread her hands. "These children are all that I care for. Why can't you see that?"

"Oh, I do. That's exactly why you're needed."

"Enough." Khavad darted forward, surprisingly quick on his feet, and swung his cudgel.

The sensor lights revealed a figure at the far end of the corridor. She was of average height, with grey dreadlocks pulled back from a sharp, austere face. A silver snake head capped each dreadlock and they rasped together as she strode towards me. Her skin was covered in a layer of grey clay and ash, so I had no way divining her origins. The body beneath her grey T shirt and matching yoga pants was lean and muscled. We locked gazes and I shifted perception, trying to understand what lay beneath her human shell.

The field surrounding her was a void just like the one that had surrounded Metamorphoses. She smiled as I studied her. Grey plumes lifted from her aura. They whipped around her limbs and torso, spinning like dervishes. Reality peeled away from her presence and I belatedly understood why Sophos had named this thing the Tempest.

The grey streamers settled, and she continued her steady pace towards me.

"Did they give you any choice?" I asked in a raised voice. "Hephaestus and the others, I mean. Do you retain any will, or are you just a puppet with clever strings?"

She tilted her head and studied me with dark, pitiless eyes. Her pace never wavered.

"Not even speech, I see. Well, your masters don't like servants who have thoughts of their own." I lifted my scaled hand and drew upon the power of the pocket in my satchel. A section of the ceiling above the Tempest cracked and a shower of rocks and dust collapsed upon her.

Moments later, the fallen debris melted away in a slurry of sandstone to reveal her whirling streamers. Once she was clear, she lifted a fist from her side and twisted her wrist until her knuckles faced the floor. Her clenched fingers sprang open, revealing a single scale nestled in the palm of her hand. A heartbeat later, my scales ruptured.

I staggered backwards, blood streaming from my neck, chest and arm.

The Tempest closed in.

I side-stepped Khavad's cudgel and ducked under the follow-up swing. Each step took me closer to Esmeray, who hadn't budged. I no longer possessed the time to be gentle.

Khavad swung again, narrowly missing my head. I slid under one of the trestle tables, rolled and sprang to my feet on the far side.

"Please," I said, throwing up both hands in surrender. "There's no need for this. I'll leave."

Khavad placed a foot on the bench, clearly preparing to spring across the table.

"We were colleagues once," I said to the former agent. "Surely you remember, Khavad?"

Esmeray lifted a hand and Khavad paused, clearly displeased by the interruption. "The exit is that way." She pointed towards the double doors.

"Yes, it is." I edged away from Khavad, who was still glowering at me. "And I'll be on my way. I just need to show you one thing."

I had imagined this moment more times than I'd care to admit. In every scenario I had indulged in, Esmeray and Khavad had been grateful at being reunited with their true pasts. What I was about to do couldn't be further from that pleasant daydream. Yet I no longer possessed the luxury of other choices.

I ran my fingers through my hair, down the back of my neck, and across my chest. My fancy clothes dissolved beneath my touch to reveal my true form. Esmeray back-pedalled, a look of shock fracturing across her face as the extent of the scales covering my skin was revealed.

Khavad drew in a shocked breath and the nearest children squealed.

"Demon! A scaled demon!"

The cry swirled around me, rising until it became piercing. After everything I had done for humanity—after everything I had been forced to become—it was inevitable they would reject me. I had known this from the beginning. Accepted it, even. And then buried it as I built the Order and wrestled with the Archetypes over the years, so desperate to fashion a better future I had forgotten about the flawed foundations my efforts rested upon.

"Enough." I silenced the terrified children with a chop of my good hand. "I'm sorry, Esmeray. For everything before, and for what's about to follow."

Her look of horror softened into confusion. I marched back to the double doors and grasped each brass handle. Concentrating,

I pictured the Order's hidden hospital beneath the earth and yanked hard. The doors tore from their hinges with a metallic squeal of protest. The alternate reality Esmeray had crafted tore open as well, revealing a long stone corridor and an approaching ghost that refused to flee in the glare of harsh, artificial light.

"There's your demon," I said, stabbing a finger at the Tempest, who had almost reached my bloodied figure, staggering towards us.

I dropped to my knees as my blood spattered across the stone. My body was failing, and with it, my hold on the mortal plane. The strain of fracturing my awareness across two realities was too much. I had to trust that the rent in Esmeray's alternate reality would hold, allowing her to see what stalked us both.

The Tempest paused, studying the rift that had opened behind me. Did she perceive Esmeray and Khavad staring through? Or was this merely another obstacle to overcome to eradicate me?

I decided I didn't really care.

Marshalling my dwindling strength, I pictured the vacuum of space surrounding the Tempest and summoned potentiality from the pocket. Ice feathered across her bare skin and she tried to draw in a breath, her chest hitching with the effort. The grey tendrils lifted from her field and whirled, slicing through the vacuum like razors through wet paper. Air rushed back in and she drew in a long, deep breath.

I pictured the crushing weight of the deep ocean trenches. Focusing on the Tempest, I lodged that pressure in her chest and inverted it. Her eyes bulged and her spine bent backwards until I thought it must surely snap. A snarl of effort flashed across her face as the tendrils whirled again, this time wrapping around my pocket of altered reality in her chest, containing it. She straightened and continued her advance, unhindered by my best efforts.

It occurred to me that every incursion I had foiled over the centuries was an opportunity for Hephaestus and the other Archetypes to study my tactics. In fashioning the Tempest, they had anticipated every manipulation of reality I might employ.

Except, perhaps, one.

The Tempest closed to within a few steps. A light flickered at the end of the corridor behind her. I kept my gaze locked on her face, unwilling to betray whoever had dared follow her.

I could not win this battle.

Sophos had warned me of that.

Which was precisely the point.

The Tempest raised an ashen hand towards my face, a surprisingly gentle gesture, like a mother soothing a restless baby. Her proximity drew my memories to the surface. They boiled upwards, like a violent stream of bubbles rising from a ruptured air tank on the seabed...

...paddling down a moon-kissed river while the jungle pressed in on all sides...

...smoking a cigar in a merchant house of faded glory while people danced in cobblestone streets to celebrate the overthrow of a tyrant...

...leaning against a tree, soaked in blood, as the Fraternum tumbled their dead into a mass grave.

The Tempest's plumes shivered in delight as they feasted upon the memories of my many lives.

It would have been easy to cease struggling—to let this abomination expunge all my failures and successes, and to absolve me of all guilt in the process. For an agonising moment, I contemplated that complete and utter surrender. After all, no one could accuse of me not trying. Yet, I could not give in, regardless of how pointless any further resistance might be.

Instead, I said, "I suspected you might enjoy all that death." Her eyes widened a fraction and I lurched backwards, tumbling through the rift into Esmeray's alternate reality.

The Tempest threw her head back and howled in frustration, the snakeheads in her dreadlocks spinning in a silver arc. After a brief hesitation, she followed.

I stumbled and collided with the corner of a trestle table. My left leg from the hip down went numb. "Don't let her touch you," I cried, limping away from the rift.

Esmeray yelled at the children and they scattered, the majority heading for a set of stairs at the far end of the hall that presumably led above ground. Khavad leapt over the trestle table and dragged Esmeray away from the ragged tear from which I had just emerged.

The Tempest leapt through the gap and landed lightly on her feet. Immediately colour seeped from the tiles beneath her and the nearest children twisted and evaporated in a cloud of ash, like dry leaves caught in a fire. Esmeray screamed in anguish.

The cudgel in Khavad's hand morphed into a shotgun. He pumped the stock and fired a round into the Tempest. The sound was deafening in the hall, and for a fleeting instant, I was transported to the ancient cistern under Istanbul.

The Tempest staggered under the blast, but the pellets didn't appear to penetrate the clay covering her skin.

Esmeray's shapeless shift and hijab dissolved into black security overalls and she moved to the right of Khavad. Bringing both hands up together in a practised motion, a revolver appeared in her hands and she fired six rounds in quick succession. Tears leaked from the corners of her eyes, but her hands remained steady.

The whirling grey tendrils surrounding the Tempest absorbed each bullet.

Khavad fired his shotgun again. The Tempest turned towards him and tossed the trestle table aside like it was made of paper.

"Lead her away from the children," I yelled.

Esmeray glanced at me and her brow furrowed as a glimmer of recognition flickered across her face. She let the revolver fall to the floor. Her gaze roamed around the hall, as if she no longer recognised where she was.

The Tempest darted towards Khavad, who was loading his shotgun with salt encrusted shells.

"We can save him," I called. "Together."

Esmeray nodded.

I limped towards her and reached for her hand.

She caught my wrist in a frantic grip. "Do what you must," Esmeray said in a voice thick with emotion.

This was Esmeray's reality, not mine. It would cease to exist once she released it. Drawing upon the strength of Esmeray's field, I sent the trestle tables and heavy wooden benches flying towards the Tempest. They slammed her into the stone wall so hard, pieces of plaster fell from the ceiling.

"Let's go," I called to Khavad, waving to him frantically.

He stared at the pile of splintered wood in astonishment. Pieces were already crumbling to ash as the Tempest struggled to her feet.

"Khavad!" Esmeray's piercing yell broke the spell. He raced towards us as the Tempest heaved aside the shattered timbers.

I swung Esmeray around and sent her stumbling towards the rift. Khavad caught her elbow and together they ran towards the breach, spurred on by some of the foulest language I could muster.

The Tempest rushed towards us, fury making the snakes writhe about her head. I glimpsed Metamorphoses in that moment, always wanting to tear down the world and build it anew. I caught sight of Hephaestus too, the tortured misfit whose cunning inventiveness could never win him acceptance. And the Tyrant howled at me, incensed by my continued defiance.

Grabbing the ragged edges of this reality, I pulled them together like heavy curtains and squeezed through the gap. The Tempest made a desperate lunge and caught an edge. I mustered all of my strength to force the breach closed, but in my weakened state, it wasn't enough. She forced the tear open, a wild, triumphant look dancing in her black eyes.

Behind her, a dull fog rolled in through the crescent windows. Dust shuddered from the ceiling and cracks appeared in the stonework.

"Almost," I said with a gasp.

Releasing the edges of the rift, I grabbed my battered leather satchel and ripped it open. The pocket siphoned from the Ladder spun between us, a ball of mercurial potentiality. Thrusting both hands into it, I imagined this alternate reality sealed by seamless, impenetrable walls with me standing on the outside.

Light burst along the edges of the rift, searing the image of the Tempest's fingers reaching for my face onto my retinae.

I lay on the ground, staring at the ceiling. My body was numb and stubbornly refused to respond to any command. Blood leaked from my wounds. Thankfully, pain was a distant thing, belonging to someone I used to be. I knew this lethargy, this dreaded slowing of mind and body. I had died before, of course, but never without a tether.

No return this time; not with at least two of the Tenders' seals broken.

Just a one-way ticket.

How very human of me.

I laughed at that. At least I tried to; it was more of a gurgle. This wasn't the ending I had imagined—alone, already buried beneath the earth and ready to be forgotten. Surely, I had earned some kind of ceremony.

I called for Esmeray, then Khavad. I couldn't form the names properly in my treacherous mouth. Or perhaps I hadn't earned the right to speak them.

The ceiling stared back at me. Seconds ticked by—countless grains shifting on the shores of eternity. My heart slowed, the beat almost coming to rest.

A face swam into view. Pale skin. Freckles. Ragged strands of auburn hair.

Delaine.

Beyond her, the lean outline of Harkins and two other shapes I couldn't quite make out.

Delaine said something. Probably one of her incessant questions, although I could see concern etched into her features.

I blinked in reply. It was the best I could muster. I just needed to know whether Esmeray and Khavad had survived. That was all that mattered now.

Delaine leaned closer and wrapped my hand around a cold piece of metal. That seemed important for some reason. I pushed back at the lethargy, a solitary candle flame of hope stuttering in the darkness.

I told my eyes to focus and they obeyed reluctantly. My hand clutched the base of a staff wrapped in copper that had turned green with age. Two opposing snakes curled around the staff, each connected to the main shaft by six struts.

The Rod of Asclepius.

Delaine had found my staff in the archive after all.

Another face framed by long, tousled black hair appeared above me. Behind her, the large frame of a loyal bodyguard. It took a moment for me to recognise them both.

Esmeray said something. The words couldn't get past the ringing in my ears. My gaze darted to Delaine, who nodded once and gently wrapped Esmeray's hand around the top of the rod, just above the fanged mouths of the opposing snakes.

The transition was instantaneous.

I stood in the centre of the seal of Ophiuchus carved into a rock plateau almost eight hundred years ago. The Rod of Asclepius thrummed in my left hand, replacing my trusty satchel. Esmeray faced me, a look of complete bewilderment etched into her face.

"Welcome back," I said.

"Back?" Esmeray looked around in astonishment. "Zeite, where are we?"

"Please, call me Ophiuchus."

"I don't understand. What is…all this?"

"This," I replied, gesturing to the darkness pressing in on all sides, "is a pocket of memory. And before you ask, I brought you here to conduct what can only be described as a long overdue handover."

"What are you talking about?" Esmeray planted her fists on her hips in a gesture I remembered only too well. I couldn't help but smile.

"A lot has happened since you and Khavad saved me from Metamorphoses."

"The cistern. Yes, I remember." Esmeray shot me a searching look. "What does 'a lot' mean, exactly?"

"Well, two of the Tenders' seals that tether me to this plane have been shattered. My satchel was destroyed. And I'm bleeding out as we speak. That covers the key points."

Esmeray stared. Eventually she said, "Zeite, I need you to be serious."

"Ophiuchus."

"All right, Ophiuchus, then. I still need you to be serious."

"I am. Deadly serious, in fact." I raised a hand to forestall her next question. "Here is what you're going to do: when you return to your body, you're going to tell what's left of the Order that I have nominated you as my successor. Of course, you'll have the Rod of Asclepius to prove it. Next, you're going to appoint the woman you're kneeling next to—Delaine Kearney—as Head of the Fraternum. After that, you'll speak to Delaine's father, Cormac. He's a pale, nervous-looking chap with thinning red hair. You will convince him to give you my memoir. Finally, you'll read my book and make your own decisions from there." I snapped the fingers of my free hand. "Simple, really."

Esmeray stared at me in astonishment. "*You* wrote a book?"

I shifted uneasily. "Well, a memoir. More of a diary than actual prose."

She shook her head. "This is absurd. When did *you* find the time to write a book?"

"Diary." I shook a finger at her. "Look, it wasn't easy, but you make time for things that are important. Think of it as an insurance policy."

"Are you finished playing games?" Esmeray arched an eyebrow.

"Yes," I replied with the most sober expression I could muster. "I am finished. One hundred percent."

Uncertainty clouded her expression. "You mean...all those things you said are true? About the seals, and the pocket, and..." Her gaze darted to my chest, searching for signs of injury.

"I'm afraid so. It's time to pass the baton."

Esmeray took a step back. "I can't take over from you. That's ridiculous."

"Is it?" I ticked off points on my fingers. "You perceive the threads of reality. You possess a fierce desire to protect those in need. And you inspire loyalty from the people who know you best. Look at Khavad, for instance."

"That's not enough. I couldn't possibly...I mean, the very thought." She shook her head again.

"Esme, we've had almost eight hundred years of patriarchy

under my stewardship. Yes, there have been advances. But there has also been far too much corruption and conflict. The world is crying out for more compassion, empathy and equality."

Esmeray stared. "You're really leaving us? For good?"

I nodded. The bereft look on her face was all the ceremony I needed.

"You'll face resistance," I warned her, "but I know you possess the strength to craft a better future than I could."

She looked up to the sky, and took a long, shuddering breath. "What will happen to you? When you return to the Ladder?"

"Ah, yes. That." I pursed my lips. "It will be awkward. No denying it. There is a faction amongst the Vices that wants to strip away my memories to make me more pliable. That's what the woman who attacked us was designed to do. However, I have a feeling that some of the Virtues privately approved of my initiative, if not the manner in which it was accomplished. Better to beg for forgiveness than ask for approval, right?"

"I'm not sure that really applies here," Esmeray said in an uncertain voice.

I hefted the Rod of Asclepius. "I want you to take this. It's a manifestation of the Ladder, of course, and by extension, an aspect of me. Between my memoir and this staff, you'll always be able to reach me if needed. Opposite ends of the same bridge, if you like. And through that bond, the Archetypes will never be able to purge my humanity. Even if they wanted to." I thumped the rod on the stone. "Just remember that it's the tool of a healer, not a warrior."

Summoning my very best smile, I offered to it to her with only the faintest of tremors.

After a long moment, she gingerly accepted it.

And finally, I let go.

Every book must have a final page, even my memoir. As you can see, I have left it largely blank for you, dear Reader.
Pick up my pen.
Picture the reality you wish for.
Hold it in the frame of your mind until it is steady, then release the

potentiality that lies within us all.

The future is not a mystery, it's merely your vision waiting to be summoned. Hold to that, and you'll set us all free, human and Archetype alike.

Ophiuchus.

Afterword

I have a bad habit of taking on large themes in my fiction, especially in the shorter format. There is always a risk, of course, in not satisfactorily tying off all the threads you've woven into your story.

With this final chapter of Zeite's journey, I wanted his personal arc to be resolved, but to leave the future open-ended. Some will be content with that, others perhaps not. In the end, as Zeite notes, the real story is about what our species will do next.

Acknowledgements

Writing fiction is not quite the solitary process many people assume it is. I have been fortunate enough to be influenced—and helped—by many generous and talented people along the way. So with this in mind, some heartfelt thanks are in order.

Firstly, I'd like to thank all the editors who have helped me improve my craft. A special shout out to Angela Challis, Shane Jiraiya Cummings, Sarah Endacott, Russell B Farr, Stuart Mayne, Amanda Pillar and Keith Stevenson. Thank you all!

Like most authors, I've had a support crew who've been kind enough to endure my early drafts. Foremost amongst these is my wife, Liz, who is always my first reader and greatest source of encouragement. I'd also like to thank my daughters—Liana and Brielle—for their encouragement. A doff of the hat must also go to Matt Filkins for outstanding field research and navigational skills; Simon Burrage for always taking an interest in the latest project; Terry Black for logistical and promotional support; Oliver Palmer for internet domain mastery; and Darren Weiskop for regularly suggesting ideas that I will never write about. Medals of bravery (based on the sheer volume of words read) should be awarded to Karen Beilharz, JJ Irwin, Anne Mok, DK Mok, Rivqa Rafael, Angie Rega, Susan Wardle and Wendy Waring.

My thanks and gratitude also go to the fantastic team at IFWG Publishing. I'll be buying the first round for Gerry Huntman for publishing this collection; Greg Chapman for the superb cover; Noel Osualdini for his thorough editing; and Steve McCracken for proofreading.

I'd also like to acknowledge the authors who were generous enough to say kind things about this collection: a heartfelt thank you to Jo Anderton, Karen Brooks, Richard Harland, Ian Irvine, Stephen M Irwin, Jason Nahrung and Keith Stevenson.

And finally, I'd like to thank *you*, dear Reader, for travelling with me for a while.

Nathan Burrage
May 2022.